The Inn of the Healer
Sarai's Journey, Book 2

By Michelle L. Levigne

M Zion Ridge Press LLC

Mt Zion Ridge Press LLC
295 Gum Springs Rd, NW
Georgetown, TN 37366

https://www.mtzionridgepress.com

Copyright © 2020 by Michelle L. Levigne
ISBN 13: 978-1-949564-81-5

Published in the United States of America
Publication Date: April 1, 2020

Editor-In-Chief: Michelle Levigne
Executive Editor: Tamera Lynn Kraft

Editor: Deborah Cullins Smith

Cover Art Copyright by Mt Zion Ridge Press LLC © 2020

Author's Note:

This is entirely a work of fiction, a product of my imagination. An early version of the first book, **Heretic's Daughter***, was originally published with By Grace Publishing as* **The Price***. The germinal story was sparked by long hours sitting backstage with the cast and crew of the Easter pageant my church produced for thirteen years in a row. We occasionally discussed other approaches to telling the story of Easter. One was the viewpoint of the people whose lives Jesus changed. In continuing Sarai's story past the original story told in* **The Price,** *I make no claim to any biblical/historical accuracy, when it comes to actual people and events beyond what is stated in the Bible. Church history most likely disagrees with me on the movements and fates of real people mentioned in these books. My knowledge comes from Sunday school lessons, Bible trivia contests, and efforts to research Bible-era geography and terminology.*

Chapter One

Jerusalem felt too quiet, as if it had been wounded and lay waiting for healing or death, like a wild animal. Sarai looked up and down the street from the doorway of what had once been her home, and she shivered. There was only enough light for her to make it most of the way to Norah's home before nightfall. Not all the way. Not even if she ran. She doubted her strength to do that, after the long day of painful sitting, waiting, and pacing.

Turning back was impossible. Lingering in the darkening streets would be more than dangerous. Anyone who saw her would wonder what a young woman was doing out after dark, alone. Depending on who saw her, she could be attacked or even arrested. No one was safe from either suspicion or accusation, after the strange events of the day. Would Jerusalem ever be the same, now that Jesus had been crucified?

Sarai headed down the street. She needed to move, to get as far away from Simon's door as she could. Distance was more important than shelter, at least for a short time. She would walk quickly while trying to conserve her strength and beg Adonai for protection and the ability to keep going until she was safely under Norah's roof. Maybe Malachi would have more details of the events of the day. She thought Norah's father might even have been brave enough to go to the hill of crucifixion outside the city. He could answer her questions.

"Rabbi Nicodemus," she whispered, as she thought through the far-too-short list of people who would have had the courage to stand with Jesus in His last moments. Sarai stumbled even as she smiled. She would go to Nicodemus' house, which was much closer. He had to know what had happened to Jesus. He would have answers for her.

More important, Nicodemus would share her belief that despite the tragic events of the day, the brutality and injustice, Jesus was still the Messiah. Despite His death, He would triumph.

Sarai wasn't sure how. She didn't want to face the questions.

She just needed to hold onto the bruised, aching faith that remained with her, and find shelter with others who still believed.

She turned her path to Nicodemus' house, only a few streets away from the home that was no longer hers. Hadn't he said he would stand as her father? He would shelter her, even if all Jerusalem declared she was as much a heretic as her father had been.

Leah, the daughter of the cook, answered the door and let Sarai into the house. Nicodemus was not there. He had come back shortly after the earthquake, made sure those in the household were all right, then left again. The servants weren't sure where he had gone. Perhaps he was making sure of the safety of some of his elderly scholar friends. Laila, however, was there. She had come back to the house with Nicodemus and he had left instructions for her to be taken care of. She came to meet Sarai and embraced her and led her to the courtyard. They sat in silence for a while, as the daylight faded. The air cooled and the sky seemed to bleed with a blaze of glory that seemed like a silent protest.

Then Sarai told Laila what had happened to her, from the moment Simon caught hold of her arm and led her away, until she decided to come to Nicodemus for shelter. She thought perhaps later she would be amused at how few words she needed to relate the destruction of what had been a safe, secure life. Neither of them cried, but Laila held her, cradling her as they sat in silence, and waited.

Nicodemus returned when a few fading streaks of crimson burned in the clouds on one side of the sky. On the opposite side, framed by the walls of the house, stars were just starting to glimmer. He wore the same clothes he had worn to the Passover meal. They were just as mud-stained and bedraggled by the storm as Simon's clothes had been.

"Rabbi Nicodemus? Are you all right?" Sarai asked as he paused in the doorway of the courtyard.

"Sarai?" He moved toward her and Laila with all the slow caution of an old man who had been bruised all over. "What are you doing here? Does Simon know where you are?"

"Simon has divorced me."

"No!" He spread his arms wide and gathered her in close. "Oh, my poor child. Why?"

"I believe Jesus is the Messiah, even though He is dead. Tell me -- is Jesus truly dead? Is there no hope?"

"Yes, Jesus is dead. I helped bury Him, just a short time ago. A friend had built a tomb for himself, intending to be buried in Jerusalem. He wanted to believe in Jesus as the Messiah, but … he was justifiably afraid." Nicodemus guided her to the bench and they sat. He kept hold of her hand and reached over her with his other hand to grasp Laila's.

"Will that be all we know from now on, if we choose to believe despite everything that has happened today?" she mused.

"We must hold fast." He sighed. "No matter how we ache, no matter how tired we are, no matter …" Another sigh.

"You need to eat. I know you have gone all day without food," Laila said, getting up from the bench. "Hephzibah was making a nice, hearty stew. I'll see if it's ready. Unless you want to wash before you eat?" She cupped his cheek for a moment. The tenderness in her gesture put a sob in Sarai's throat. "Such injustice today … I must believe that Adonai's hand is in it, despite the pain, because otherwise the world would shatter."

"Be careful," he said, his lips twitching as he tried to smile. "I might be tempted to keep you here to look after me."

Laila chucked softly and hurried out of the courtyard on her errand.

"Where is your friend now?" Sarai asked.

"We are both old men. He has gone to his lodgings to rest. To mourn. We are both ceremonially unclean, after dealing with the dead, but …" He sighed. "What does it matter? How can we continue to celebrate Passover in the face of all this?"

"How can we?" she echoed. "So you buried Jesus? In a tomb, not thrown into a pit with the paupers, with criminals?" A sob escaped her in a little hiccup, and she realized some of the ache had left. She supposed she had been afraid, without even realizing it, that Jesus' body would go to the burning piles in Gehenna, denied proper burial.

"My friend's tomb is newly cut. He tried to laugh at the timing of it. Part of his reason for being here in Jerusalem, besides the Passover, was to arrange for his tomb. He gave it for Jesus' burial because there was no place to put Him. It is the irony of our God that His Son died between two thieves, and yet is buried in the tomb of a rich man. Yes, Jesus is dead." Nicodemus sat up straight and pulled back his shoulders from the slump that clearly illustrated his weariness. "But there is still hope."

"You still believe?" The tears came now, hot, stinging her face and awakening the aches laid on her soul.

"I still believe. Stay here, Sarai. I will take care of you like my own daughter. You and Laila both. Whatever influence and respect I retain, I will protect you both. We will wait, and we will pray, and we will see what miracles Adonai has waiting for us."

"Here we are." Laila stepped out into the courtyard, carrying a tray with cups and bowls and a serving bowl of something that steamed. "It smells delicious. You both must eat. We will need all our strength in the days to come."

"I am a foolish old man," Nicodemus said, standing. His mouth twisted in a weary smile. "Here, I insisted Laila should come back with me, so I could look after her. I felt it wouldn't be safe for her to return to Norah's house, with all the unrest in the city. Yet now she is looking after me, instead."

The stew was savory, full of flavors she had not experienced before. As they ate, Nicodemus told them about the late-night meeting he had with Jesus what felt like a lifetime ago, and the ideas and questions that still troubled him and made him think and re-assess his life. If not for the quiet, mournful spirit seeping through the city, Sarai thought they might have had a pleasant evening.

~~~~~

The next day was the Sabbath. Quiet hung over the city, despite the Passover festivities. Nicodemus, Sarai and Laila went to Norah's house. Sometimes people stopped and watched them walk past. Perhaps they recognized Rabbi Nicodemus, or they had seen Sarai and Laila yesterday at the foot of the steps of the governor's palace. Sarai shuddered in anticipation of someone raising a hue and cry, chasing them down to either beat them or arrest them for their continuing loyalty to Jesus.

At Norah's house, Malachi saw them coming down the street and came running to meet them. Sarai remembered Norah's teasing that she thought her father was smitten with Laila for her good business sense. Malachi hurried them into the house, closed the door, and led them to an inner room, rather than the courtyard or
~~~~~

to the roof to talk.

They spent the day there in quiet conversation. Somehow Norah's home became a hub for people looking for information, to exchange rumors and what few facts were known. After several stories were shared, Sarai realized what they all had in common. These were all people who wanted to believe in Jesus, despite all the condemnation of the religious leaders. They came to Norah because they knew they could speak freely and ask their questions and share their stories without being accused or threatened or vilified. Some came to relate what they had seen and heard during the crucifixion, and to share frightening and confusing stories of what other people had seen and heard during and after the earthquake. Sarai held Laila's hand when several people brought stories about how Barabbas had been freed. Jesus had died in his place. The Zealot leader had fled Jerusalem without looking back. Sarai ached for her friend, who tried not to love Barabbas any longer. Later, thinking over the constantly shifting emotions of the day, she found some amusement and wonder to realize that the woman who had been given the power and opportunity to destroy her life had become a friend, and important to her. The story between them perhaps illustrated how much difference Jesus could make in what should have been filled with heartache and anger.

Malachi left the house several times, walking down to the marketplace where people met to talk even though shops were closed for the Sabbath. He came back grim and quiet, and waited until the house was quiet again to share what he had learned. The Sanhedrin was in a vile mood, despite their triumph. They were already planning to take action against Jesus' followers and anyone who had supported Him during the trial. Anyone who protested the break from tradition and called the nighttime trial what it was -- illegal -- was considered an enemy of all Jews and rebels against Yahweh. On top of that, they were taking extra measures to assist the Romans, to express their gratitude for the removal of the threat they saw embodied in Jesus. Rumors said one of the steps they would take was to move against anyone who supported or had merely been friendly with the Zealots.

Over the evening meal, they agreed on their plan. Malachi would leave Jerusalem immediately and travel to Damascus, to personally see about some property that could be transformed into a new inn. He had been corresponding with a man hired as his agent, and the agent for the previous owners, for several months now. Yesterday's events and the rumors filling the city had convinced him the time for caution and careful preparation had ended. It was time to act, and quickly, if they would preserve their freedom. And perhaps their lives.

Acting in faith that Adonai would protect them and bless their steps, Norah would prepare for the move without waiting to hear from her father if he was successful. She would start by contacting the former inn servants and offer them a chance to go to Damascus and join the new venture. She would sell her home, and with the profits fill wagons with provisions for establishing the inn.

They wanted Laila and Sarai to come with them, to run the inn. Laila knew people in Damascus. Malachi valued her advice and experience. She would help identify the sort of people who would try to cause trouble for the new inn, so he could discourage any unsavory folk who might try to establish the inn as their domain. Sarai's skill as a healer would be a valuable asset and help establish the reputation of the inn as a safe and reputable shelter for travelers with women and children. Even without knowing the layout of the inn, they determined to have a special area designated where only women and children could go, and men could not enter. If there was a portion of the Temple where women could not go, why not a place in the inn where men could not go?

They invited Nicodemus to come with them, when he visited the next morning to check on Sarai. Later, she reflected that it was good they had made the offer first, because the news Nicodemus brought them drove all plans and other concerns from their minds for most of the day. He seemed to waver somewhere between laughter and looking dazed, as he listened to their plans and the invitation. For a few moments he bowed his head, then smiled and declined, and expressed gratitude for the invitation.

"I must stay, although I believe you would be wise to leave Jerusalem. The authorities will be in an uproar for days, perhaps weeks, even months ..." Nicodemus sighed, and his face looked flushed. "Children, Jesus is alive." His voice cracked on the last word.

He had few details to share with them and excused himself quickly to go on to the house where the disciples had gathered to hide, so he could learn more. All he knew for sure was that several followers of Jesus had gone to the tomb and verified that it was indeed empty. The authorities had sealed the tomb and posted guards after he and his friend buried Jesus, but the stone had been rolled away, the guards had fled, and the shroud that Nicodemus had bound around Jesus was left behind, empty.

Over the next handful of days, they ventured out in the shadows of early morning and dusk to gather up news, to share stories with other followers of Jesus, and try to avoid the notice of the Sanhedrin and the Romans. Laila was the bravest of them, venturing out to the house where the disciples had gone to hide. To hear directly from the ones who had seen Jesus and spoken with Him, the ones who had gone to the tomb and seen the empty graveclothes.

The stories grew strange, warped by speculations and poisoned by the lies that Jesus' enemies tried to spread. Too soon, the joy and wonder faded into fear, and then the growing certainty that whenever they moved through the city, unfriendly eyes were watching them.

Malachi left for Damascus, reluctantly. He feared for the safety of Norah, Laila and Sarai, despite admitting they might be safer if he wasn't in Norah's house. More than half of the servants who had worked at his inn were willing to throw their lot in with him and Norah, and travel to Damascus with them. As the days turned into a week and then two since news came of the resurrection of Jesus, they turned all their energies back to preparing for the journey.

Sarai encountered Deborah at the market twice, and gladly sent messages to Hannah to assure her she was well, she was safe, and was with friends. Deborah was pleased to report that Simon spent more time at home than with the Sanhedrin, and he was quiet, preferring to be alone. Then she remarked that Sarai looked thinner, paler, and asked if her belly was still troubling her. That brought some questions to Sarai's mind that she had forgotten in all the chaos and sadness and wonder.

The day a messenger came with a letter from Malachi, saying he had purchased an inn, but not the one he had hoped to obtain, Sarai went to visit the midwife, Naomi. She had had her suspicions, but constantly put them aside because of more important considerations. In this instance, she needed to turn to someone else.

Her teacher, Huldah had often said that a healer, or in this case a midwife, was especially blind when tending herself. Naomi was sympathetic, and scolded her gently when she confirmed that yes, Sarai was pregnant.

"This is good news, yes?" she said, and studied Sarai, her eyes bright and piercing in their nest of wrinkles. "I heard what your husband did, but certainly he will change his mind when you tell him. He will be sorry for his cruelty. What man can be so stubborn that he disowns his own child before he is even born?"

Sarai thanked the old woman and walked slowly back to Norah's house. It disturbed her that Naomi assumed her firstborn would be a son. She didn't want Simon to take her back on the chance she would give him a son, because what would she do — indeed, what would he do -- if she gave birth to a daughter?

She suspected that when life quieted down again, if it ever did, she would decide she did not want Simon to take her back. She would go to Damascus with Norah and Laila and Malachi, and she would not tell people she was divorced. She would tell them she was a widow and raise her child free of the poison of Simon's foolishness and arrogance.

~~~~~

Jude came to Norah's house after dark fell that night, sporting a swollen nose, smears of blood on his clothes, and a black eye. Norah clucked over him and sent a serving girl down to the well for cold water.

"Just what were you doing and why did you risk your handsome face to do it?" she scolded, as she led him to the table in the kitchen with three lanterns hanging over it.

"Is Sarai here?" Jude turned, looking around, and his face lit up when he saw her in the opposite doorway. "There you are. I should have known you would come here. Are you all right? He hasn't come after you, has he? It's what I would expect, after the argument we had."

"Argument over what?" Sarai couldn't make herself move into the room.

Jude raised a hand to probe his bruised and swollen face, tried to smile, and winced.

"What did you do to get him angry?" Norah slapped his hand away.
~~~~~

"I bought Sarai's freedom." He winced again when Norah applied the first cold cloth to his face.

"Bought my freedom?" Sarai whispered.

"I tried to. He threw the coins into my face, followed quickly by his fist." Jude closed his eyes and pressed the cloth against his eye. "I should have remembered what quick fists Simon had, when we used to fight as boys."

Sarai could see Jude was inordinately proud of his bloody nose and black eye. She couldn't stay in the doorway. Not with the way he kept looking at her. Her mind kept skittering around the entire subject of exactly why Jude had tried to buy her freedom.

What did he think would happen, if Simon had accepted his coins? What would the scribes and keepers of the law say, if presented with this situation? If Simon cast her aside before Jude came with his coins, was she still legally his property, even if she was no longer his wife? The law was clear when dealing with a maiden bought to become a wife, when her owner changed his mind about marrying her. She was to be given her freedom and clothing. Sarai didn't know if there was any law about a woman who was bought, married, and then cast aside. Could Simon hand her over to Jude, without incurring charges of adultery?

What did Jude want from her?

She didn't want to confront old, abandoned dreams.

That realization told her something. It wasn't all clear in her mind, but she was sure of one thing. She was going to Damascus with Simon's child in her womb, and the fewer people who knew about it, the safer she would feel.

Somehow, she wasn't surprised when Norah came to tell her Jude had left after only a token attempt to see her. He had given up so easily before, why would she expect him to fight for what he wanted now? Sarai tried to laugh at his weakness and be glad he had never taken her as his wife. Perhaps he wanted her to come to him. Since Simon didn't accept his money, he couldn't claim he had purchased Simon's slave-wife. If Jude wouldn't say outright what he wanted, if he wouldn't take decisive steps and risks ... what made him think she would want to be with him?

The sooner Sarai left for Damascus, the better.

~~~~~

Sarai and Laila decided it was wise to avoid the marketplace
~~~~~

during the days of preparation. Norah and the serving women always returned with more stories than supplies for the inn. People claimed they had seen Jesus. Other stories told of the frantic attempts by the Sanhedrin to hush the witnesses. Rabbi Gamaliel had supposedly cautioned Caiaphas and the other leaders to be calm, to ignore the tales. Supposedly he advised them that fighting to quell the stories would only give credence to them. Treating them as worthless gossip and children's tales, unworthy of their attention or concern, would encourage reasonable people to ignore them. Some rumors claimed that soldiers had been assigned to guard the tomb, and when Jesus returned to life, the soldiers had seen Him. The rumors claimed the Sanhedrin had paid the soldiers to lie and accuse the disciples of stealing the body. Yet as far as anyone knew, the soldiers hadn't been punished for failing in their duty. Even just two trained soldiers with spears or swords could have stood against a handful of disciples. So what was the truth? What did the Sanhedrin fear would happen?

Sometimes Sarai let herself wonder: What if Simon saw Jesus? Would he believe? Would he come for her? Would he apologize and ask for her forgiveness, and take her back as his wife?

"Don't be a fool," she told herself each time, and each time scolded herself not to think of such things.

Ruth came once to Norah's house, to pass on all the gossip swirling through Jerusalem. Everything she said was heavily interwoven with sarcastic remarks and doubts. She paid no attention to the packing and other preparations filling the house, asked no questions, and no one told her anything. Finally, Ruth left, flushed with irritation, her piggy eyes sharp, and she didn't come back. Norah confided in Sarai later that she wouldn't put it past Ruth to go running to the Sanhedrin with greatly exaggerated stories. Maybe she would even put words in Norah's and Malachi's mouths, to make herself look good and perhaps finally win the admiration, or at least the attention, of Reuben.

Chapter Two

Simon never came to look for Sarai, although he had to know she would go to Norah for shelter if she wasn't with Nicodemus. He didn't ask Nicodemus, who would have told Sarai if Simon had come seeking her. Maybe he was ignoring her, waiting until she had time to consider what she had done. He likely expected her to repent and come back to him, begging for forgiveness. If he made no fuss over her, told no one she was gone, perhaps he thought she could return, chastened and submissive, and he could take her back with no one the wiser? They could keep it just among the members of the household. No shame. No gossip. Simon certainly cared about appearances more than was wise.

Sarai amused herself for a few moments, considering Simon's consternation over divorcing her on the spur of the moment. If no one knew he had divorced Sarai, he could take her back without people asking uncomfortable questions or calling him a fool. He probably cared more about people mocking him if they learned he had divorced her. After all, enough of his Pharisee friends had told him, in front of Sarai, that he had made a mistake rescuing and marrying the daughter of that heretic, Eliakim ben Levi.

No one other than Jude, who only made that one visit, mentioned Simon to Sarai during those days. She was grateful. She supposed Laila felt just as grateful that no one mentioned Barabbas to her. Sarai wondered if her friend prayed for him, or at least tried to pray for him, just as she struggled to pray for Simon. After all, he was the father of the child she carried, and any blessings or curses that rested on him would trickle down to her child.

The morning their traveling party climbed into their wagons and rode down the dark, pre-dawn streets, Sarai nearly wept aloud as she thought of Hannah. How could she have forgotten Hannah? Why hadn't she tried to leave word for her, or at least meet up with Deborah in the marketplace, to make her farewells with her? Losing Deborah and Hannah, and especially not raising their children together, was truly her one regret. The aching, thick feeling in her head and throat and chest shifted into something that might have been laughter, when she thought about Simon's reaction to the idea that she would miss Deborah and Hannah, but not him.

If she never saw Simon again, and he never thought of her, she thought she would be happy. From this moment forward, her life would focus on her child. She thought of the two contrasting figures of Hagar and Sarah, the slave woman and the free woman, who had given Abraham his sons. She swore her child would not suffer the fate of Ishmael.

~~~~~

When evening came, Norah directed the men driving the wagons to continue past the crossroads. They stayed on the Roman-built road taking them north and east to Damascus. In the fading light, Sarai read the guides for travelers, carved into the stone pillar set into the hard-baked soil by the side of the road. She guessed the light in the cluster of buildings on the horizon west of them came from the inn named on the pillar. There looked to be little else here. Likely someone had calculated this would be a good stopping place for travelers. They built the inn to take advantage of hungry, cold, tired, dirty people who didn't have any food or firewood or wash water left at this stage in their journey to Jerusalem.

The lights faded in the distance as the wagons continued down into the Jordan River valley. The sun sank down so only a faint, bloody orange arc rested on the horizon. Sarai moved up between the bales and crates and jars to kneel behind Norah's seat next to the driver of their wagon. Laila had fallen asleep in the warm air collected under the canopy. The serving women and men accompanying them were in the other two wagons. No one but Eli, the driver, would hear what she said.

"I know." Norah turned and looked back at Sarai and smiled.

"Know what?"

"I'm being foolish."

Eli snorted and turned his head enough to wink at Sarai. He had worked for Malachi, overseeing the safety and maintenance of the inn since before either young woman had been born.

"Not you," the big, white-haired man said, and slapped the reins on the backs of the donkeys. They didn't move any faster. Sarai suspected that hadn't been his intention anyway.

"That inn's owners tried for years to convince travelers they were Father's partners," Norah said with a sigh of weary humor.
~~~~~

"Their patriarch tried at least once a year to persuade Father to marry me to his odious son, who is nearly Father's age. They used bribes, they used threats. Before … before Abner died and we lost the inn, they wanted to ride on Father's reputation."

"And gain you as a cook and permanent slave," Eli added. He turned his head and spat into the dust along the road for punctuation.

"Yes, there is that. Ever since, they have made overtures every two or three months, and foolishly think that mocking Father for his misfortunes will convince me to submit." She glanced behind them. The signpost was lost in the distance and shadows now. "Stopping there for the night would give them hope. They might try to perform the wedding ceremony before we could flee."

Despite the droll tone and the glimpse of a smile in the growing shadows, Sarai sensed this was a sensitive topic for Norah. After a few more jolts and bumps of the wagon, she crept back between the crates and bales to her nest of cushions under the canopy with Laila.

"I'm likely to blame." The older woman opened her eyes. "When the demons ruled inside me, my girls and I were quite well known at many inns along the Roman roads. Especially where we could encounter legions and their commanders. Norah likely thinks to spare me some embarrassment, and her some trouble, by avoiding them."

"You are an entirely different woman since Jesus healed you," Sarai countered. "Even if you weren't wearing a veil, they wouldn't recognize you. Your face, the way you move, your voice … Made new. No jewelry, no cosmetics, and your hair is braided. With the veil across your face, no one would know you."

"Despite everything, you are still such a sweet, innocent child." Laila reached across the cushions that made the bumpy, jolting, swaying journey bearable. She caught hold of Sarai's hand and squeezed it, and the two smiled at each other as the shadows deepened with every creak of the wagon's wheels.

Their journey would take six days, just a day less than it would take to walk straight from Jerusalem to Damascus at a brisk pace. The wagons moved almost slower than a small group of men would walk. Sarai remembered her journey from Jerusalem to the Decapolis to be sold as a slave, then the long, meandering journey back to Jerusalem after Simon rescued her. Damascus was part of the Decapolis, but she hadn't been taken that far north to be sold.

The wagons finally stopped near the edge of the road, in a safe place partially screened by scraggly trees. Eli had traveled this road often for Malachi, and he knew where to find small wells that the occasional travelers didn't know about. Larger merchant caravans didn't bother with them because they were so small. This well provided enough water to take care of the donkeys pulling the wagons, to cook and wash and fill their water skins for the next day's journey.

Sarai joined the women in drawing water and lighting lanterns while the men arranged the wagons for shelter. The women would sleep within the partial walls formed by the wagons, with a canopy of tent fabric spread over support poles and ropes stretched between them. Curtains of blankets hung down the wagon sides would give more than enough privacy for sleeping and washing and would serve to block the night breezes. The men would sleep in the wagon beds, and take turns standing guard. Everything would be proper and neat and sensible, and no one could accuse them of immodesty or breaking any laws. Malachi had been proud of the high, moral reputation of his inn. He had been first hurt, then infuriated when Caiaphas and his underlings accused him of relaxing Jewish laws of cleanliness, both physical and ceremonial, for the sake of doing business with Gentiles, especially Roman soldiers and officials.

Much of their safety and success when they reached Damascus would rest on Malachi's reputation and Norah's cooking. Women ran inns the world over, according to Norah, but they had a far harder time than women who ran other types of businesses as the sole support of their families. People seemed to naturally expect that a woman involved in the operation of an inn provided bed services with the beds. In many cities, a woman wasn't referred to as an innkeeper, but a harlot, even if she was a married woman, covered in veils, and guarded by five sons who never let a male stranger within ten steps of their mother. Laila had hesitated to accept Norah's offer to come with them and find a fresh start in Damascus because of that. She feared people would assume all the women in the inn were harlots, if she was recognized.

The largest uncertainty ahead of them was the reception waiting for them in Damascus. How would other innkeepers react when they learned Malachi would turn the building from warehouse back to an inn, which it had been years ago? What about the reactions of the merchants who regularly stored their wares in the building when they learned it was no longer available? That subject came up when the camp had been assembled. They all settled down on cushions and crates around the small fire and the massive clay pot that was heating to cook their evening bread.

"I don't anticipate it being an easy change." Norah gave a final flourish to the mortar and pestle where she ground herbs to season the oil for dipping their bread. "The merchants won't like having to make new arrangements. Father has learned that some of them were customers of his. Some of them are genial enough when they get what they want. Make them accept changes, and they could become opponents, perhaps even complain to the city officials. The best we can hope from some of the troublemakers is that they will expect special privileges, to make up for the inconvenience."

"What right do they have to oppose your father using the building any way he chooses?" Caleb yanked the thick pottery stopper coated in wax from the neck of the oil jar.

"Newcomers, even property owners and freemen, have fewer rights than residents and citizens." Norah watched him pour the oil into the bowl, and paused her words until she lifted her hand, signaling him to stop pouring. "According to the law, my father has rights and privileges as a landowner. He paid the back taxes that led to the building being seized by the authorities. He has earned some goodwill from the landowners on the street and neighboring streets just for making repairs and hiring boys to kill vermin. However, we are newcomers. We are changing the ranking among the merchants in that district of the city. Many landowners and merchants will oppose us, likely in hopes of being offered bribes to earn their good will. At the very least, other inns will stand against us, even if they are ten streets away, and even if our presence does not affect their business. They will consider us rivals."

"Especially when they taste your cooking," Laila said.

"You'll have a dozen suitors from rival inns," Eli said with a snort and a grin.

The night passed uneventfully, with a chill in the air that was refreshing when they left their blankets at sunrise to resume their journey. Sarai acted as scribe, recording all the ideas for making the inn stand out and letting travelers and residents know they were there. The building sat in a district between the outermost city wall, and the next wall inward, six streets away. Damascus had several concentric circles of walls, clearly marking the outward growth of the city. The inn sat up against the inner wall, and Malachi had managed to buy the house built on the other side of that wall, abutting the inn. The plan was to break through the wall and connect the house to the inn, with a sturdy metal grill to clearly mark the line that customers could not pass. The women would live in the house. The kitchen would be expanded to fill up the lower level of the buildings on both sides of the wall. The men would live in the inn, providing security and a strong arm to control customers, enforcing civility and good manners.

The former inn had been built as a caravansary, and part of it would provide those services again: storage for merchants' wares, stabling for their animals, fodder, and cooking facilities. They could sleep in the courtyard, safe within the walls, and the gates would be guarded. For a little extra money, they could rent rooms on the upper level of the caravansary side. The inn had the advantage of two wells, in opposite corners of the courtyard. That negated the drudgery of walking a street or two or even farther away multiple times during the day to obtain the water necessary for the inn. Those wells had to be emptied of the rocks and rubbish that had been tossed into them during the time the building and courtyard had been used for a warehouse.

Blocking wells made no sense, but no one seemed to know why that had been done. When Sarai asked why the inn had closed and been used as a warehouse for several years, Norah had no answers. Her father had said in his last letter he was investigating, and he feared there would be some unpleasant surprises. There was no turning back now, and they would simply have to work around those difficulties when they appeared.

On the other side of the wall dividing inn from caravansary, the inn would provide meals, a courtyard for people to meet and gather, and rooms to rent on the upper two levels. Merchants could conduct business in privacy, or people lacking sufficient space elsewhere could have celebrations there. Norah would provide food for them, and as her reputation grew, she would again offer her services to arrange feasts for families and businesses throughout the city. Eli and Mattias would be charged with ensuring that those who rented the rooms did not use them for illegal or immoral activities, while at the same time ensuring privacy for those who desired it.

As the wagons trundled down the road through the Jordan River valley, the travelers called back and forth to each other, planning their new lives and work. They made lists of the chores that needed to be done, and the order in which to complete them. The supplies they would need to purchase. The repairs and rearranging of walls and floors and stairs, shutters and doors, within the inn building, to transform it back from a warehouse. Norah declared that Sarai should be in charge of the accounts and records for the inn. They would be a wonder for ten streets in any direction, having an educated woman handling the accounts. They amused themselves imagining the sort of trouble businesses and officials would make for themselves, coming up against Sarai. They would try to take advantage of a woman handling money and tallies, paying for supplies and paying servants and taking payments from customers. Always, the hopeful cheat came off the worst in the stories spun by the men driving the wagons. They had experience with merchants and former employers who tried such tricks on them. The women who rode in the other wagons laughed and called back and forth, telling stories of getting the better of thieves and cheats. Sarai was grateful they found something amusing in such situations. The talk during the long days of riding certainly proved educational.

Laila educated them on the authorities and men of wealth and power and influence in Damascus. The ones who could be their patrons and supporters and even defenders, if necessary. The ones who would stand with Norah and the inn if it benefited them. The ones who would play games, causing trouble, spreading gossip, supporting false stories, just for the amusement of putting turmoil in others' lives. Granted, Laila hadn't been in Damascus in nearly two years, and some of those men might have died or fallen out of power. Or the political power and wealth might have shifted hands since she was last there. Still, what she remembered provided a foundation for the members of the inn household to build on. They had a basic understanding of the hidden connections, the way things were done, how problems were resolved and decisions made, sometimes totally ignoring the Roman authorities and laws.

Their second and fourth nights of travel, they spent in small inns, where the women shared one cramped room and the men stayed with the wagons in the yard. Eli spoke for all of them, and Norah kept silent. No one mentioned their purpose in traveling to Damascus. The inns were small and neat but gave an impression of chill and darkness despite the lamps everywhere. Norah had warned them all before they left Jerusalem, to be careful when they stopped at inns along the road.

Inns established far from villages had reputations for cheating traveling parties, stealing from them, and even accusing them of stealing in turn. Roman soldiers were always near at hand in such situations, and notorious for demanding bribes before they would dispense justice. An innkeeper who made false accusations was likely on good terms with the captain or magistrate or judge who came to investigate a disagreement or charge. Usually, such authorities would side with him against the traveler.

If the innkeepers knew the wagons were loaded with supplies to establish an inn in Damascus, they might try to profit in some way from Norah's hard work and planning. They might even claim some of the serving women and men were their slaves who were trying to run away. Whenever someone actually asked, Eli claimed they were a family, fleeing more oppression from Governor Pilate. That was easy to believe, after the deaths of the worshippers on Pilate's orders, slaughtering them so their blood mixed with their sacrifices on the altar.

The third and fifth nights, their party made camp along the side of the road, and everyone's spirits were better for it. On those nights, they shared stories of what they had seen Jesus do, what they had heard Him say, or stories they had heard from those who had seen Him after He rose from the dead. Sarai wished she could have lingered in Jerusalem long enough to see Him just once more. She tried not to speculate and imagine what change could come over Simon if he encountered Jesus. To occupy her mind, she tried to remember everything she had learned from and learned about Jesus, and wrote down those memories, to share with others. Norah had packed strips of parchment and papyrus sheets that had been scraped clean or bleached with fuller's earth, to re-use them for inn records or receipts. She encouraged Sarai to record the stories and put no limit on the ink and scrolls and scraps she wrote on.

Sarai finally confided in Laila about her baby, and her need to ensure Simon could not find her and take the child away someday. Her friend thought over it that night, their final night on the road.

"You should claim to be a widow," Laila said, the next morning. She and Sarai stood by themselves, watching the men harnessing the donkeys to the wagons.

"I did consider that the easiest way to explain my child but no husband."

"There is some respect accorded to widows, even ones as young and pretty as you. Some protection. Your child shall protect you, as well. Women who don't trust their husbands and sons will always accuse a pretty girl of setting out to trap them, but if you are devoted to your child, they will see the two of you as needing their protection. Be warned, you could be besieged with suitors, having proven you are not barren."

"I will never marry." Sarai tried to laugh. "Even if I were a widow in truth, I would never want to marry again."

"Do not make such vows." Laila slid her arm around Sarai's shoulders. "There is always someone to hear and set out to make you break them."

A little chill curled through Sarai's middle. She suspected Laila meant the demons who had nearly destroyed her life.

~~~~~

Tobiah, the friend who had served as Malachi's agent and host in Damascus, had posted his son and two nephews at the gate of the road from Jerusalem, to watch for the arrival of their caravan. The oldest nephew, Nadab, knew Eli and Norah, having come to Jerusalem several times on his uncle's business. He sent his brother and cousin running to fetch Tobiah once he had met up with the travelers in the churning crowd trying to enter the gate. The noise of people talking and wheels creaking and donkeys braying and camels groaning was nearly overwhelming. Sarai thought Nadab was just a year or two older than her, with a dusting of golden-red beard on his cheeks and his shoulders thrown proudly back as he welcomed them to Damascus. There was something amusing, yet endearing about the young man's mannerisms, his broad gestures, as if Damascus were his to gift to them all. Sarai tugged her veil over the bottom half of her face to hide her smile.
~~~~~

The light moment passed quickly, in the weary eagerness to get out of the wagon. Sarai perched on the bench behind Norah's seat, where she could hear the conversation between Eli and Nadab. The young man led their wagons around the wall of Damascus, rather than going through the center of the city. They had come to the southeastern gate, but their destination sat in the northern quarter of the city. Going around, while a longer route, would take less time. No maneuvering around and being stopped by other wagons and people on the streets or detouring to streets wide enough for the wagons.

The gate they eventually passed through to enter Damascus was taller and wider than the gate that straddled the road from Jerusalem. Nadab led the first wagon through the gate, then let go of the bridle of the lead donkey and gestured for Eli to turn the wagon to the side, out of the main flow of incoming traffic. He hurried back to speak with the drivers of the other wagons. They stopped outside the gate. Before Nadab returned to them, a sweaty, dust-streaked man, with a headcloth sliding off his bald head, hurried out of the room built into the wall on the left side of the gate. A soldier in leather armor, his bronze helmet hanging from a strap at his belt, walked with him. Two men followed them, with shaved heads, clean-shaven faces, bare chests and slightly grimy white linen wrapped around their waists and hanging to their ankles. When they drew closer, Sarai saw the dark lines painted around their eyes, and the writing boxes slung over their shoulders. Egyptian scribes. Her father had told her about such men, but she had never thought she would ever see one, let alone two. The man approaching them had to be some city official, important enough to warrant two scribes. Most likely he was here to inspect them and question them about their business and what they were bringing into Damascus.

"Egyptians," Eli muttered. "Probably some fancy trick. Write in their pictures that make no sense to an ordinary man, cheat us somehow."

"I don't suppose you write and read Egyptian?" Norah said, turning to Sarai.

Before Sarai could respond to what she hoped was a joke, the four men met up with Nadab just a few steps from the front of the wagon. Sarai thanked Adonai that Tobiah had sent the young man to guide them, because he bowed and gestured and made introductions and explanations before the city gate official could say one word. The soldier took a step back, and one corner of his mouth turned up as he shifted his gaze back and forth between Nadab and the official and the lead wagon. Sarai stayed behind Norah with her veil pulled close around her face. She flinched every time it seemed the soldier's gaze met hers. He never paused, never reacted, so she dared hope he hadn't noticed her enough to react.

"So you're here to change that warehouse on Harvest Moon Street back into an inn, are you?" The official stepped away from Nadab to approach Norah's side of the wagon. He wiped his face with the trailing edge of his headcloth, further dislodging it, then gave it a yank to straighten it. He jammed his fists into his hips and tipped his head back to look up at her.

"That is our plan, yes," Norah said, after a pause and a glance at Eli.

Where she sat against the side of the wagon, Sarai felt Eli tense, saw his fist clench around the guide reins. She held her breath. Would this gate official be a troublemaker, castigating Norah for speaking instead of Eli, even though he had directly addressed her?

"I've had four complaints lodged against your inn already, claiming you've stolen business from better, more honorable men." He took a step back and swayed to one side, to look down the length of the wagon, then to the other wagons waiting outside the gate. "I fail to understand how an inn that doesn't yet exist can steal business from anyone."

The soldier said something, his voice pitched low so Sarai couldn't hear. The official chuckled, his face brightening so he seemed to be an entirely different man.

"The centurion is right. Men who complain about crimes that haven't yet occurred fear being robbed of treasures they don't possess. Tobiah ben Amram has boasted about the good food and clean beds of the inn on Spindle Street in Jerusalem. How can you guarantee you will provide the same here?"

"I can guarantee it because I am the daughter of Malachi ben Joachim, and the terror of every farmer and merchant who tried to sell us flawed goods." Norah tucked her veil tighter around her neck and shoulders and grasped the side of the wagon seat to slide down to the pavement.

Sarai caught her breath. Norah stood just a little taller than the city official, who had yet to give them his name. Nadab stayed on Eli's side of the wagon, looking stricken. Norah's nose was even with the official's eyes, and Sarai feared he would turn out to be one of those men who hated to be shorter than those he faced.

"Terror, eh?" The official tipped his head up to meet her gaze. "Did you bring the cook that Tobiah boasts about?"

"I *am* the cook."

"No wonder the complainers are afraid." His smile returned, a little wider than before. He gestured for the scribes. One stayed with him, while the other hurried out to the other wagons.

Somewhere in the middle of asking about the contents of the wagons, the names of the people in their traveling group, if they were freemen or slaves, Roman citizens or what nations they hailed from, he gave his name. Jasper. No surname or family name. Sarai thought his friendly sort of curtness was honest, rather than a mask he wore to hide his true intentions. He wasn't trying to trick them into relaxing and saying or doing something that could be used against them later.

Later, Tobiah informed them that they couldn't have met anyone better among the gate officials, when entering Damascus. Jasper had a reputation for honesty, and was admired for it, despite admitting openly that he protected his reputation just for the fun of frustrating those who kept trying to bribe or intimidate him. The man's family claimed to trace their roots to the kings of ancient Persia. They prided themselves on the scholarship and high government postings of their sons, and the politically astute marriages of their daughters. Nadab had taken them to Jasper's gate to make their entrance inspection as pleasant as possible. Shortening the trip to get to the inn and Harvest Moon Street was a secondary consideration.

Jasper didn't speak to any women other than Norah. He nodded to Sarai and to Laila when they climbed down from the wagon to allow the scribe to look through some of the chests and crates, but otherwise politely ignored them. Sarai found that somehow comforting. She only flinched a little when Eli named the members of their party, and stated she was a widow. Had Laila told him what they had decided that morning? She was grateful, and wished she had thought to tell everyone in their traveling party about the person she would claim to be from now on.

The centurion's gaze seemed to land on her more often than anyone else while answering questions for Jasper's records. Sarai hoped she only imagined it. What if Laila was wrong about widowhood protecting her? Perhaps men like the centurion considered her easier prey because she had no husband, father or brother to protect her. Should she add to the lie, and ask Eli or one of the other older men to claim to be her uncle or cousin, someone with authority over her? Malachi had already stated he would stand as father to her, but wouldn't she be safer if she had someone claiming a closer tie? Or would the weight of lies add up sooner, and bring disaster down on her head?

"What name are you giving your inn?" Jasper asked, once everyone had climbed back into the wagons.

"The Inn of the Three Sisters," Norah said without hesitating.

"Ah. A warning, I assume?" Jasper's sweaty face brightened with an amused smile.

"And a promise." Norah nodded to him. He chuckled, and so did the centurion. They stepped back and Nadab caught hold of the donkey's lead rein to get the team moving again.

"I should have thought of that," Laila said, once they had left the open square at the gate.

"I don't understand," Sarai said.

"It's a series of old stories, about three sisters in a wealthy family. All the men of their family lost everything through foolish choices. Finally they lost their lives. The sisters turned their huge, splendid home into an inn. All sorts of greedy, dishonest men and thieves and adventurers tried to take advantage of them. In every story, the sisters bested them and profited, and even inflicted punishment on the foolish men." Norah smiled, but her voice was weary. "Of course, the stories all agree the sisters died old and alone, with no children or grandchildren to look after them. Women aren't permitted to triumph completely, no matter how clever and brave they are."

"If they were brothers," Laila said, "you can be sure the story would have ended with them living to a good old age, surrounded by adoring wives and children and grandchildren, and no condemnation for the wealth they obtained."

"It's one thing to obtain wealth." Eli glanced back long enough to wink at Sarai. "It's another to hold onto it and use it wisely. When I've seen a man live to good old age and wealth and comfort, he's always had a good wife to look after him, and he's smart enough to treasure her."

Chapter Three

Tobiah and Malachi were waiting at the inn, which had finally been emptied of the last stored crates and jars just two days before. The walls and paving stones had been scrubbed with water and brooms and lye. A pile of tables and benches waited in one corner. From their battered condition, some of them were likely furnishings left from the previous inn. Others in better condition sat in another corner, and Sarai guessed Malachi had just bought them. Norah hugged her father in greeting, and Eli stepped up to clasp Malachi's hand.

Malachi happily announced the workmen had already built the bracing framework and broken through the wall, to connect the inn with the house on the other side. A decorative bronze grill had been commissioned to fill part of the hole. Norah and those in the inner kitchen would be able to monitor activities in the inn's central courtyard without needing to constantly step into the inn side of the kitchen.

While the men got to work unloading the wagons and the women scurried to inspect the cleaning job and assign living quarters, Norah inspected the work already done. She, Malachi and Tobiah settled at a table close to the hole in the wall, and she asked Sarai to bring the writing case full of drawings she had made along the way, with ideas for arranging the inn. She wanted a long table extending out from the kitchen wall into the inn courtyard, and shelves on either side of the opening, to hold dishes and baskets and cups. Over that would go a long canopy, to cover the table and provide shelter from the sun and rain, to protect the food and those who came to eat. They could start with a thick cloth covering at first, and if it worked out as she hoped, they could later build a permanent one of wood and covered with roofing tiles.

"We will also maintain all the inn's records here within the walls of the house," Norah said, after Nadab and the other two boys, Caleb and Elias, headed out on the first of what would be many errands.

"That will certainly provide security and put a halt to those who would like to cause you trouble," Tobiah said. "Did you bring a scribe with you, or do you need the names of several honest young scholars to hire?"

"I brought my own." Norah smiled at Sarai. She gestured at a wide opening in the wall, with a low stone sill, to be fitted soon with shutters. "I think we should build the table even with the sill, so we can slide dishes in and out easily enough. No risk of tipping something and spilling. We can build a platform under the table, to raise it."

"Won't that make it easier for people to climb into the house?" Sarai asked. "When the door into the inn is closed, how can we keep people out if they can still see in and climb inside?"

"I suggest a decorative screen." Laila pulled herself up onto the sill and sat looking down at them. She wasn't that high off the ground. "One that will swing out, with a bar on the inside for reinforcement and to lock it down. Is there a skilled ironworker nearby? Perhaps one who knows how to do decorative work in bronze?"

"Several." Tobiah nodded and leaned against the sill. "Make the screen of iron, and decorate it with bronze, so no one guesses how strong it is until they try to break in and steal."

"And the same screens on the other windows, to close up at night, or if guests become rude or troublesome. It will be expensive, I fear, but we will certainly earn some appreciation from city officials if we make it hard for people to evade the soldiers at the gates by going through the house. The harder we make it for people to turn the inn into a weak spot, the better friends we will have among those in power."

"You speak like a soldier." He bowed to her, smiling.

"I have had occasion to listen to soldiers speak of their work, the things they must consider." Laila's lips twitched as if she weren't quite ready to smile. Sarai ached for her friend, even as she was grateful for Laila's experience, providing insight into things she had never needed to consider before.

"We can be grateful she escaped that awful life," Norah confided to Sarai later that evening, as they shared a jar of water for washing. "To think that I would ever be grateful for friendship with a harlot -- former harlot," she hurried to say. "So much wisdom from bitter experience, and willing to share with us. I thought I knew all I needed, to safely deal with travelers and patrons of the inn. Father always made me feel that I was quite as capable as a son. I think now I was sheltered."

"I think people treated you with respect because of your father, and because you earned it," Sarai offered. "Who would dare insult you, and find themselves barred from eating at your father's table, or gathering with their friends in the courtyard?"

"True." She sighed and sopped up more water in the cloth, to rub over her arms and chest again. "We must rig some sort of screen on the upper level, not just walls and a canopy, but a solid roof to stand in all weather, to allow women to bathe with all protection for their modesty. I don't like the high walls leaning over us. Like vultures."

"The soldiers on the wall stopped often to watch while we were unloading the wagons. For a taste of your cooking, they could be asked to help protect our customers."

"The soldiers could be our worst offenders. I want our inn to be a place of safety and comfort for travelers with families. If we offer something the other inns don't, and we discourage the rabble and carousers, then we won't have jealousy problems. They will disdain us for considering the needs of women and children." Norah dropped the wet cloth in the basket set aside for dirty clothes. "Let them. A good reputation will protect us."

Sarai reached for the towels and handed one to Norah. She understood the things her friend didn't want to speak. Laila had told her more unpleasant stories than she had wanted to hear, to protect and prepare her. Even with Mattias and the other men to protect the inn's women, some men would be angry and offended when they were refused fleshly services. They would force themselves on the women, and insist they were willing, no matter how fiercely the women resisted and even screamed for help.

The best defense for the Inn of the Three Sisters was a reputation of refusing such services, and the open support and esteem of the city officials. If Sarai wasn't mistaken, the gate official, Jasper liked them. Perhaps he just appreciated the irritation they provided other inns and the troublemakers or arrogant folk who owned them, but she would take all the friends they could find and thank Adonai for His gifts.

~~~~~
~~~~~

There were three synagogues in Damascus within a reasonable walking distance of the Inn of the Three Sisters. The inn sat several streets away from the meandering edge of the Jewish quarter of the city. Malachi judged they would have their pick of which synagogue they would attend without anyone having any right to criticize or consider themselves slighted. That didn't mean they wouldn't come up against trouble from the synagogue leaders and leading families in each. Eli remarked that the chances were better they would be asked not to return, as soon as word went around the city that the newcomers belonged to the new inn, rather than anyone offended if they didn't choose one particular synagogue.

The major difference between the three synagogues was size, and that was how Sarai thought of them, even after making one visit to each. The largest synagogue, on Marketplace Street, was twice the size of the medium-sized one, which sat one street closer to the inn, at the Court of the Phoenix Fountain. The smallest synagogue sat farthest away, the opposite direction of the largest, on Kiln Street, and was perhaps a third of its size.

To be fair, the inn household agreed that they would visit each synagogue at least twice before coming to a decision, and Malachi announced he would not require them to all attend one synagogue together. That could end up being a hardship for the women if they preferred one location for worship, while the men preferred another. As strangers, the women certainly couldn't walk to the synagogue without at least one man for escort. Even after they became established and known in Damascus, it might not be safe for the women to walk far without men for company. That would have to be dealt with when or if the problem ever arose.

The Phoenix Fountain synagogue made the most favorable impression on Sarai after just one visit to each of the three, and she tried not to express her opinion until after the agreed-upon two visits. The building was plainer than either of the other two synagogues. Rabbi Amos, the leader, greeted Malachi in the market a full week after the household's first visit and asked when he could come visit. That was a longer time to make contact than the leaders of the Marketplace synagogue took. None of its leaders asked when it would be convenient for Malachi to speak with them, but simply walked through the gates of the inn without being announced, two days before the next Sabbath. Sarai's strongest impression of the six men was irritation that Malachi didn't come running to greet them. At the time, he was out in the city, trying to find men to clean out the wells. The visitors stopped just short of gathering up their robes and stalking out of the busy courtyard, when Norah and Eli approached them in welcome. They wanted to speak to the owner of the inn, not his daughter, not his right-hand man. They warmed up slightly when they tasted Norah's apricot bread, but Sarai thought they were far too concerned with their dignity and establishing their authority over the newcomers. According to her father, and Rabbi Nicodemus, such men spent so much energy on ensuring they were respected, they had little left for being good leaders and teaching those within their spiritual responsibility.

The leaders of the Kiln synagogue didn't visit the inn at all. The leading women confronted Norah as she was leaving the women's gallery, on the first Sabbath visit the inn household made. At the same time, the sons of the four leaders asked Malachi and the other men to stay back and wait to speak with their fathers. The eagerness of these people to learn everything about the newcomers bothered Norah. Laila and Eli agreed with her that something rang false in the apparent friendliness and welcome. They did not return to Kiln Street for a second visit.

Sarai decided what she liked best about the Phoenix Court synagogue after the second visit. The others agreed that one detail somehow summed up the atmosphere, and the hearts of the people and their leaders. The stairs going up to the women's gallery were placed inside the building, instead of outside. The attitude implied by the outside stairs at the other two synagogues bothered many of the inn household, the more they discussed the differences. It wasn't just a disregard for the safety and modesty of the women. How could the men thoroughly immerse themselves in the worship of Adonai if they could be so easily distracted by the presence of women passing them to reach the stairs and climb to the gallery? Sarai's father had been of the opinion that men who feared distractions so greatly were men who hadn't learned proper discipline. He disdained people who blamed everyone around them for their mistakes or flaws or failing to reach their goals or accomplish their dreams. Looking back, Sarai decided her father had been somewhat harsh, practicing his own kind of self-righteousness, but that didn't mean he was wrong.

Rabbi Amos asked thoughtful questions about Malachi's plans for the inn when he visited. The changes to the structure, the differences between how the Three Sisters would conduct business and how other, established inns already did so. He smiled and looked genuinely interested as he walked about the inn, and made a visible effort to stay out of the way of the workers. He asked everyone's name and introduced himself, which indicated he didn't expect everyone to know who he was or remember his title and position immediately. He didn't demand that Malachi drop the many tasks resting on his shoulders to escort him, and he asked permission to walk about the inn as it was undergoing repairs and changes. Most important, he didn't look as if he had been offered a rotten fish, when Norah spoke directly to him and answered his questions, instead of deferring to her father. Sarai liked him, and she felt certain that worshipping with Rabbi Amos' congregation would be a comfortable experience. She was relieved when several members of the inn household expressed their choice of the synagogue at the Court of the Phoenix Fountain, before Malachi asked.

~~~~~

The most important item of business was to hire men to clear out the wells. The sooner the inn could use its own water and not have to spend time and sandal leather walking to the nearest well, the better for everyone. Hiring workers should have been simple and quick, even for newcomers. Enough people had looked in through the gates of the inn courtyard while the wagons were first being unloaded and the cleaning work began. Enough people had asked what kind of work they would be hiring people to do, and if there was regular work available after the inn was open for business. Word should have spread at least through the contiguous districts of Damascus. Malachi and Tobiah went down to the marketplace to hire workers as soon as the household had unloaded and settled into their quarters. At first, the men who were seeking work gathered around them and looked eager. Then before Malachi quite realized it, all the workers had drifted away. On the following days when he had hired carpenters and stonemasons and men for other tasks, he couldn't find anyone willing to clean out the wells. Soon, when they approached other knots of men, those either walked away or turned their backs to him and Tobiah, clearly not
~~~~~

interested in working for them.

Laila went to Jasper for information that perhaps the inn's neighbors on Harvest Moon Street weren't willing to share. She came back with her shoulders hunched and her fists clenched. Eli chuckled and gestured for Sarai to be quiet, when she was about to call out and ask what Laila had learned. They waited a few moments, then followed her into the inn. Malachi was busy marking places on the wall of the kitchen where he wanted the carpenter to build shelves once he and his sons had finished their current task elsewhere in the city.

"Did you ask *why* the previous inn closed?" Laila said, just as Eli and Sarai stepped into the room. Her words started Malachi. "Did you keep asking," she hurried on, when he stopped and turned around with the measuring rod in one hand and the charcoal stick in the other. "Did you keep asking until you got an answer? No, you didn't. Not a clear answer. Did you?"

"You found out something," Malachi said, after several long moments of studying Laila.

"No one wants to work here. Every single person you've hired has other work to do before they can come here. Didn't that strike you as odd, after all the men you talked to? It's not because there is more work to be done in the city than there are workers. The fact that so many men are waiting in the hiring market square every morning should have told you otherwise. They don't want to work here, but it's easier to lie than anger you. Or maybe they enjoy laughing at you behind your back. They don't want to work *here*, especially not cleaning out the wells, because the water is poisoned. That's why the inn closed, why it's been a warehouse. Why the wells were filled with trash." Laila flung up her hands. "How could you allow yourself to be cheated? I thought Tobiah was a clever and well-connected man, but either he is an oblivious fool, or he cheated you! Which is it?"

Malachi's mouth opened and closed a few times. His brow furrowed and Sarai wondered if she would finally see him when he was truly angry. She had seen Malachi handle rude and vicious and even dangerous people with calmness and sometimes humor. She had only *heard* tales of how he could destroy a man with mere words, when the situation warranted. He could cut through the haze of wine with a look of disgust and fury, and send drunken brutes stumbling out of his inn before they could harm anyone.

Eli touched her shoulder and beckoned with a sideways tip of his head for her to follow. Sarai obeyed. Her ears seemed to ache with the effort to hear what Malachi said next, or even what Laila would say, as she followed Eli outside and across the inn courtyard, to the well closest to the gates.

"There are many ways a well can be poisoned." The big man looked down into the darkness. The rocks and broken boards and pottery that had been dropped there during the years this had been a warehouse and safe storage place were visible, piled high so no water could be seen. "Or made to *seem* poisoned. Norah says you are a healer. Is there a way to heal a poisoned well?"

"Even if there is, proving it is wholesome again will be the challenge, won't it?" The question slipped from her lips before she could really think. Then Sarai caught her breath as an idea came to her. She shook her head.

"You've thought of something."

"From scripture. Tales of the prophets in the days of the kings. When Israel was still a great nation, even after it had been divided into two countries by foolishness and ..." She sighed. Eli led her over to one of the tables and benches that had been set up in the cleaned portion of the courtyard. "The prophet, Elisha, healed a spring of water that was considered poisoned. There were miscarriages and other maladies attributed to it."

"How?" He settled on the end of the table while she took one of the benches.

"Scripture just says that he tossed in salt from a clean bowl, but my father always maintained that he must have prayed long to Adonai, for mercy and grace and healing. It is simply assumed or understood that prayers and the mercy of God undergird any miracle," she hurried to add. Sarai had the awful feeling that light in Eli's eyes meant he was going to ask her to try the same thing. Who was she to attempt to recreate a miracle from the glory days of Israel?

"That's one idea ..." He nodded and swung one muscular leg, making her think of a little boy plotting mischief. "Perhaps we should ask help or at least advice from the local healers. Even Gentiles are gifted by God," he added, with a wink and a nod. He slid off the end of the table and looked at the open gates. "Give me until noon tomorrow, yes?"

"If only I had my scrolls. I'm sure there would have been something in them about how to determine if a well is truly poisoned. What kind of poison. And yes, how to cleanse it and drive away the source."

"What kind of scrolls?" Eli asked, pausing only a few steps away from her.

Sarai told him about the scrolls Ebed had found for her father, to give her. All the writings from different countries and cultures and the lore of healer temples dedicated to foreign gods. Norah came out to join them, and she listened and reminded Sarai of a few times when they were younger. They had tested the efficacy of some of the potions and powders and pastes on sick animals.

"I have several recipes Sarai gave me, that I use to this day for headaches and sore muscles. That mint salve I give you came from the writings of a Roman physician who spent years in Gaul," Norah added.

"So if we could find scrolls, not just talk to local healers," Eli said, brow furrowed, "we could find a way to heal the well."

"I hope so, but we might just learn that the previous owner went to the healers and couldn't get help." Norah glanced over her shoulder, back at the doorway where Malachi and Laila had yet to emerge. "I pity Tobiah when Father catches up with him. I pity the merchant and the records keepers for the city who played games and thought they could trick him." She sighed. "Did trick him."

"Have you considered that the healers refused to help?" Sarai offered, and wished she hadn't thought of that, almost as soon as the words left her lips.

"Then it's a good thing we brought our own healer," her friend retorted, with a nod for punctuation.

~~~~~

By the noon deadline Eli had set, he found several merchants who claimed to have scrolls discussing healing practices. He had also located two healers within five streets of Harvest Moon Street, who were willing to talk with Sarai and give her advice. He gave her a warning, after they had left the merchants and bought three scrolls she thought would be useful. He suspected the healers agreed to let her come more out of curiosity than any real willingness to help. They were intrigued by the thought of a Jewish
~~~~~

woman, daughter of a rabbi, who could not only read and write but was willing to consult the lore of other nations.

The first healer was a fat man whose features were lost in rolls of fat, even on his face, giving his eyes a strangely slanted look. He seemed to be jammed into the massive, thronelike chair set against the wall farthest from the door of his shop. Sarai wondered if he ever got up from it. From the smell filling the dark room, she suspected he was unable to wash properly or regularly, and used incense to cover the odor of his filthy body. His head was shaved, but for a patch at the top, from which sprouted a long braid of hair. His robes were dark, with hints of crimson in the light from numerous tiny lamps that hung from the ceiling. He had three assistants, all with the odd look to their eyes and a golden cast to their skin. They dropped to their knees and touched their foreheads to the thick matting that covered the floor when Eli announced their names from the doorway.

The healer didn't give his name, and Eli didn't tell her. He was more interested in Sarai's education, the scrolls she had studied, the healing work she had done, than he was interested in the inn's poisoned water. She tried to be patient during the string of questions, spat at her one after another. The stink of incense and all the other aromas that made the air thick awakened the queasy feeling in her belly. She had to wonder what all these foreign herbs and combinations, the incense itself, the filth under the rich, cloying aromas, could be doing to the baby in her womb.

Finally, the man paused long enough Sarai thought she could start to ask her own questions.

"Are you a virgin?" the man said, when she inhaled in preparation to speak.

"She is a widow," Eli said.

"That does not answer my question."

"Why do you ask?" Sarai said.

"A wise healer always looks for an apt pupil. The best pupil is pure of heart and mind, and that is ensured by a pure body."

"I am not looking for a teacher, I am looking for information, for answers to help my friends." She decided to be grateful that the fat old man hadn't offered either of them seats, but left them standing, with several cubits of floor space between them. When her patience and endurance finally snapped, she could merely turn around and flee out the door.

He laughed. She wanted to slap him. One of his assistants giggled and crossed his eyes at her when she glanced at him.

"I heard a rumor that you know more about the poisoned wells than anyone else," Eli said, spacing his words apart in a way that made Sarai shiver a little. As if he were making a threat. Or more accurately, an accusation? "Perhaps the wells were poisoned from above, rather than below."

"When you are ready to submit to your proper role as a student and leave off posturing as a healer, then perhaps you will find those answers," the fat old man said.

"I think there are answers you will never give," Sarai said. "Please, Eli, may we leave? The stench of this place is disagreeable to my child." She rested her hands over her belly, which was still flat, mimicking the gestures of hugely pregnant women in their last months.

The fat old healer let out a shriek more appropriate to a six-year-old girl having a temper tantrum. He spilled words in some foreign tongue that seemed to emerge from his nose rather than his throat. Eli wrapped an arm around Sarai and half-carried her away. She didn't need to know the language to know the man cursed her. Laughter fought with the queasiness trying to climb up her throat. Maybe he hadn't been impertinent, asking if she was a virgin -- maybe her pregnancy somehow violated his ideas of cleanliness?

"I'm sorry," Eli said, when they finally slowed their steps, and the lingering miasma from the shop had faded from their clothes. "I think that one consorts with demons to perform the healing miracles attributed to him."

"Did you really hear that? That he might be party to poisoning the wells?"

"I've picked up many rumors. A rival innkeeper wanted to buy your inn, and several of his friends and men in his family spent some time there before people started falling sick. Some of the people I talked to mentioned he was furious when the previous owner sold the inn to a merchant, to use as a warehouse, rather than to him."

"Why would he want to buy an inn that had poisoned wells?" she mused aloud as they turned a corner. "Unless he knew the source of the poisoning and knew how to cure it."

"Why indeed?" Eli bared his teeth in a fierce grin that would have made Sarai shudder if she didn't know how loyal he was to Malachi and Norah, and by extension, to her.

That gave her ideas, so when they reached the home of the second healer, a woman named Istra, and she wasn't there, Sarai wasn't too disappointed. She saw the designs painted on the doorframe that indicated what services the woman performed, all relating to needs of women. The largest sign, of course, was that of a midwife. Chances were good this woman was tending to an expectant mother or delivering a baby.

When they returned to the inn, Nadab had come back from his own mission, asking questions of people who had been patrons of the inn years ago. His information confirmed what Eli had heard. When asked, two young men came to talk with Sarai, and described how the people had fallen ill, and could even remember the smells that no one had paid attention to until after the fact.

Chapter Four

Sarai consulted the scrolls Eli had found for her and proposed a plan to Malachi and Norah. It would be expensive, because of the rare herbs she needed to use to brew the antidote. It would also take some time to complete, and she couldn't guarantee success. While they waited for the well to heal, they could concentrate on setting up the inn, making the changes and additions. They would have time to obtain good furniture and dishes, rather than taking what was available to meet the immediate need. They would have time to remake the house on the other side of the wall to please themselves, instead of having to settle for what they could do in a limited amount of time. However, all that work would be wasted if her proposed plan for cleansing and healing the wells didn't work.

"Salt heals and cleanses," she explained. "Roman physicians use it in cleansing wounds and preventing the rotting of damaged flesh. Salt destroys plants that thrive in fresh water, molds and slimes and such, that could be poisoning the water."

"So all we have to do is throw barrels of salt into the wells?" Ebenezer asked. For once he looked more confused than his usual skeptical expression.

"That is my theory for the healing of the well in Elisha's day, but I am sure Adonai expanded on the effect. I believe poison was poured into the well, and it clung to the rocks. Perhaps it was a plant of some kind that ..." She shrugged. "I think it somehow multiplied. We need to cleanse the water thoroughly and haul away what has been tainted. We need to remove layers of rock and soil, as well as all the rubbish dropped into the wells over the years." She sighed. "And then pray to Adonai for His blessing and protection and healing, after we have done all we can."

"And then," Malachi said, "we need to convince people that we are relying solely on our own water, and we stay healthy, so they will be willing to come in."

First, Sarai and Norah worked to brew the antidote, and dosed the four men who would be climbing down into the wells to haul out the rubbish and scrape the filth off the stones. Sarai hoped this was wasted effort, and the men would show no signs of falling ill. She dosed herself when she and Laila and Seth examined the dirt scraped off the stones and the buckets of muddy water pulled up from both wells, looking for signs of unwholesome growths. Sarai found greenish-gold clumps that could have been mold or a slimy kind of lichen. The men who brought it up said they found it a handspan or two above the water level. She took that for a good sign -- it wasn't thriving in the water itself, and it wasn't predominant throughout the wells. Still, she insisted that the stones be scraped clean and smooth. The bottoms of both wells needed to be dug out, to remove nearly a cubit depth of mud and dirt that might have become contaminated by the poison over the years. Then the insides of the wells were painted with a mixture of harsh, sour wine and the antidote, to cleanse everything and fight off the slightest spore of the lichen that might have remained.

During all this, the gates of the inn were left open, so anyone passing by could see and remark on the activity. The women who went to the marketplace to buy provisions, to search for cloth for the beds and matts for the floors, for new dishes and copper and iron cauldrons for cooking, were encouraged to talk to everyone, and to answer any questions people asked. They were specifically instructed to give even more information than anyone asked for about what was being done to heal the wells.

Norah was furious, the morning she woke up before Sarai and caught her bent over the vessel for night soil, waiting for her regular morning queasiness to fade. She accused Sarai of letting herself be poisoned. When Sarai admitted to her pregnancy, Norah was even angrier.

"And what would we have done if you had lost the child, if you had risked your child or even your own life, for us, for this place?" She gestured around their shared bedroom, indicating the entire inn building.

Most of the other women came running, roused from their beds or from the kitchen by her angry, raised voice. The early risers in charge of breakfast were already at work. When the news of Sarai's pregnancy spread, most of the reactions were joyful and surprised. Several who knew Simon had divorced her promised that word would never get back to Jerusalem, and he would never know. They congratulated her for being wise enough to claim she was a widow. Several of the older women just laughed and claimed they had guessed weeks ago about the child.

"It makes sense now," Judith said, as she brought the first loaf of bread out of the new baking oven. It had been finished three days ago, built double the size of normal household ovens, in the wall between the inn and the house. "Why you tell people you're a widow. Imagine the slander if people heard you were divorced. They would think the child was the reason why that stupid man cast you off."

Before breakfast for the household of the inn had finished, everyone knew. Several of the young men gave Sarai reproachful looks, while others looked relieved. Sarai overheard some of the woman laughing over this. By listening carefully to their comments, she realized some of the young men hoped to ask her to marry one of them, once the inn settled into a daily routine. Were they frightened off by learning she was divorced rather than widowed, or because she carried a child?

Finally, enough time had passed for the antidote and cleansing to take full effect. For three days, the men drew out and carried away enough buckets of water to remove all traces of the antidote and salt used for cleansing. Norah was aghast, when Sarai insisted on being the first to try the water. Malachi understood, even if he looked suitably concerned.

"If a healer doesn't trust her own work, how can anyone else trust her?" he said, after Norah and several other women tried to convince Sarai to let someone else drink the first cup of water. "I trust in the grace and protection of Adonai, and the healing gift given to our Sarai."

~~~~~

During the cleansing of the wells, the work to prepare the inn for business continued. Years of neglect and using the building to safely store merchandise required repairs and improvements, such as digging new, deeper trenches to carry away waste and wastewater. During the cleansing, they built up the mouths of the wells and installed grates over them, to prevent any rivals or enemies from trying to poison them again. Malachi had a cistern dug within the inn itself, so they could store water against drought, and as added security against poisoning. Eli and Mattias were the head builders, and were up before dawn every day, cutting wood
~~~~~

and climbing the walls and on the roof. They replaced and extended the roofs of the rooms surrounding the courtyard, reinforced and decorated the main gate, and replaced wood that had been damaged or rotted. The most important building project, however, was Norah's idea. They dug a hole in the wall of the kitchen, and fashioned a thick wooden door, hung on sturdy iron hinges, with a strong lock. The records for the inn and the money chest would be locked up in that sturdy cupboard. The chest would be anchored to the stone sill of the cupboard with two iron chains, and have a lock as well, for double protection.

Sarai was stunned when Norah handed her copies of the keys for both locks. Her friend laughed and closed her hand around the bronze keys.

"Haven't you been listening? You are our scribe, aren't you?"

"Yes, but --" Sarai closed her mouth hard enough her teeth clacked. "You want me to handle the accounts for the inn. I'm sorry. I thought ..."

"My father taught me years ago that Elohim does not give gifts of mind and body and soul by mistake. You know how to handle accounts. You can read and write and cipher, and you are here. I hold you far more trustworthy than any man with the same skills. The man who handled those tasks on Spindle Street left Jerusalem after the Romans closed Father's inn." Norah spread her hands. "Besides, I know you. I don't know any of the managers and scribes who have come knocking on our door, trying to impress or intimidate me into giving them work."

"Thank you." Sarai opened her hand to look at the keys. "I will need a chain to hang these on. Safest around my neck, or perhaps attached to my girdle."

"I trust you in all things." She patted Sarai's cheek and then sighed, smiling, as she turned to handle yet another question called into the kitchen from the courtyard.

Laila dealt with several visits from men in rich clothes, some wearing the chain or shoulder decorations marking them as city officials, and just as many visits from soldiers. Sarai was busy each time with cleaning or comparing a new delivery of purchases against the list Norah had made and the list sent by the merchant. Sometimes she heard Laila's rich, low-toned laughter cutting through the voices and laughter of the men as she talked with them in the inn courtyard, and once in the doorway of the house. When she was truly happy or amused, Laila's laughter now was sweeter, lighter than when she had been the Rose of Sharon. Sarai always said a quick prayer, thanking Adonai for her friend's freedom from demonic control. Then she gave more thanks that Laila knew how to handle people who could cause the inn trouble before it even opened.

Several times she caught Norah and Laila in somber conversation after such visits. Norah never explained what problem had come up against them, but Sarai trusted that she wouldn't say anything if the complaint or request or question had been dealt with. Laila never called in any of the inn's workmen to stand with her when those city officials and military representatives came to visit, so that had to be a good sign.

~~~~~

"I won t truly rest easy until we are officially doing business," Norah confessed one evening, as they were preparing the meal. "All we have had to deal with are whining complaints with more imagination than substance, and rumors with even less substance. Two merchants were told we would try to do all business on credit, and they were pleasantly surprised to find we send coin with every order. If they share that news with the ones who are telling lies about us, I don't know. Is it a good sign that those who consider us a threat don't come to us themselves, but let the authorities speak for them?"

"My father dealt with some scribes and rabbis who treated him that way," Sarai offered, after she finished patting another round of bread into shape and laid it on the hot surface of the cooking pot.

This one was bronze and heated far faster, and more evenly, than the clay one they had brought with them from Jerusalem. It was also far easier to take outside and empty the ashes from the cooking fire.

"They were Hellenists, and Father confided in me that he thought they were offended before they arrived in Jerusalem, and ready to blame everyone for any ill treatment they received. He was amused, a little, by the whole ugly, ridiculous situation, so I wasn't worried." She contemplated her hands, then reached for another handful of dough to shape into a flat round of bread.

"They didn't come to our house to speak with him. Depending
~~~~~

on who Father talked to, either they stayed away because someone told them he refused to deal with Hellenists, considering them rebels against Moses' commands. Or they were extremely delicate about being Hellenists, and so feared Father's reputation as an expert in the law that they didn't want to offend him. All their questions came to him through messengers. He was quite irritated with the whole mess before they left him alone."

Norah shook her head. "I can understand how our people, no matter how devoted to the laws of Moses, would take up the ways of the Greeks and other nations they live among. Sometimes I feel as if all the world hates the tribes of Israel. What is wrong with changing your style of clothes and your language and your name, just to be a little less visible, and a little safer?"

"Where does it stop, though?" Sarai murmured.

Would Norah someday suggest they renounce the teachings of Jesus, and their belief that He had risen from the dead, for the sake of safety and comfort?

"Father never despised the Hellenists," Norah continued, "even if he found some amusement in seeing them come to the inn wearing Greek-style clothes, take a room, and emerge a few hours later in new-made clothes, to conform to Hebrew tradition. He sometimes joked that they needed to change their names from Greek to Hebrew as well, if they wanted to curry favor with the priests and scribes."

~~~~~

Malachi and Eli and the other men made certain that everyone knew the wells at the Inn of the Three Sisters had been cleansed, and the household was drawing their water solely from them. There were plenty of witnesses. People who made it their business to be near the gates of the inn saw them draw water, most of it in the morning, but throughout the day as there was need. Others who lingered in the street outside the door of the house waited to see if the women went to the nearby wells and fountain squares to draw water. On especially hot days, some of the younger men among the inn folk made a point of coming to the well closest to the gate and drawing up buckets of water to pour over themselves, when they were sweaty and dirty and hot from their labors on the roof or elsewhere outdoors.

In the week before they planned to declare the inn open for
~~~~~

business, anyone who went to the well to draw water made a point of offering some to the people who lingered outside. Finally, a brash young man who wore his beard braided in the Phoenician style took the dare. Or perhaps he was shamed into it by the teasing of the other young men who waited farther away from the gates. He took one small sip and his eyes widened. He paused, and Rebekah, who had offered him the dipper of water, said later she thought he was going to spit it out on the cobblestones. Or even on her. Then he took another, longer drink from the dipper. His eyes closed and he swallowed slowly, then he took a third drink, dropped the dipper on the ground, so it clattered, and walked away, shaking his head.

Istra, the healer woman and midwife Sarai had never been able to visit, came to the inn that afternoon. A number of people followed in her wake, some dressed in foreign styles, some looking important enough to be city officials. Sarai was in her bedroom, resting and indulging in some self-pity. She had dreamed of Hannah the night before, and wanted badly to be able to compare her symptoms and experiences as her pregnancy grew. Dinah came for her, saying the healer woman wanted to speak with her.

"The water is sweet," the tall, big-eyed woman announced as Sarai crossed the courtyard to the well closest to the gate. She wore her thick, stark white hair braided into a crown on the back of her head and she stood straight and strong. "How have you made it even more wholesome than it was before?"

"El Shaddai has honored her with the gift of healing, as well as wisdom and scholarly skills," Laila called from the walkway on the second floor, close to the gates.

"Yes," Sarai said, grateful for the help. All the people gathered in the front of the courtyard, and spilling out into the street, reminded her too much of the square in front of the governor's palace, even though they were for the most part quiet and attentive. "The healing came through the grace of El Shaddai. I was blessed to be the vessel of His power."

"Hmm, perhaps," the woman said. Then she introduced herself, and laughed, gently, when Sarai apologized for never returning. She had been invited to visit and consult with her, after all. "The gods work through us, but we are required to do more work than they do, to earn blessings from them. What did you do?"

Some of the crowd had left by the time Sarai fetched the scrolls she had consulted for the antidote, and invited Istra to sit. Malachi joined them, and then several of the men who had cleaned out the wells, to explain their part. By the time Istra had the full story of all the work involved, the herbs, the precautions, most of those waiting by the gates had drifted away, likely bored. Sarai suspected some of them had hoped the revered healer woman would condemn what they had done to heal the well, or even declare it was still poisoned.

Istra and several men and women, leaders of different guilds of crafters, accepted Norah's invitation to join them for the evening meal. Sarai had to laugh, when Malachi led the way in performing many evening worship rituals that the household in general had neglected since leaving Jerusalem. She supposed that her and Laila's words, giving praise to Adonai for the healing, had influenced him. Maybe he felt guilty, or maybe he simply felt required to support what they had said. She was surprised that Istra was familiar with many Jewish practices.

She was even more surprised, and a little amused, when from that day forward, she heard people refer to the inn as the Inn of the Healer, almost as much as they did the Inn of the Three Sisters.

~~~~~

Jasper came to visit the day Malachi sent Nadab to request that the Inn of the Three Sisters now be listed at all of Damascus' gates as open for business. Sarai was alone in the house, because Norah and Laila were occupied with painting the last decorations on the doors of the upper level rooms around the courtyard. She was expecting a delivery of grain and a new upper millstone for the hand mill to be installed in the courtyard, for the use of guests, so she didn't hesitate to open the door. Jasper didn't smile, he wasn't sweaty, and he wasn't accompanied by the centurion, whose name she still hadn't learned. She didn't recognize him for a moment or two. Four men in the short tunics and leggings of Phoenician workmen stood behind him. Their arms were bare and bulged with muscles and scars. Two wore bronze rings around their upper arms that made her think of bronze bindings for doors, to reinforce them.

Adonai, please, protect us.

All she could think in those few seconds, when her heart tripled in pace, was that Jasper had come regarding some complaint
~~~~~

he finally believed. Had he brought these men to ransack the house, to look for proof of the claims against the inn?

"Gatekeeper." She gave him a head-and-shoulders bow and spread her arms in welcome, as if this were her own home and she were once again a lady of some standing. "How may I be of service?"

"You are not the woman who runs this inn." His frown deepened, making her heart skip a beat, then she lost her breath when he smiled. "No, you are the little widow." He made a waving gesture. "Forgive an old man who can't remember the names that go with pretty faces."

He hurried on before she could do more than nod, and give the four stolid, dark-tanned workmen behind him another glance. Why were they there? If this was an official visit, wouldn't he have brought Roman soldiers? Was this an unofficial visit, with some bullying or threats?

"Tell me, you came from Jerusalem, yes?" Jasper took a step closer, and without thinking Sarai took a step back.

She wished she knew where the closest knife was, but the kitchen was in the next room. Could she run fast enough to reach the kitchen and shout for help before someone caught her, dragged her away or did worse things to her?

"Yes. Why?"

"Have you received word of what has been happening in Jerusalem?" Now he glanced at the man standing to his right.

"No. Nothing. Why?"

"What have you heard of that troublemaker rabbi?"

"Gatekeeper, my father was a rabbi of some high standing. He often remarked that every self-proclaimed rabbi and self-appointed prophet was destined to come to Jerusalem to cause some kind of trouble, because it was against the law of Elohim for a prophet, false or true, to die anywhere but Jerusalem."

That earned a chuckle from Jasper. Sarai could only look at one face at a time of the men behind him. One flinched at her words. He looked more disappointed than angry. Something coiled tight inside her relaxed. Just a little.

"Meaning Jerusalem is filled with troublemakers, especially those who claim to hear the voice of your One God." Jasper nodded. "I am thinking of the one called the Galilean or the Nazarene. Why two names?"

"Nazareth is a town in the territory of Galilee. Jesus had many followers among the Galileans, especially fishermen on the Sea of Galilee." Her breath caught and her voice broke on the last word, as the four men all seemed to stand taller, more alert.

"Ah, then you do know of whom I speak. Have you heard anything new about this man? Jesus, you said?"

"There was much turmoil at Passover. While we were making preparations to come here. The Sanhedrin had Him arrested on charges of blasphemy and turned Him over to the governor to be executed."

"That was more than two months ago. Haven't you heard anything new?"

"Jesus was executed." She clenched her fists, hidden inside the long sleeves of her tunic, and silently begged Adonai to either drive these men away or send someone to rescue her.

"Is that all you have heard?" the man standing on the far right of the four blurted.

"Do you know anything of what happened at the Feast of Weeks?" the man next to him growled.

"Please, I don't know what you want. Why are you asking all these questions?" Her voice cracked again.

"She doesn't know anything," the man standing behind Jasper said, his voice pitched low. "We're frightening her."

"She's wise to be afraid, after all the things that have happened," the man next to him said. He offered Sarai a crooked smile and looked away.

Maybe that was his idea of an apology? That was little comfort, with her heart racing and stealing her breath.

"Gatekeeper Jasper?" Tobiah appeared behind them, coming from the street. He nudged aside two of the men. "Is there some problem?" He gave Sarai a wide-eyed glance, as he stepped into the doorway and put himself between the five men and her.

She wanted to smile, she wanted to shake her head and laugh like Laila did, and say nothing was wrong. Her mouth was dry and her lips trembled, so it was all she could do to press them flat.

"These fellows are new to Damascus." Jasper stepped back and gestured at the four workmen. "They had some questions about events in Jerusalem, and since the innkeeper came from Jerusalem

..." He spread his arms in a gesture of defeat. "I thought they would have more recent, more sure news and information."

"You heard her. She is the daughter of a rabbi." The first man gave Sarai another glance and then turned his back on her.

She had never been so relieved to be summarily dismissed as beneath notice.

"Whatever she knows, it isn't what we need to know," he added.

Tobiah nodded to Sarai and stepped outside again. She hurried to close the door. Gently, as quietly as possible. She leaned back against it and closed her eyes and listened to her heart slow its frantic fluttering, so loud she barely heard the voices of the men speaking outside. She was grateful when they walked away.

~~~~~

Sarai wasn't sure what she expected, once the Inn of the Three Sisters had opened its doors for business. Norah couldn't really tell her, because the inn on Spindle Street had been established before she had been born. Malachi had inherited the Jerusalem inn from his father, and his grandfather before him. News spread quickly, and many of the same people who had lingered in the gates, watching all the work over the course of nearly a month, continued to linger, to look in, to ask questions. Slowly, new arrivals in Damascus came to use the caravansary side of the inn. Gradually, men came to make use of the rooms available for meetings. Business increased when word spread that Norah and her women would provide feasts, the food either prepared in her kitchen or in the kitchens of the homes where the celebration would take place. Twice, large parties hired the upper level for long meals with multiple courses. Gradually, men made it a practice to come to the inn to sit in the shadows and cool at the end of the day, to relax and talk, drink wine, and enjoy the food Norah prepared.

They knew the Inn of the Three Sisters had become established and accepted in Damascus when Norah was hired to cook for a wedding feast. The fathers of both bride and groom had eaten three times at the inn's table while conducting business with visitors to Damascus. They were pleased and intrigued by several dishes they had never tasted before. Tobiah had done business with both families in the past, and he urged Norah to consider the request because it would be good for the inn's reputation. Also, he vouched
~~~~~

for both fathers as honorable men. What did it matter that they were Gentiles? Norah and her people were living in Damascus now, a vital crossroads city for many trade routes, and they would only harm themselves if they held too tightly to Hebrew traditions and laws and practices of separation.

Sarai was just as excited as everyone else, when Norah shared the news. She had also brought back a heavy purse of coins to purchase all the food for the feast. Tobiah was right, of course. She pushed aside that little niggling fear that had lingered ever since the four Phoenicians had come to the door with Jasper. To survive, the Inn of the Three Sisters had to do business with everyone who came with honorable requests. Insulting their neighbors would bring them the wrong kind of notice.

Sarai turned away from the happy crowd of inn workers to go into the house to put the purse away for safekeeping. A man came through the gates into the courtyard. He stood tall, dressed in good clothes that hinted at wealth and high social standing, with a Grecian style to his mantle and the neat trimming of his beard, yet wearing a prayer shawl, embroidered with Hebrew letters. A Hellenist, then. She put on the smile she had learned to give to all strangers, which welcomed and yet promised nothing.

"Welcome to the Inn of the Three Sisters," she said, spreading her arms as she approached him. The purse hung heavy in her left hand, but that couldn't be remedied now. "How may we serve?"

The man smiled, his gaze traveling over her, and he nodded. Sarai shivered, though she had no idea why. The sensation of a whisper coming from over her shoulder, indecipherable and yet oddly clear, made her think this man was no danger. And yet she was afraid, chilled, for two heartbeats.

"I come to you in the grace and peace of our risen Lord, the Christ," he said, and gave her a head-and-shoulders bow of far more respect than any innkeeper would ever expect.

"Do you?" slipped out before she could think. Fear surged up harsh and hot in her throat.

The man took a step back, eyes widening in surprise. Then he smiled and shook his head. His expression turned to that warm mixture of compassion and amusement that sometimes had made her want to slap her father, when he had turned it on her.

"Child, there is good reason to fear, but not to live in fear.

Indeed, our Master has spoken to me through the Spirit that was given at the Feast of Weeks and instructed me to come here. I am to share the message Peter spoke and encourage all of you in the service to which He has called us."

"How can we be of service?" Norah said, stepping up next to Sarai.

"Ah, yes, you are Malachi's daughter. You have his eyes."

"You are not a familiar face … how do you know my father?"

Sarai choked on the need to protest that he could have been making a guess.

"I met him infrequently when I went to Jerusalem on business. He can vouch for me."

"I will send for him to come momentarily," Norah said, and that only added to Sarai's sense of uneasiness. Malachi had left Damascus on business three days ago.

"You cannot send for him, because he will not return until tomorrow morning." The man smiled, neither looking offended nor upset, nor even threatening.

"Are you saying my father met you while he was away on business?" She turned, gesturing further into the inn courtyard. "Where are my manners? Be welcome."

"Perhaps I should state who I am, before you allow me any further inside?"

"Yes, you should," Eli called, crossing from the dispersing knot of inn workers to join them.

"My name is Ananias, and Damascus was my home at one time. I heard the news of the rabbi from Nazareth, and I went in search of Him, to learn if prophecy was at last being fulfilled. I tested Adonai, much like Gideon, by selling my home and business, in anticipation of spending the rest of my life traveling with and learning from the Master." He shook his head, his smile twisting just a little, into what Sarai could only label a wry or rueful look. "I thought never to return to Damascus, and yet the Spirit has led me back here."

Sarai heard footsteps and leaned to look around him. Two men leading three donkeys, all pulling carts, came into the gates of the inn. Before she could say anything, Timaeus hurried past the four of them and greeted the newcomers. Norah gestured with a tip of her head and led Ananias to the shelter of the serving table. The four sat on benches, away from the table but still under the cover of the canopy, before Ananias continued.

He told them how he had traveled with the core group of Jesus' disciples for more than a year, and how he had been sent on an incredible adventure of learning faith and feeling the power of El Shaddai work through them. Seventy of the disciples had gone out with nothing -- no spare clothes or food or money -- and ministered to the needs of the people they met. The power from Adonai flowed through them to heal and to cast out evil spirits, and to share Jesus' words to the people of Judea. Ananias admitted freely his disappointment that he wasn't invited closer, to be part of the inner circle, the twelve who surrounded Jesus day and night.

Chapter Five

"The Master had to teach me humility and to put aside my pride. I thought I was a highly educated man, worthy of the position." Ananias shook his head. "I wrestled with disappointment and jealousy on the night of the Passover feast, because I wasn't included among those who sat at the table with the Master. I wasn't there when they went to the garden for prayer, and the betrayer led the soldiers in search of our Lord. Always, I have stood several steps back from where I wanted to be. I was there, but far down the hillside when Adonai took the Master up into the clouds and restored Him to His side in the heavenlies."

Sarai flinched. Norah caught hold of her free hand and the two shared wide-eyed glances. She hoped she had mis-heard Ananias. Did he truly mean Jesus had left? He was no longer in the world? What would they do without Him? Sarai had cherished some small hope that someday, she would see Jesus again, be able to talk to Him, perhaps ask some questions, gain some small understanding and peace.

"Always, I was one among many, and the Master has had to teach me to be glad in my humble position. To serve willingly and with joy no matter how menial the task. Now my greatest test has come. May I prove worthy. May I prove that I have learned my lessons well. May I not fail Him." He looked from Norah to Eli to Sarai. "At the Feast of Weeks, the Spirit from El Shaddai fell upon us, as was spoken by the Prophet Joel. We spoke in languages none of us ever learned, and Jews from many nations who were in Jerusalem for the feast understood us. The Spirit filled Peter, and he spoke with power and confidence, in the same wisdom and strength that the Master displayed while He was with us. That day, hundreds were added to the ranks of those who believe in and obey and serve the Christ. I had hoped to spend the rest of my days learning from those who walked daily with Jesus, serving them, using my worldly wealth to provide for their needs."

Ananias sighed and his smile widened. He shook his head. "I must learn never to make plans that will please me without considering first what will please the Spirit that Adonai has gifted to me. As soon as I made those plans, as soon as I set myself to devise a strategy to gain that position of what I thought was full humility and service ... the Spirit spoke in my heart. Almost an audible voice in the room. Yes, almost an audible voice. Frightening and yet comforting. Terrifying, to know just how small I am, standing in the presence of the Almighty. And yet exhilarating to know that He finds me useful, and He knows my name."

"Jesus sent you back to Damascus?" Norah guessed.

"Exactly." He laughed, spreading his arms, as if inviting them to join in the joke. "Yes, you are quite right to doubt me," he said, nodding to Sarai. "You wonder what kind of profit I can find in deceiving you."

Her face burned in sharp contrast to the chill that flashed through her. Ananias spoke her thoughts almost before they were clear in her mind. Was this proof that the Spirit of Adonai spoke to him? Was he a prophet?

"Spiritual treasure, not worldly wealth. I am to serve the Master's disciples who come to Damascus. My duty is to prepare, to gather disciples and teach, to strengthen, and to wait." He shook his head. "For what, I do not know. The Spirit's proof that I heard correctly was to give me the name of this inn, but not its location. When I asked, I heard all the news I needed to confirm our Master's guidance in this matter. Imagine my surprise and delight, to learn my friend Malachi was here. Truly a gift from Adonai."

"Have things changed for the better in Jerusalem?" Norah's voice cracked.

"When God moves, a wise man prepares for Satan to retaliate. When I left Jerusalem, the disciples stood in the favor and admiration of most of Jerusalem. They are performing all the miracles that Jesus did when He was among us, speaking and walking in the full power of the Spirit. I know the leaders of our people and the Romans will not be intimidated by public feeling for long. When they strike ... well, perhaps you were sent here, unknowing, to prepare a sanctuary for any who escape and flee here to safety."

Ananias told them a few more details of the day the Spirit flooded over the gathered believers before inn business intruded. He apologized for taking up so much of their time and promised to return that evening, when they could talk uninterrupted. Then he left, after raising his hands and praying a blessing on each of them. Sarai couldn't shake the oddest impression, until long after he had departed, that he had lingered twice as long over her blessing. She had shuddered when he spoke of her being fruitful in her exile. Yes, everyone knew she was a widow, but how many people, outside their small trusted family of the inn, knew she was pregnant?

Norah and Eli had their doubts about Ananias, and they were visibly worried that he claimed to be a friend of Malachi. What if he said that because he not only knew Malachi was away, but would not be returning? Sarai put the purse of coins away securely and was in and out of the kitchen a dozen times over the next hour, while Norah worked and spoke with Eli. She listened but didn't catch all their conversation, just enough threads and fragments to know they talked themselves into deeper doubts.

"There could be some truth in what he's told us," Eli said later that day, as he and Norah worked over the tally of supplies they would need to create the wedding feast. "Enough truth that he's trying to set himself up as a leader." He glanced at Sarai, who settled down on a bench nearby, where she could check the numbers once he and Norah were finished. "That sort of thing has happened hundreds of times through the centuries. A prophet arises, gathers followers, is destroyed by evil rulers, and then his followers scatter. They separate into small clusters, with each teacher sharing his own version of what the prophet taught."

"But Ananias admitted that he has been learning humility and not to seek a position of authority," Sarai offered.

"What better way to convince us that he is a humble man?" Norah ground her knuckles into her temples, a sure sign of a fierce headache threatening to attack her. "What better way to trick us into wanting him to be our leader, because we think he doesn't seek power?"

"True." She sighed. "There is just one problem."

"What is that, little one?" Eli put down the wax tablet he and Norah had been scribing on, smoothing the figures to erase them, and starting over multiple times.

"All the other prophets you mentioned did die, but Jesus returned to life. What good will it do His followers to separate into groups, each making their own changes to His teachings, when He is here to correct and rebuke them? How can you hide your betrayal from the very Son of God, and hope He will not come to correct you?"

"Yes, but that could be part of the truth Ananias told us. Jesus returned to Adonai in the heavens."

"Why would He do that when we need Him to lead us and teach us?"

"He is the image of the Unseen One," Norah said. "Who are we to understand His ways and reasons and plans?"

"I can't believe that He would simply abandon us."

"Neither can I." She sighed and gestured at the cauldron of water constantly kept sitting over a firepot. "Will you make me that willow bark tisane? Whatever you do, it works better than when anyone else makes it."

Eli raised himself from the stool with a grunt and a groan. "We would be wise to walk about the city, speaking with our friends, and learn what people here know about Ananias."

He stepped through the door to the next room, heading for the door of the house. Sarai paused in setting up the mortar and pestle to grind the dried willow bark. Norah sat in silence, watching him until he pulled the door closed behind him.

"I can't help thinking about those four men the gatekeeper brought to our door a few days ago," Norah said. "They were trying to find out about something that happened in Jerusalem. What if something did happen, reason enough for Ananias to come back to Damascus?"

"I'm sorry."

"For what?" She tried to smile, but winced and pressed her fingers across her closed eyes.

"I was so afraid, I didn't think to ask any questions or learn what they were trying to find out from me."

"No, you were wise to tell them nothing. Until friends come to us from Jerusalem, or my father returns, how can we be sure of anything? How can we know who to trust?"

By nightfall, Eli and the other men had learned that Ananias indeed had once lived in Damascus. Tobiah confirmed that the other man had made his living as an inspector for merchants and city officials, with a reputation for honesty and integrity, invulnerable to bribery or threats. Several sources had repeated the same proverb about him, nearly word-for-word: when dishonest workers or lower-level officials heard Ananias was coming to inspect their work or their records, they confessed immediately, rather than be shamed by having their misdeeds or mistakes revealed in public forum.

Ananias had returned to the city four days ago. He had visited his former acquaintances to tell them of the teachings of Jesus of Nazareth. The Jewish leaders who had always criticized him for being a Hellenist, accusing him of allowing Greek ways to dilute his Hebrew upbringing, had not yet condemned him for following this new teacher. Those who paid attention to such things expected it to start soon. They were still gathering up the news of what had been happening in Jerusalem and judging for themselves what to believe.

"I find belief hard, even as I want to believe him," Norah admitted, when the women had gathered in the kitchen to eat the evening meal. The men usually ate in the courtyard with the guests, to hear what news had come from other cities. "To have someone among us to whom the Spirit of the Living God speaks ... that would be a blessing and great comfort."

~~~~~

Sarai was alone in the courtyard, filling a jar of water from the well after dinner. She heard the scrape of a sandal on the cobblestones and turned, bracing to be accosted by one of the guests. One man had watched her a little too intently when she helped bring the long baskets of fresh bread, herbed oil, and olives to the men who had gathered around the brazier to eat dinner. His face was unfamiliar among the growing number of regular customers. Sarai didn't yet have enough experience with the behavior of men to predict how they would treat her, depending on what they heard about her. She had yet to decide if Laila was right, and being known as a widow would protect her, or it made her an even more desirable target.

"Our Lord bless you." Ananias smiled and gave her a little head-bow.

"May His grace shine upon you," she murmured, and let her jar settle back on the lip of the well. "If you wish to be seated, I can run for Norah, or perhaps you wish to speak with Eli?"

"In time. What I have to say to you is best done in private."
~~~~~

"Say -- to me?"

"You doubt my testimony, the calling and leading of the Spirit." A brief chuckle startled her, so she stayed still when her first reaction should have been to flee. "That is wise. I fear during the brief time when the disciples stand in favor with the common people, there will be many who claim to be with us, in the hopes of profit. In hopes of influencing seekers, leading them astray." His smile faded. "I know who you are. "

He raised a hand slightly to quiet her when she opened her mouth. Sarai wasn't sure if she intended to deny his words or perhaps call for help.

"The Spirit told me you were the daughter of Rabbi Eliakim ben Levi after I had left this place. You do well to doubt me. But hear me, Sarai, so cruelly cast off in punishment for your faith. I give you proof that I have been sent by the Spirit, and that I will stand beside you in the days of questioning and doubt. Your joy will be tempered with doubt and fear and anger. Hold fast, daughter. Be strong. Do not let your faith waver. Trust our Master, who has sent you away to safety among friends who will defend you and uphold you with their loyalty and love."

She reached for the jar, intending to snatch it up and flee. Where was Norah or Eli or any of the dozen others who should have noticed someone had entered the slowly emptying courtyard, and come out to investigate? If they were her defenders, why weren't they here now?

"Rejoice, as Hannah and Sarah rejoiced." He reached out and lightly rested his hands on her shoulders. Sarai couldn't move her feet, though her body trembled and she thought her knees might fold and tumble her to the stones. "You carry a daughter, and you are to name her Pearl, in memory of the story you heard the Master tell, when you first saw Him on the road to Jerusalem. Her name will be a reminder for your husband, to break his spirit and awaken him to his foolishness, and begin his healing."

"I have no husband," she said, her voice a rasp like sand blowing across stone.

"What Adonai has joined together into one person, no one can separate. Do not fear," he continued, as she stared into his eyes. "As the psalms tell us, the joy of our Lord is our strength. That joy will be your strength. Your child will be born at sunset on a rainy day, as sign and seal and surety that I have been brought here to teach and to help and to guide, and to prepare for the bitter days that surely lie ahead."

Then Mattias' voice rang out across the courtyard from the floor above them, calling greeting. Sarai trembled and tried to swallow. Her mouth felt like sand filled it. Somehow, she found the strength to step back. Ananias nodded to her again, his smile softening, and turned to greet Mattias as he hurried down the stairs. Sarai gathered up her jar, clutching it to her chest instead of bracing it on her shoulder. She only got as far as the steps up into the kitchen, before she had to set the jar down on the threshold. She sat down on the bottom step, her arms wrapped around her middle, and watched as Mattias greeted Ananias and led him to one of the rooms off the courtyard, to meet with the other men.

The scraping of the jar being dragged off the stone sill startled Sarai, so she leaped to her feet and nearly fell off them again. Laila paused, the jar braced in one arm, and started to laugh. Then her expression darkened to concern.

"Little one? What's wrong? What happened?" She held out her hand.

Sarai staggered through the door with Laila's guidance.

"What has happened?" Norah stepped into the kitchen, holding a lamp high.

"Ananias has returned." Sarai wished the wineskin from dinner was still lying out, but someone had put it back on its peg in the cool chamber in the foundation. She needed something to moisten her mouth.

"What did he do?" Norah nearly dropped the lamp in her hurry to put it down on the nearest table and catch hold of Sarai's other hand.

"He told me ..." She shook her head and turned to glance over her shoulder into the courtyard. The door hung half-open, but she couldn't hear any voices coming through the evening quiet. "He gave me a sign that he was sent by Adonai. I can scarcely believe him, but ..." She shook her head and tugged her hands free to press them against her face. It felt cold. Likely white and bloodless.

Perhaps if this announcement had been a happy one, if she had been giving the news to Simon, she might be flushed, blushing with joy.

How could this be a happy announcement? She was a divorced woman with a child in her belly. When her belly increased, someone would accuse her of adultery, would point to the child as proof that she had been justly cast off by her husband.

Ananias had told her to rejoice, as Hannah and Sarah had rejoiced when they conceived after years of barrenness. How could she rejoice?

"Little one?" Laila nudged her toward one of the benches against the table and made her sit. Norah joined them. "What is this sign, and why does it distress you so?"

"He told me I will birth a daughter, and I am to name her Pearl."

Strange, how easily the words came out, when she thought her tongue would freeze or even break off before she got the words past her teeth.

"But how --" Norah shook her head. "Someone gossiped. Though we asked everyone to be quiet, to spare you, someone knows, or they guessed. How hard is it to pretend to prophesy?"

"Who are we to question the means and choices and tools of El Shaddai?" Laila said. "Well, that is one fear relieved. If Simon ever hears that you bore his child, he won't go to all the trouble of coming to Damascus to take a daughter from you. Not like he might with a son."

"True." Sarai thought she could breathe again.

~~~~~

That Sabbath, the household headed for the synagogue to worship. Sarai walked half a step back from Norah and Laila, encouraging the other two to speak without fully including her. She found it hard to participate in any conversations that didn't spin out more tangled thoughts, like uneven threads coming off an unbalanced spindle. Ever since Ananias had come to them with his signs of proof that the Spirit of Adonai had indeed spoken to him, her mind and her emotions had tossed about like a ship on a stormy sea. She was relieved that the chances of Simon taking her child away had nearly disappeared -- that is, if she really did birth a daughter. Ananias' words awakened the anger she thought she had put aside, if not released. She didn't like knowing she was still angry with Simon. More disturbing, she thought that some of the men who worked for Malachi now looked at her differently, when
~~~~~

the news about her child became common knowledge. After all, her child would provide proof that Ananias had been sent. Everyone in the household knew now. She couldn't interpret the expressions of some of the men, especially the younger ones, but they treated her differently. Some were distant, some even looked hurt at times. She blamed Simon for that, and her anger increased, along with the awful feeling that she might be in the wrong.

Eli and Jonas moved up on either side of the three women, catching her attention. She dropped back another step, to allow the two men to speak with them. Mattias startled her with a hand on her shoulder as he fell into step next to her.

"Walk faster," he said, and gestured with his chin for her to watch Eli. "Someone is following us. They were waiting as we came through the gates and have been catching up, a few steps at a time, every time we pass another street."

Sarai barely caught herself before she looked over her shoulder. Letting the followers know they had been seen would be foolish, and perhaps encourage them to move even faster and catch up with them.

"Who could they be?"

"They don't look like Jews. Not even Hellenists." He nudged her shoulder, nearly making her stumble before she picked up her pace and moved closer between Norah and Laila.

Sarai scolded herself for being so wrapped up in her thoughts that she hadn't paid attention to their path through the city or their surroundings. Especially the men who had been waiting when they came through the inn gates. She looked ahead, since it was foolish and would slow her pace if she looked behind. Ananias was coming toward them.

"Our Lord bless you and keep you and make His face shine upon you," Ananias greeted them. He raised both hands, fingers spread in the sign of Shaddai. Then his gaze slid beyond them and his smile widened. "Ah, good, you found them."

"Found who?" Eli said, turning. His words ended on a growl as his thick brows lowered.

Sarai turned and had to lean to the right to see around Mattias.

For three racing heartbeats, she didn't recognize the four men who quickened their pace for maybe ten more steps, then stopped just outside of arm's reach of Caleb, who walked in the rear of their household group. The four men bowed to them. A gasp escaped her as the tallest one, on the far right, met her gaze. She remembered those deep blue eyes. Now she knew them. They were the four Phoenicians who had come to the door with Jasper, asking if she knew about events in Jerusalem.

She couldn't look away, caught in that blue gaze, and barely heard as Ananias introduced his four friends to them. Alexius, Cosimo, Kratos, and Iason. Kratos had converted to belief in Adonai almost a full year ago, and managed to persuaded his cousins and brother to accompany him to worship on the Sabbath at least once each month. He had seen the inn household at the synagogue where he had chosen to worship, and where he went with questions about Adonai. Rabbi Amos welcomed his questions and said he enjoyed their friendly arguments, especially when his brother and cousins joined in.

"We find this new prophet, Jesus of Nazareth, most interesting," Alexius said, after Ananias suggested they all resume walking, since they were heading to the same place.

"Less painful," Cosimo said. That earned a glare from his brother, Kratos, and a snort from Iason and Mattias, who walked together, several steps behind Sarai.

"Do you follow His teachings?" Alexius continued, after several steps of silence.

Sarai looked up and found he had maneuvered to walk beside her. She swallowed hard and fought the urge to tug her veil completely across her face. Why wasn't Mattias hurrying to put himself between her and this Phoenician? He didn't accept and trust him, simply because Ananias called these four men his friends, did he?

"We have much to learn," she said, nearly tripping over her tongue and her own feet.

"I apologize."

"For what?"

"We frightened you. My brother was rude."

She glanced back at Iason, and a tiny sputter of laughter escaped, surprising her, when she remembered the comment he had made.

"He was right, in a way. My father was a rabbi, a teacher of the law, and ordinarily that would mean you could learn nothing from me."

"If he was a Pharisee like most of them," Norah said. "Which he was not. Rabbi Eliakim ben Levi was condemned and cast out of the synagogue and the Sanhedrin. He chose to believe the Messiah would not come as an avenger and destroyer, but first as a good shepherd. No, the daughter of a Pharisee would know nothing about the Law and the Prophets or prophecy. She would not know how to read or write." She wrinkled up her nose at Sarai, who widened her eyes and shook her head slightly, silently begging her not to say so much. Certainly not about her. "No, Sarai is our scribe and our accounts keeper at the inn. She can read and write and cypher and she has already caught two merchants trying to cheat us, believing she didn't know the difference between a bath and a bushel."

What was wrong with Norah? She was as chatty as Ruth, though not as sharp-tongued and critical.

"What are you talking about?" Eli moved up on Sarai's other side, so she felt just slightly trapped between the two men, both of them more than a head taller than her.

Kratos laughed and hurried to explain the visit they had made several days ago. They had been waiting for Ananias to return from Jerusalem, as promised by messenger. Merchants and messengers had told too many conflicting stories about the events in Jerusalem. Having heard from Jasper about the Inn of the Three Sisters, and the people who had come so recently from Jerusalem, and having seen them in the synagogue, they had thought to find more accurate stories and facts instead of just speculation. He apologized again for frightening Sarai.

"I want to believe this teacher did come back to life," Iason said. "That gives us all hope. Have any of you seen this Jesus since that day?"

Only Ananias had seen Jesus since the resurrection, and then only from a distance. Sarai thought something in his grave expression, his reluctance to say much on the subject, hinted at a great deal more to the story. From the expressions on her companions' faces, they had the same thoughts. She thought about the conversation several time during the worship in the synagogue.

Rabbi Amos, the eldest of the synagogue leaders, read from several prophets. Later, Sarai couldn't recall which ones. That spoke eloquently enough of her distraction. She stayed as still as she could on her bench in the women's gallery and tried not to hear the whispering among the women and children all around her. Why had the lack of focus in those surrounding her never bothered her until now? Had she always been able to ignore them, but now that she couldn't focus, she blamed them for her lack of discipline?

Sarai barely heard the announcement of the psalm to be sung. The women around her stood and she had to hurry to get to her feet. Laila hooked their arms together and patted her hand. Sarai didn't dare look at her, even knowing she wouldn't be condemning. If anything, her smile would be sympathetic, inviting Sarai to laugh at herself.

When they descended from the women's gallery after worship, Norah stepped away. Sarai didn't have time to wonder where she had gone, when three women approached her, wanting to know if the rumors were true and she was not only a trained midwife, but she had the approval of the healer, Istra. The trio were Anna, Michal, and Miriam, a young woman, her mother, and aunt. Anna had just learned she was pregnant, and she did not want to have to depend on the aging midwife who lived closest to their home. The woman was rumored to have turned into a drunkard since the deaths of her husband and son. Sarai was sure some other social currents were involved. She hadn't been in Damascus long enough to be aware of all the gossip, the hierarchies, and who to trust and who to snub and who to dismiss as a habitual liar. Laila came to her rescue and suggested they all meet to talk on another day. It was the Sabbath, after all. They agreed, and Sarai saw all three women looking over their shoulders as they left the synagogue. Most likely, she suspected, they were afraid the old midwife was close enough to hear they didn't want to use her services.

She had just thanked Laila for her help when Norah came looking for them. She announced she had invited Ananias to come eat with them. Fortunately, only Ananias. Sarai wasn't sure what she felt about the four Phoenicians. Ananias' trust in them didn't quite vouch for them, because she wasn't sure yet she trusted him.

Several of the inn's men had gone home ahead of them, to deal with any business that might have appeared while they were away. Only half the household could go to worship on the Sabbath, and they took turns. There would likely be new customers to be settled by the time they returned to the inn. Perhaps this was the Sabbath, but the Inn of the Three Sisters still worked, whatever needed to be done, even if sundown and the end of the Sabbath was still a handful of hours away.

They were two streets away from Harvest Moon Street when Chillion, an orphan boy Ebenezer had taken in, met them, urging them to hurry back to the inn. A merchant and his six servants and two wagons had left three days earlier than planned. Norah had given him a slightly reduced price because he planned to stay so long, and because he brought another merchant to the inn.

The second merchant, his five servants and six camels were packing to leave, again several days early, as their group stepped into the courtyard. Ebenezer came running, distraught, to report that the first merchant had argued with him about the price he had agreed on with Norah, and wanted more of his money returned than he was due for leaving three days early. Ebenezer was not good with numbers, but he was very good with sending messengers running for soldiers and other authorities, to accuse the departing merchant of thievery. The man had stopped demanding his coins and fled with his servants.

Eli stomped over to where the second merchant was now haranguing his servants with doubled intensity to pack and leave. Norah apologized to Ananias and told Mattias to take two men to search the inn's supplies, to see if anything had been stolen.

"Do you think they chose now to leave, despite what they said before, because they know we are Jews?" Laila said, as she and Sarai led Ananias over to the table under the canopy. They would take care of their guest while the others attended to inn business.

"Everyone for several streets around knows how hard Norah is to bully and browbeat, and how clever Sarai is with numbers," Ananias offered. "Yes, if those two men wanted to cheat you, they would wait until you were gone, and try to confuse the servants."

"He couldn't have gotten any money," Sarai said. "I keep the key to the chest with me, and the copies are hidden, and no one knows where the money box is hidden."

"We *think* it is hidden," Laila said. She and Sarai exchanged wide-eyed glances, then she apologized to Ananias and they both hurried through the inn and into the house.

Nothing looked disturbed, and Sarai was afraid to move

benches and tables and open doors, just in case someone watched from hiding, to see where she checked on the household valuables. Later, those who had stayed to take care of the inn affirmed that no one had gotten into the house or anywhere near where the money and account books were stored.

However, they discovered a possible explanation for the first merchant's hasty departure and his willingness to leave after only a token argument about returning his money. Myrtle, a new servant girl, was missing. Rhoda said she had seen her flirting with the merchant. Myrtle's older brother escorted her to the inn every morning and came for her every evening when she finished her duties, washing clothes and helping with the sewing and mending that brought in more income for the inn. Her daily earnings were given to her brother, and Mattias reported that he had heard Myrtle argue with him over that three times, just in the eight days since she had started working for them. Myrtle had arrived at the inn before the household left for the synagogue, but she was nowhere to be found now.

Chapter Six

"I will speak with her father." Eli stomped away on his errand, just moments before one of the errand boys returned with Sylvanus, the captain in charge of the gates where the merchant had tried to leave the city.

Sarai thought Norah came near to tears when the soldier reported that Jasper wanted her and Eli or Mattias or someone with authority to come to the gates. A girl had been found hiding under the cloth that covered the contents of the first merchant's wagon. A man who assisted Jasper with inspections insisted the girl, Myrtle, was betrothed to his cousin. The merchant claimed the girl was his niece. Another man helping with the inspection said that he had seen the girl working at the Inn of the Three Sisters. Jasper hoped Norah or someone else in the household could bring some sense to the clashing stories.

Sylvanus had eaten three times at the inn and had been more polite than Sarai expected from a Roman soldier with any authority. He confided in them that he already believed Myrtle was running away. Whether she had fallen in love with the merchant, or she was simply taking the first opportunity to flee, it didn't matter to him. He didn't blame her running away, because he knew the man who was supposed to be her betrothed. He was more than twice her age, and had already been married twice. One wife had died in childbirth, the other had simply vanished.

Through all this, Ananias waited patiently, quietly, and stayed away from the knots of activity and talk, negating any fear of eavesdropping. Sarai hurried to serve him and make him comfortable while Laila sent another boy to find Eli and give him the news, if he wasn't already on his way to the gates with Myrtle's father. The second merchant finally left, after Caleb and several others searched the bundles on the camels to ensure that nothing belonging to the inn had been taken. The man didn't bluster with self-righteous indignation or threaten to ruin the reputation of the inn or bring charges against them. Sarai wondered why. Was he frightened? Did he feel guilty? Or did he fear he would be blamed or held responsible for whatever the first merchant had stolen?

"The girl was foolish to trust that man," Ananias observed, when Sarai had brought him a cup of wine, fresh bread, olives, and cheese, and finally sat down on the bench opposite him. There was nothing else she could do, and she felt it her duty to attend to the guest in their household. "He could have lied and pretended to be sympathetic, offering to help her. He could have intended to make her a slave, after wooing her with sweet words. Where did she think she could go, once she had left the city?"

"Sometimes the unknown is far less frightening than what we see lying ahead of us," Sarai offered.

"True." He made a gesture of blessing over the basket of bread and tore one of the flat loaves in half, offering her the larger piece. "Child, do not let your heart be troubled."

"Oh, I am not worried. Myrtle is no innocent. She seems so … worldly-wise, perhaps?"

"I did not speak of the foolish servant. The Master has given you your child as a blessing. A gift. Just as El Shaddai protected Moses when Pharaoh slaughtered the innocents, He will protect your child, and you."

"How can I be sure?" Her throat ached with the sharpness of her blurted words.

"I know a little of your husband. When I consider what I have heard about your father, and the varying stories of how and why Simon cast you aside, I think that he cares over-much about what others think of him. He will make himself appear a fool if he takes you back. He will make himself look even more foolish if he takes the child from you, because that will be admitting you did not commit adultery, as I am sure many of his peers will claim. As long as he cares more about staying in the good will of the leaders of the Sanhedrin, his wisest course of action will be to ignore you, and any reports of you that come to him."

"The same pride that made Simon cast me out will protect me from him." She could understand that simple common sense with her mind, but accepting that in the trembling, weeping place deep inside would take some time. "Thank you. Why did I not think of this before?"

"I am sure you would in time." He reached across the table to rest his hand over hers. "Be sure, child, that though I have had no direct guidance from the Master, you may consider me your protector. He would not have led me so clearly to this household, to you, if not for some specific task, some part in the grand weaving of His will. I would have chosen to stay in Jerusalem and fellowship with the disciples and all the new followers of the Master, but the Spirit sent me home to Damascus for a purpose. What that is, only time will reveal."

Norah and the others returned sooner than Sarai expected. Myrtle's father had heard about the ruckus at the gate before Eli reached him, and to Norah's relief, was far more understanding and lenient than expected. The man who claimed Myrtle was his betrothed had overstepped himself, because her father had not yet agreed to the marriage. The hopeful bridegroom had bought up several debts Myrtle's father owed, to force the man to hand over his daughter. He had the money and goods to repay the debts, but had been delayed in returning to Damascus in the time specified. Several witnesses testified that he had repaid his creditors after they sold his debts to the unwanted bridegroom. They were in the process of dealing with an advocate and a mediator to untangle the ugly mess. Myrtle's brother escorted her to and from the inn to ensure the man didn't kidnap her. The dishonest creditors were part of the problem, telling a different story to each party involved. Myrtle had overheard the wrong gossip, as well as threats against her family's safety. She thought that running away would solve everything.

Clearing up the mess of lies and evasions took nearly two weeks of arguing back and forth. All Norah cared about was that no one had any claim against the Inn of the Three Sisters, and their reputation did not suffer. Malachi returned the day after the problem at the gates, and he agreed with her. Fortunately, many people heard about the inn through the ruckus, and came to investigate the good cooking, to use the large bread oven Eli and Mattias had built in the courtyard, and to hire Miriam and Dorcas as seamstresses. When several people saw Sarai working on the inn's records, tallying expenses and comparing the inventory of supplies with the actual contents of the storage rooms, word spread about the woman who could read and write and cypher and was willing to use her skills for others. By the end of the month, eight men had come to her, asking her to write letters for them, to attend to business in other cities. She was proud to add a few coins to the strongbox and increase the profits of the inn.

All this felt like a blessing, perhaps a gift to comfort them, after the news that Ananias shared that Sabbath afternoon. When everyone had returned from trying to deal with the problem of runaway Myrtle, the entire household gathered in the courtyard of the inn. Sarai helped the younger servant girls distribute cups of wine and rounds of bread, cheese and figs to everyone. Then Ananias stood and raised his hands in blessing and prayed to El Shaddai before he sat down to relate the news from Jerusalem.

Sarai listened and wished she had thought to gather up papyrus and ink, to write down some of the things Ananias said. He told about the various encounters people had with Jesus in the month after He walked out of the tomb. Some of the stories she knew, because they had been shared among the small community of believers before the inn household left for Damascus. She wished, just for a little while, that they hadn't been in such a hurry to evade the anticipated trouble from the Sanhedrin. Perhaps she might have had a chance to meet Jesus again. She nearly didn't hear two of Ananias' stories, lost in the wonder of imagining that encounter.

Something tightened in her chest as Ananias told the story of everyone gathering on the Mount of Olives, as Jesus had instructed. He gave them, as best he could, Jesus' exact words as He taught His followers and gave them instructions. Orders. Ananias related Jesus' command to spread His teachings to all the world. Sarai held her breath, sure she would cry out in protest, as his voice rasped and his eyes widened in wonder as he related how Jesus rose in the air and vanished among the clouds. Sarai released that breath as he described the angels who appeared among them, to gently scold and promise they would see Jesus again.

A sob caught in her throat. Her imagined encounters between Simon and Jesus dried up like a badly made pot, and crumbled. Yet amid the pain, there was a sense of lightness. Perhaps relief?

"You are a selfish, fearful child," she whispered, and nearly laughed aloud when insight burst upon her. If Simon did not face the truth and repent, the threat of him coming to take her away had ended.

She didn't want Simon to take her back. She didn't want to be his wife again. She couldn't forgive him. Not yet.

Perhaps that was petty and cruel of her, to be glad that he would not repent. She told herself she didn't care. Or rather, she cared too much. She still hurt.

Then she realized Ananias was still talking, and she glanced around the gathering. Who could she ask to relate to her what she had missed while she indulged in her hurts and fears? Sarai shook her head to clear her thoughts and focused on listening to Ananias. Just listen. Later she could think about what he had told them.

He mentioned the Feast of Weeks, the activities in Jerusalem leading up to it, the preparations and ritual cleansing. She thought some of the things he said were references to encounters with different rabbis and teachers of the law as the day of the feast approached. Not encounters Ananias had, but reported by other followers of Jesus.

Before Ananias related the day when the disciples were gathered together in prayer, hiding from the Sanhedrin, at the height of the Feast of Weeks, he paused. He shook his head and smiled, looking off into the distance for a moment.

"The Spirit of the Living God … fell on us. Drowned us in … blessings ... I suppose that is the best word. I thought I had experienced wonders when I went out among the seventy to be an instrument of blessing and miracles. This was a thousand times more marvelous. And frightening. The enormity of the burden, the stewardship placed upon us."

He took a slow sip of the wine, tipping the cup up far enough that Sarai realized it needed refilling. She couldn't make herself rise from the bench to handle that little task of hospitality. Norah gestured to one of the boys who cleaned up after the camels and donkeys and cart oxen. He hurried to pick up the skin of wine and refill Ananias' cup. The man thanked him and took another, longer sip, while the boy went around the gathering and refilled any cup held out to him. Sarai thought Ananias hesitated because he had trouble finding the right words. She felt sorry for him. Somehow, that eased the aching deep in her chest and helped release the muscles in her legs and hands, which had seemed to lock, holding her in place.

"We had gathered together. As many as could fit in were in the upper room and on the roof where they could hear the voices raised in prayer, coming through the open doors and windows." Ananias put down the cup and clasped his hands in his lap. "A loud, swirling wind fell upon us. I was sitting in the doorway. I tried to lean out to look up at the sky, but I couldn't move. I felt the pressure of the wind, but no hair or clothes moved. How can nothing move when we are surrounded by a wind so strong it threatens to pull the very air from our lungs? I have no explanation. That is only how it felt, in those few seconds of utter confusion." He bowed his head, a curious, twisted smile parting his beard in those moments of introspection. Then he raised his head again.

"Seconds of utter glory, when the hand of Adonai rested on us all. All of us saw fire. Like tongues. Cloven tongues. Writhing flames. They rested on each of us. I can't tell you what I felt when the flaming tongue touched me. Not because I can't remember, but because words escape me. All in an instant, everything changed. A crude attempt to describe just a part of what I experienced ..." He sighed. "I felt as if I were a barrel in which years of filth had been collected. With just a touch, like when the seraph touched the Prophet Isaiah's lips with the coal from the altar -- with just a touch, all that filth was removed from me. I was scrubbed and scorched clean and filled with new wine. Yes, a potent, new wine such as the world has yet to taste. A new wine that will change all the world, if people are only wise enough, brave enough, faithful enough to taste it."

After another pause, during which Sarai thought Ananias' face took on a soft glow, he continued with the tale. How everyone gathered there ran out into the streets, speaking words that were poured into them by the Spirit of Adonai. How they discovered they spoke in the languages of everyone who could hear them, every tongue and nation and land, who had come to Jerusalem for the feast. Just as many marveled at what they heard as those who mocked, either from jealousy or fear or because perhaps their ears were stopped up by their own refusal to understand. Ananias admitted that he had thought many times about the events of that day, and even now he thought he had only a fragment of understanding. Perhaps it would take the rest of his life to fully grasp the implications, the details, of what had happened to them.

Up until then, Peter had been too quiet among the disciples, wallowing in the guilt of how he had acted when Jesus had been arrested, and later when confronted during the cruel pretense of a trial and mockery of justice. Sarai had heard some whispers of how the disciples had fled when the soldiers confronted Jesus in Gethsemane, and later how an unnamed disciple had denied knowing Him at all. She ached for Peter, even as something went hot and bitter inside her. How had she, a mere woman, been able to stand up in her faith, when one of Jesus' closest followers had turned against Him in fear? What had given her the strength, and why hadn't Peter had it that night?

Pride, she scolded herself. *Pride will raise me so high that the fall will dash me to pieces. Adonai, protect me from pride. Help me pity him.*

She held her breath as Ananias related how Peter had stood up in the fountain square near the gathering place and proclaimed the truth of Jesus' resurrection and the fulfillment of prophecy. The Spirit of Adonai had given him strength and courage and put words in his mouth, just as Jesus had promised. Then hundreds upon hundreds had joined the ranks of the disciples.

"These are glory days among the followers in Jerusalem, and I would have been glad to spend all my days there, learning from those who speak as they are led by the Spirit," Ananias said. "We have lived in such unity, such sharing and harmony. We merely smile when we hear of the grumbling and threats of the Sanhedrin. We have too much joy in the Spirit to laugh at their foolishness and rebellion and blindness. Rather we pity them." He sighed and looked around the gathering, with a smile of blessing, touched with just a little sadness.

Sarai knew then that leaving Jerusalem had been painful for him, if the fellowship among the believers was as sweet and nourishing as his words and voice implied.

"Yet the Spirit guided me to leave there, to come here, come home. I have a duty awaiting me, and a time of preparation ahead of me. What I am to prepare for, I know not. I can guess, however, that I was sent to find the Master's people here, so far from Jerusalem, and ensure that they, you, we, all join together in fellowship and community. No matter how glorious the blessing that now protects all believers and keeps us in high standing, how long can that last? How long until the fall begins, and we are attacked, and the good will of the people turns against us? We must be ready. Perhaps Damascus shall be a sanctuary for those who flee for their lives. Perhaps Damascus is merely the first step in obeying the Master's command to spread the good news to all the world."

~~~~~

After that day, the household of the inn became the center of a growing fellowship. At the core were those who had seen Jesus and heard Him teach, and a blessed few who had seen Him after the resurrection. They were joined by those who had heard about the rabbi from Nazareth and were curious, needing to sort through all the stories and rumors and learn the truth. They usually gathered in the evening after the Sabbath had ended with sunset. The Gentiles among them were finished with their day's work. The Jews were freed from whatever Sabbath activities their families and synagogues practiced.

The word went around that Sarai was recording all the memories of Jesus' teaching that anyone wished to share with her. Soon, members of the fellowship came to her, asking her to read to them what she had recorded, or to add their stories to the slowly growing pile of parchment and papyrus sheets.

Word also spread that she was pregnant, along with doubts about her widowhood. No one mentioned Simon's name, so Sarai knew her inn family kept her secret. She could only surmise that everyone else chose to believe she had never been married.

That was soon proven by the reactions of the people living and doing business in the streets surrounding the inn. People yelled mockery from the gates, and then ran so they could not be identified. Men who had never come to the inn before came to take a room and tried to force the serving girls to share their beds. Malachi had to repeatedly throw them out of the inn and command them never to return. They refused to listen, until he complained to the soldiers who patrolled the streets. The men still tried to return, and then protested that they were being ill-used when the soldiers arrested them.

The situation came to the breaking point when three women who were married to known detractors of the inn came to speak to Norah. They had always refused to speak to her before when they met at the synagogue. This day, they expressed concerns about the moral standards of the inn, which they said seemed to be all lip service. Norah and Malachi went to see Rabbi Amos. He arranged for a meeting of all the synagogue leaders. He invited all their
~~~~~

wives, and the leading families in the synagogue. Sarai was grateful she didn't have to attend the meeting. She imagined having to stand before all those people and swear on the scrolls of the Torah that no man had taken carnal knowledge of her since she last shared her husband's bed.

Laila created the story that she, Norah and Malachi brought to the leaders of the Jewish community, in hopes of settling the rumors.

No, no one spoke of Sarai's husband, because they were tender about her feelings.

If Laila had her way, Sarai's husband would never be mentioned, to protect her.

She had only begun to suspect she was with child when the chaos erupted in Jerusalem, resulting in her losing her husband. She had never had a chance to tell him she carried his child, and now he would never know.

That was entirely truthful.

Sarai didn't know whether to laugh or cry or cringe in a queasiness of both body and spirit, when she realized how much truth and deception were interwoven for the sake of protecting her. She was grateful and yet she couldn't help wondering when the growing structure of the lie woven about her would grow top-heavy and fall, crushing her.

Norah laughed later, recounting Laila's performance before the synagogue leaders and all the self-appointed arbiters of truth and justice in the Jewish community. She played the part of concerned and frantic auntie to a slightly scatterbrained young widow -- Sarai. She feared for the "poor, distracted child," weighed down with grief. Now she faced the added burden of unjustified slander and accusations, on top of her "terrible, wasting grief" after the "astounding, terrifying events that took place at Passover."

Laila had treated everyone to an earful of her interpretation of the events that took place at Passover. She focused on the horrible injustice against the kind rabbi who had performed verified miracles through the power of Adonai. When she was finished, everyone agreed it was kindness to Sarai in her grief never to ask her about her husband. No one asked his name, or if he had a family who should be caring for Sarai. Norah and Malachi emphasized that they were now her family and protectors. If anyone were to try to slander her with false accusations, or even mention the idea of marriage until her child was weaned, it would be taken as rudeness to everyone in the Inn of the Three Sisters. Meaning they would not be welcome at Norah's table.

"I think that frightened them more than anything else." Malachi ended on a weary chuckle, after he and Laila and Norah recounted the entire meeting to the rest of the household.

"What weighs on me is the heavy load of lies we're all telling. My father was right," Sarai confessed later to Mattias as they worked together.

No matter the crises that kept striking them, the business of the inn had to keep going. Today they were taking an inventory of supplies so Norah and Eli could go to the market in the morning to replenish them.

"It takes far more effort to keep the fabric of a lie whole, than it takes to simply tell the truth," she said.

"We don't need that," he said, and put down a barrel of flour with a thump and a grunt. "You're not out there, hearing the arguments and judgments everyone passes on everyone else. You think women are cruel, criticizing each other all the time?" He grinned and gestured with his chin at the water jar. Sarai got up to fill the dipper and hand it to him. "The moment some of those graybeards hear you are divorced, they'll send the fastest couriers to Jerusalem to tell that idiot Simon. Or worse, bring you up on charges before the city magistrates and send you back to Jerusalem in chains."

"What charges?"

"Stealing his child." He shrugged. "Man doesn't deserve you, after the way he treated you. He's an idiot, not to believe in Jesus. How can anyone hear the stories Ananias has been telling us, and not believe? No, Sarai. We're your family now and you're safe with us and that's where you'll stay. Doesn't matter how many lies we have to tell to protect you and your little one. You're safe here."

~~~~~

Sarai wasn't sure when she was able to breathe normally again, and not flinch every time a stranger stepped through the gates of the inn and his gaze met hers. The change, the relaxation, the acceptance of safety came gradually. It grew more quickly than her belly, she realized one day with a little bubble of humor. And
~~~~~

gratitude.

Then Laila responded to a knock on the door at midnight. After a whispered conversation with a woman who sounded like she was weeping, she came to fetch Sarai. That night call for help shredded the cocoon of warmth and safety she had painstakingly woven around herself.

Sarai stepped into the room on the second floor used by the inn women for relaxing and talking in privacy in the evenings. The woman Laila had brought inside stood in the center of the room, washing with a basin and a handful of rags. At first, Sarai didn't see the blood in the water. All she saw were the henna designs painted on her arms, her exposed chest, her exposed legs, her long neck, her face. The multiple bracelets circling her bared arms. One in the shape of a coiled snake, with emeralds for eyes. The anklets of coins.

Laila had brought a harlot into their home. From the looks of her, a successful, popular one, judging by the wealth of jewelry and the fine material of her clothes.

Then Sarai saw the blood. In the water of the basin. Soaked into the shredded, fine material of her clothes. Trickling from her broken and swelling nose. The cuts on her hands. Bruises formed on her legs and arms. Blood trickled down the inside of her leg. She realized where that blood had to be coming from, the brutal treatment the woman had endured and the pain she had to be feeling. It all stabbed Sarai in her belly and took her breath for a moment.

Her eyes met the woman's, and behind the mask of henna designs she saw a girl younger than herself. Green eyes like jewels were wide with terror. And pain. And a struggle for control and strength. Sarai knew, as if a storyteller were whispering over her shoulder, this girl expected to be thrown out of the room, treated with disgust. Instead of pity, she expected to be told the injuries she had suffered, the fear she felt, were deserved, earned, her own fault.

"Sit down," Sarai said. "You are among friends."

The girl dropped the rags, hitting the water in the basin with a soft splash. She trembled, but didn't sit.

"Marakata," Laila said from the doorway. "This is our little healer. Don't fear." She stepped around Sarai and came into the room with a tray of jars and pots and soft, clean strips of cloth for bandages.

The girl reached with the hand that had been holding the rags and braced her other arm as she slowly settled on the edge of the couch. She winced and her skin paled, making the henna swirls and stars and other designs stand out starker by contrast.

"What did he do to your arm?" Sarai didn't wait for an answer. She sat next to the girl and gently tugged back the last few layers of sheer cloth. They were darkened and stuck to her arm with blood.

Nausea hit her belly like a fist when she saw the torn flesh and the bone protruding from Marakata's arm, midway between elbow and shoulder. Sarai took several deep breaths to fight the need to shriek fury. Interwoven with that was fear that the man who had so brutalized the girl would break through the door any moment and attack them all.

"I need the poppy elixir." She cupped Marakata's face with both her hands, making the girl look at her so she could gaze into those emerald eyes. "I won't put you to sleep, but I will make you so sleepy, you won't feel the pain as I tend your injuries. Trust me."

Tears made those eyes glisten like jewels. The girl nodded. Her gaze turned to Laila. One corner of her mouth tried to twist up in a smile. Then she closed her eyes and didn't open them again until late into the day. She drank the poppy elixir Sarai held to her lips, and she lay back and held as still as she could. Her trembling could have come from pain or cold or fear or all three. It continued long after the sleeping draught should have sent her into a limp, half-dreaming state.

Sarai sang psalms under her breath as she worked, for her own benefit, to calm her hands and help her to think, as well as to assure the battered girl in her care. The only time she paused was to ask Laila to bring her what she needed. Bandages. Needle and thread to sew up torn flesh. Balm. Wine to cleanse the wounds, salve to soothe and protect and promote healing. Thin, strong strips of wood to brace the broken bone. More water and cleansing lotions, to wash Marakata once she was healed and the dirty, torn, bloody clothes removed. And finally, a clean robe.

Dawn had nearly arrived by the time Sarai was finished. Several of the inn women had awakened. Either they were getting up to start the morning baking, or they sensed something unusual happening in the house. Maybe Laila dropped something as she went to and from the room where Sarai compounded and stored her potions and pastes and powders. They stood in the doorway, whispering and watching. Sarai nearly wept, when no one hesitated or protested Laila's request for their help in putting the sleepy girl in her own room and bed.

Finally alone, trembling took Sarai, so she fumbled the tray of pots and jars she carried back to her storage room. She caught all but one pot. The stinging aroma of a paste used to fight off flesh rot seemed to leap from the broken pot on the floor and drill into her nose. She sagged against the wall and covered her nose and mouth with her sleeve and blinked away tears. Fury and fear and a strange emotion she couldn't identify, confusing and chilling, made her choke on the need to weep. She feared if she allowed the tears to come, she might cry aloud. Maybe shout.

"Forgive me, little dove." Laila stepped past Sarai and shoved the broken remnants of the jar into the storage room with her bare foot. Then she wrapped her arm around Sarai and led her away, down the stairs, out through the kitchen, to the open air of the inn courtyard. The fresh air swept away the heavy, clogged feeling in Sarai's head, her lungs, the sensation of weights tugging at her limbs.

A few men moved around on the far side of the courtyard, near the arched gateway into the caravansary. Likely tending animals, taking food to the merchants who wanted to make an early departure.

"I reminded you of the fate you almost suffered." She guided Sarai onto a bench at the table under the canopy and sat down facing her.

"You never would have allowed a customer to treat me like that." Sarai swallowed, the taste in her mouth bitter.

"You think too well of me. You only know the woman who was cleansed of demons. For the sake of coins, for the sake of spying on the Romans, I would have let a dozen men use you in one night, and not wept a single tear if their pleasure killed you. As long as I profited. Or the demons were amused and entertained."

Sarai raised her head and gazed at Laila in a frozen kind of horror. There was sadness in her friend's eyes, but far stronger was a weary, somber acceptance.

"You said you would have kept me just to tend the others."

"Yes. At first. As long as my customers didn't see you. As long as they didn't know about you. Nothing makes a man hunger more than being told no, that's not for you. As much as my normal, sane mind and heart might have treasured and wanted to protect you … perhaps *because* I would have wanted to protect you, the demons and my idiotic hunger for profit would have eventually convinced me to turn you over to them. Especially if I thought it would serve Barabbas and his war against Rome. Even if it hurt my profits, because you wouldn't be there to heal the other injured girls."

"Why are you telling me this?"

Chapter Seven

"Because I need your help. Because no one knows better the terrors and darkness and loneliness of the harlot's life than one who has lived it and escaped. Or one who stood on the brink, looking into that living hell. I hope you can feel some pity for them, and you will not condemn them and say their injuries are justified."

"That is what you do, when you are gone for hours at a time, before dawn, and after sunset." Sarai shivered and something aching uncoiled and relaxed inside her. "You look for harlots. To help them."

"I thought no one noticed." A bit of a smile caught up one corner of Laila's mouth.

"I don't think anyone else has, but … With all the accusations, the people who insist we only speak loyalty to the law, but we act in the dark for profit …" She shrugged, unable to find the right words. She had feared, if only for a few moments, that Laila had returned to the life that had invited the demons into her soul.

"Yes, I seek out those few who will listen to me and hope. The ones who long for escape and haven't let that yearning turn to poison and bitterness." Laila closed her eyes and her breath hitched. "She could be my own child," she whispered, as a tear slid from the inner corners of each eye.

Sarai stopped herself before insisting Laila never would have sent her own daughter into harlotry. Hadn't she just confessed what she would have done despite her promises of care and protection?

"I conceived twice, when I was younger than you. I was a favorite of the richest customer of the brothel, and reserved for his use alone, so we knew the child was his and no one else's. The first, I lost early." Laila bowed her head, her fists pressed against her forehead, elbows on the table, and her voice grew softer as she spoke. "That changed him, the father. He pampered me. His wife had never conceived, and I think he was delighted that I had proven he was able to breed. When I conceived again, he bought my freedom and promised he would marry me if I gave him a son.

Everything would have been so different if he gave me my own home. But no, he insisted on bringing me into his household, and gave me servants, and pampered me even more."

"Surely his wife couldn't have liked that."

"She raged and she went to witches for potions to kill me and charms to curse him. I turned to the witches too, for charms to protect me. When the wife died, poisoned by her own hand, her own stupidity and mistakes, I thought the charms worked, and I went back for more. My lover, my owner, because I most certainly was not free, even though he had bought my freedom ..." Laila raised her head and lowered her arms to the table, reaching across to take Sarai's hands. "He didn't marry me. I saw that he only cared about the child in my womb. And in my rage, I listened to the voices whispering to me that I could have my justice and my revenge. He was killed by bandits, and since I carried his child, and he had boasted to everyone that the child would be a boy ... I was allowed to stay in the house and keep all his properties. For his heir. That was what his few relatives claimed, when in truth they were terrified of the demons that told me what they were thinking, and what they said and planned in dark, closed rooms."

She swallowed hard and her eyes seemed to go dry, her gaze distant. Laila squeezed Sarai's hands.

"When I lost the child, torn from my belly by the demons who gave me wealth and power, I didn't mourn. I hid the truth. Then I sold everything and took the money and traveled far beyond the reach of anyone who knew the story. I listened to the demons and I bought girls to turn them into harlots and gave what remained of my heart to Barabbas." Her breath caught and she blinked away the hint of tears. "Marakata was the first child born in my household. I treasured her as if she came from my womb. She was the darling of all the women." A strangled, bitter laugh escaped her. "What little love we were able to find in ourselves, we lavished on her. Yet when my world was shattered and I lost everything, I wept not one tear after Marakata was snatched off the streets and sold."

"You are weeping for her now," Sarai whispered.

"I saw her five days after we came here. I was terrified, and sick with guilt. Then I prayed for Adonai's mercy that I would have a chance to right some of the many thousands of sins and crimes weighing on my heart," Laila whispered. "I have the money to buy her freedom, but until tonight, she scorned my help. She had a patron who promised to free her and surround her with wealth and power." A snort escaped her. "She believed him until tonight. He turned on her, as if all the demons who ever tormented me had come to reside in him."

"Anyone would expect her to die of those wounds, if she couldn't get help," Sarai said, squeezing Laila's hands in turn. "Truthfully, who would help a harlot who had been so badly used? If she never goes back, she will be considered dead and lost, won't she? No one will look for her in the refuse heaps, will they?"

Laila went utterly still, so Sarai thought she didn't even breathe. For many long moments they stared into each other's eyes. Then a sob escaped the older woman and she smiled.

"You will help me? You will work with me to heal them, and free them, and give them new lives, as Jesus gave new life to me?"

"As you said, who knows better than one who looked into Hell and escaped?"

~~~~~

Malachi argued against letting Marakata stay with them after she healed. He had been angered and worried by the gossip and the insistence of some men that every inn housed harlots, there for the taking. No matter how loyal the members of the inn household were, eventually someone would learn about the girl's past. Then the battle of reputations and gossip would resume. While he said he sympathized with Marakata's plight, his fear and his concern for the inn's reputation, and keeping all the other women safe, were far stronger. He only spoke once about the danger of the girl's owner or the patron who had nearly killed her finding her at the inn. Laila promised him that enough people had seen her arguing with Marakata, and heard the abuse the girl threw at her, no one would expect her to provide help now.

Norah said nothing about sending Marakata away. She made it clear that she didn't expect the former harlot to become part of the inn family, simply by asking what she would do, how she would live, once she was healed. Sarai tried not to be angry with her friend. She understood the fear. What she couldn't understand was the reticence of Norah and many of the inn's women. While they helped tend the injured girl, they wouldn't speak to her, or sit with her, or sing to ease her discomfort and calm her nightmares
~~~~~

and delirium dreams.

Didn't any of them understand that only a few bad months of business stood between them and facing the choice of being beggars or harlots?

"They understand," Istra said, when Sarai confided in her, during a visit to discuss a new salve recipe. "Like the gods hate their half-blood offspring, they hate the women whom they could become. Fear turns so easily to hatred. They don't want to admit they are afraid, they don't want to admit they look down on someone whom they should pity, so it turns to loathing."

Eli understood better than anyone, Sarai learned. The injured girl was still suffering from fever and bad dreams when he came to Sarai and Laila with a plan. He took them to a small house near the southern gate. It was built into the city wall, the rooms so narrow the house inside it was barely detectable. It had a door on the inside of the wall, and the only windows looked out from a single room each on the second and third floors. Two rooms on each floor, with an equally narrow, almost treacherous flight of stairs that were little more than bricks embedded in the wall. Eli proposed moving Marakata to the house and sheltering other harlots there who wanted to leave the life. He had money saved up. He would buy the house and contribute for the women's food and clothing. They could stay in the house and hide and heal. When the time was right, they could join safe caravans and go to other cities, where they could start a new life.

"You are a blessing, a gift from Adonai," Laila said, embracing him hard.

Sarai didn't think it was the strength of Laila's arms that made Eli turn red. She had always felt some affection for the man, but now she loved him with a fierceness that made her ache.

"Why are you doing this? Don't you need your savings, for when you're unable to work?" Sarai had to ask.

"My mother ..." Eli shrugged. The sideways jerk of his head, the way he wouldn't meet their eyes for a moment, told Sarai all the things he couldn't say. "Malachi's father helped her get free. It was for my sake. I was headed for the slave market when I was weaned. Mother asked me to pay our debt by helping someone else in danger someday."

Soon, Marakata grew strong enough to be by herself in the

little, dark, hidden house. And just in time. Eli moved her in the night, and Sarai and Laila came back from visiting her the next morning to find Rabbi Amos waiting at the inn. He had come in response to gossip saying a harlot was living under Malachi's roof.

Later, Sarai reflected that the big innkeeper's relief was almost amusing, when Norah offered to let the synagogue leader walk through the entire household and all the rooms of the inn, to assure himself the gossip was false. Obviously, though Norah knew Marakata had been taken to new shelter, she hadn't told her father yet.

After a month, Norah insisted on going with Laila in Sarai's place every three or four days, to tend to Marakata. Part of it was from a sense of guilt, and to apologize for being not sympathetic enough. Part of it was because Sarai's pregnant belly seemed to soak up more of her strength, the larger it became. All the women in the inn had to offer her advice. There was some amusement in how they argued over what foods to eat, what foods to avoid, what lotions not to use, how to ward off morning illness and leg cramps and pains in the back and influence the child's skills and intelligence. Sarai might have gone mad with the cosseting and interference and downright bullying if she hadn't found some humor in it all. She knew her inn family loved her, and she loved the huge family she had gained to make up for Simon casting her aside. Still, she sometimes wept into her pillow and longed for the quiet household she had left behind, and the support of Hannah and Deborah.

~~~~~

Fall brought harvest festivals and celebrations. Norah had more requests to oversee and cook for feasts than she could handle. She had to hire several people to help with the increased business. That was a blessing, but many feasts were in honor of more pagan gods and demi-gods than Sarai had ever heard of in all her scholarly reading.

Norah and Malachi consulted Rabbi Amos about the appropriateness of taking payment for work that would essentially be worship of false gods. He advised them that Adonai knew the heart. He believed Norah's good cooking and the kindness and hospitality of the Inn of the Three Sisters contributed much to peaceful relations between the Jewish community and the other
~~~~~

nations. Perhaps more than any official declarations of alliance or friendship. He surprised them when he said that he had enjoyed more friendly discourse with the leaders of other communities over wine and spiced bread in the inn's courtyard than any other location. People who refused to come to his house, or the home of any acknowledged Jewish leader in Damascus, were quite willing to meet with him at the inn.

"We will change the world and ensure safety for our people more certainly with the smells of fresh bread and roasting duck than we will with the aroma of holy incense in the air." The elderly rabbi shrugged and offered them a crooked smile. "I admit, I am more willing to listen to people who are not poised to knocked me off my feet with the heaviest scroll of the Torah."

Ananias came to the household to lead in worship and study of scriptures, in a search for the prophecies that spoke of Jesus' arrival, His ministry and His suffering, death, and resurrection. The habit became regular meetings after sundown had ended the Sabbath, or early in the morning on the first day of the week. Many of the followers of Jesus who came to Damascus came to the inn first, seeking Ananias. The numbers of those who met for worship and study grew slowly. But again, faster than Sarai's belly.

Istra the healer had made herself Sarai's mentor. She opened many doors to scholarship and obtaining scrolls to replace the ones the Romans had confiscated. She also opened the doors for Sarai to be accepted as an equal and acknowledged as a trained healer among the midwives and healers of all nations throughout Damascus. Sarai had many fascinating evenings, sitting against a wall and listening to healers four times her age as they discussed herbals and legends and healing practices. She became very popular when other healers knew she could read several languages. They needed help translating scrolls they had inherited from their mentors, but could not read. Istra allowed other midwives to offer their advice as Sarai's pregnancy advanced, but it was understood that she and Laila would be attending the birth. She assured Sarai regularly that just because her belly was small was no reason to worry. She should be grateful that she carried high and lightly. What woman, she reasoned with a droll tone and a rolling of her eyes, wanted a child as big as a two-year-old when it came time to give birth?

She came to the inn several times, as the months slid by, to listen to the Christ-followers sharing what they learned. She asked Sarai to read to her some of the memories of Jesus' words she had recorded. The old healer woman's interest didn't surprise Sarai. The quest for knowledge made perfect sense.

However, what did surprise Sarai was the reason that brought Rabbi Amos to the inn one Sabbath. The shadows of sunset reached the halfway point in the inn courtyard, and Sabbath was officially over. She didn't leap up to greet him as she would have even a month ago. Despite the worrying smallness of her belly, she wasn't as light and quick on her feet as she used to be. Dorcas ran to greet the rabbi, while Sarai walked to the doorway into the serving area of the kitchen and called in for Mattias or Malachi or someone to let them know Amos had come. Then she went through the central hallway to the doorway from the inn to the house, to fetch her scribe's box. Ananias had promised her that a newcomer to Damascus would be joining them tonight, and he had a memory of Jesus' teaching to relate that he was sure she hadn't put into her collection yet.

When Sarai came out, Rabbi Amos was sitting at the central table, chatting with Ananias. His usual cup of sweet herbal infusion for his aching joins steamed in front of him. From his comfortable posture, he had no intention of leaving any time soon. She laughed at herself later, at the mixture of apprehension and surprise. Rabbi Amos was a reasonable man. Why did she fear that he would stand against Jesus and His followers like the Sanhedrin had in Jerusalem?

After that, he was a regular participant in the sharing of memories and teaching and studying the scriptures. If "regular" could be defined as once or perhaps twice in a month.

Life was kind, and Sarai wondered later if she should have been worried by the slow relaxing of watchfulness. Perhaps it didn't come from accepting her safety and relative anonymity among all these different languages and nations and cultures and teachings. Perhaps it was simple weariness. And the growing weight of the baby in her womb.

A familiar face appeared in the gates of the inn, midway through a hot, dusty, dry afternoon when she was sure that summer would turn around and descend on them again. Weariness kept her from recognizing Jude when his gaze slid over her multiple times as he crossed the courtyard. Part of that could be excused by her sitting in the shade and resting, in the short dip in activity between noontime meals and evening. She had just come back from overseeing a midwife in training, while the woman training her was busy delivering twins. Her weary contentment put her mind into a haze. She watched Jude approach, knew she recognized him, but felt no alarm that she couldn't put a name to the handsome, tanned face smeared with dust from the road. Besides, he didn't seem to either notice or recognize her, so she reasoned that she only imagined the familiarity.

"Is this the inn of Malachi ben Joachim?" he asked, when Dorcas stepped out from the kitchen, her arms full of two baskets of bread and a small amphora of wine.

The sound of his voice brought his name to Sarai, but the weary haze dulled the shock of recognition. She sat back and marveled at how the months and distance had somehow refined Jude. His cheekbones looked a little sharper, his beard had darkened, and a somber undertone had scrubbed away some of the light readiness for laughter in his voice.

Dorcas frowned at him, and Sarai nearly laughed aloud. She understood the serving woman's momentary confusion. Malachi rarely used his patronymic when doing business in Damascus. Not like he had done in Jerusalem. Usually he was introduced or sought by simply saying "Malachi from the Three Sisters."

"This is the Inn of the Three Sisters," Dorcas said. "If you will take a seat, I will be back with you shortly." She didn't wait for Jude to respond, but headed across the courtyard, to a table of merchants. They had been negotiating a trading pact when Sarai left to attend the birth, and were still negotiating when she returned just a short time ago.

"Yes, Malachi ben Joachim and his daughter, Norah, run the Inn of the Three Sisters," Sarai said. "He is tending to business, but Norah is in one of the upper chambers, if you are willing to speak with her." She stood slowly as she spoke, reaching out to brace herself on the wall behind her. This spot against the wall, under the canopy, had become her favorite spot to sit, just because she could brace herself for support as she got back to her feet. Sometimes it felt as if she carried twenty talents of gold between her hips.

"Thank you, that would --" Jude's gaze slid from her face downward. His mouth slowly dropped open and he caught his breath before he could yank his gaze upward again. "Sarai?"

"Adonai's blessing on you, Jude ben Boaz," she said, and hesitated before offering her hand in greeting. Sarai honestly couldn't remember if Jude's family was one of those who avoided touching pregnant women, for some finicky rules of ceremonial cleanliness.

"Sarai," he said, a little louder. "I have come -- you -- how can you --" He flipped his fingers at her belly, and seemed to go pale for a moment or two under the dust of the road.

"If you do not understand how children are conceived, it would be unseemly for me to instruct you. Shall I call for Mattias or Eli?" She stepped away, out from under the canopy, and tipped her head back to look for one of the inn's headmen. They were always somewhere on the roof or walls, doing repairs or planning how to add on to the upper stories of the inn.

"No!" Jude blushed when his voice echoed off the walls. He sank down on the bench Dorcas had offered him a little while ago, and laughed softly, unsteadily, as if he might be sick.

"Sarai?" Ebenezer darted through the gate leading to the caravansary side of the inn. One hand rested on the long knife that always hung from his belt. It was a simple, sensible precaution. Troublemakers were less likely to cause trouble if they knew the inn's men were prepared to defend the property, the guests, and the inn's women.

"It's all right. I think. Do you remember Jude ben Boaz, from Jerusalem?" She took a step up into the kitchen. "You need something cool, Jude. Let me fetch it for you."

He nodded, staring after her as she vanished into the shadows indoors. Sarai swore she could feel his gaze following her, even after she went into another room and walls lay between him and her. She said a quick, silent prayer that this would turn out to be amusing.

Yet as she thought over the situation, she couldn't shove away a chilly ripple of apprehension, even fear. Jude had been in favor of Jesus, but in the months since she had left Jerusalem with Norah and Malachi, there was no telling what sort of pressures the Sanhedrin had put on Jude and his father, to bring them back into obedience and loyalty. For all she knew, Jude had come here to assist Simon in finding her and bringing her back to Jerusalem for punishment. It was entirely believable that Caiaphas needed someone to make an example of, once the uproar over Jesus' death and resurrection had died away. For the sake of his position and future, she could entirely believe Simon would turn her over to Caiaphas' judgment and punishment.

Sarai sent the wine and bread and figs out to Jude with Abigail and retired to her room. It was no lie to say she needed to rest before the evening meal.

She slept, and that did surprise her, because there were so many thoughts swirling and churning through her head. Sarai didn't feel rested, though, when Norah came to wake her. Fortunately, Malachi had returned from his business dealings at the eastern gate. He took charge of questioning Jude and determining what he wanted -- and more important, if he could be trusted.

Jude had come looking for her. Sarai didn't know what she felt; if she believed him or disbelieved him, if she was glad or afraid or even angry. What was that breathless feeling and the sensation that she couldn't go to face him, yet couldn't make herself run away?

"Did you expect this, or did you fear it?" Malachi asked. He went down on one knee in front of the low bench where she sat in the inner room of the house.

Jude waited outside in the inn courtyard. Sarai was grateful that Malachi had come to talk to her first, before making her go out to face him. At least she had time to prepare.

Or maybe it would have been a greater mercy not to give her any time to prepare. Just lead her out there, to face him with a courtyard full of inn customers and regulars, and let him spill his message and ask the questions she had seen in his eyes. No time to be afraid, to feel she might be sick, with an odd sensation of weightlessness swirling through her, as if her feet might leave the floor at any moment.

"I do not know," she finally said, after struggling for words and to regain her breath. "He tried to buy my freedom from Simon, before we left Jerusalem."

"Yes, I remember." Malachi snorted softly. "Got himself a black eye and a bloody lip for his trouble. If he was trying to win your heart, that was not the way to do it."

"I would have been his property, just as much as I was Simon's."

"Little one." He caught hold of her hands between his. "You are my daughter, as surely as Norah. He cannot make you do anything, even if he waves a bill of sale in our faces. When Simon cast you out ..." He shook his head, letting out a gusty sigh. "Give me the word, and I will send him away. I almost hope he causes you trouble, so I can ask all the other inns in Damascus to deny him hospitality."

Sarai let out a little bubble of laughter. That helped. She could breathe again, and the spinning sensation slowed, even if it didn't ease completely.

Malachi proved his insightfulness and understanding. He tugged on her hands and when she was on her feet, he tucked her arm through his and supported her, going through the house to the inn kitchen, and outside into the courtyard. Evening shadows were thickening. Several torches had been lit, and the oil lanterns hanging from the canopy were being lit as Sarai passed under it.

They went up to the roof, where Jude had been sent to wait and they could speak in private, away from prying eyes. The noise of voices, the crackle of flames in the firepits in the courtyard, and clatter of pots and plates would make it hard to be overheard. Norah and Laila sat with Jude. Eli kept watch at the top of the stairs. Sarai caught her breath, feeling even more strongly now that yes, these people were her family. How had she ever let herself, even for a few moments, feel alone and defenseless? If she became so confused she couldn't figure out what to do, they would guard her; they would decide for her, until she was able to think clearly again.

She stumbled, catching the toe of her sandal on the top step, when she realized that yes, Jude made her afraid. Why? Had she sensed something in him to make her afraid? Istra and other healers had commended her sensitivity. Often, healers had to depend on awareness finer than ordinary people possessed, to catch the slightest signs of the cause of illnesses. Istra had laughed a little, when so many other healers claimed the insight came from their gods, but Sarai knew there was some truth in that. Adonai gave her the insight and sensitivity to heal others. She wondered if that same sensitivity warned her about Jude, or she was simply startled by his appearance. She had never thought he would come for her. She had never let herself hope.

He hadn't rescued her when the Romans destroyed her family. He hadn't come quickly enough to the slave market in the Decapolis. Then he had lied when he made his excuses. Maybe it was foolish to resurrect old resentments, yet … could she be sure of anyone from her old life? Anyone who hadn't chosen to follow and serve Jesus outright, so they had to flee Jerusalem?

"You look well." Jude stood as Sarai and Malachi approached the circle of cushions and benches around the brazier. The evenings were cool enough that a small fire was welcome for the heat, as much as the light and the pleasant aroma from the spices thrown on the coals.

"You as well." She resolved to say as little as possible. The next moment, as Malachi let go of her arm and she settled onto a bench, she changed her mind. The only way to be safe was to control the conversation. "How is Hannah? Has she had her child?"

"A boy. Micah. For Simon's father."

"Good. I'm glad for her." She knew better than to force herself to say she was glad for Simon.

Truthfully, she was glad for herself. She had to believe Ananias' prophecy that she would give birth to a daughter, but there was more safety and security for her now, knowing Hannah had given Simon his son and heir. Less chance of him showing up with no warning, with all the power of Jewish law behind him, to snatch her child from her arms. Unless she swore she had committed adultery to conceive the child, Simon had all the law on his side, and she had no voice, no power, no right to even ask for mercy, and for the law to intervene on her behalf.

"She is sickly. The last few months before giving birth were hard for her. Or so I've heard." Jude shrugged and ducked his head and couldn't look at her. "I haven't spoken with Simon since he struck me."

"You would think someone so concerned with righteousness and pleasing Adonai would take the first step to make things right with his closest friend." Norah wrinkled up her nose, as if she smelled something distasteful. "If only to make himself look more righteous."

"I have not been Simon's closest friend in a very long time. As well, I have not spent much time in Jerusalem. Or in Judea, for that matter. Father has me traveling extensively." Another shrug. "He feels it is safer for me to be out of sight of the authorities, until they forget I followed the rabbi."

Sarai caught her breath. Was that all Jude thought of Jesus? That He was a rabbi, nothing more? She wanted to demand that he explain, wanted to make him confess that he believed Jesus had returned from the grave. What had happened to her resolve to control the conversation?

"Is the boy well, at least?" she said instead.

Jude could only tell her what he had heard. Norah and Malachi took over the conversation, asking about mutual acquaintances and friends left behind in Jerusalem and Bethany, who didn't have access to a scribe to write letters for them. She was grateful when they asked about Rabbi Nicodemus, and Jude reported that as far as he knew, he hadn't suffered for his support of Jesus, or for burying Him.

As far as he knew. As far as he heard. By the fourth or fifth time Jude prefaced his answers with those words, Sarai grew sick of hearing them. Didn't Jude know anything for certain? Couldn't he have made the effort to find out details? Didn't he care about the people who had once been an important part of his life?

She felt certain that his father's influence, his fear of the criticism of the religious leaders, kept Jude on the fringes of everything happening in Jerusalem. Most likely the news Ananias had brought them or the messages sent by friends in Jerusalem from three or four months ago were more accurate than what Jude had heard. She resolved that she would write to Rabbi Nicodemus and find out from him directly how he was, if he was being punished in any way, if he was in danger. Perhaps she should speak with Malachi, and suggest he take shelter here at the inn with them? Could Rabbi Nicodemus make the long trip without harm?

That thought brought a bit of humor through the swirling, tangled emotions that threatened to knot her insides. If she could take the long, rough, hot, dusty journey from Jerusalem to Damascus without harm to her or her child, surely Nicodemus could. Sarai's hands strayed to rest over her belly at that thought. She glanced up when she realized what she did. Just like all the other times she caught herself covering the child, she caught Jude staring at her hands. He looked stunned. Hurt. Again. Or perhaps more accurately, he *still* looked hurt.

How dare he feel hurt by her pregnancy!

She owed Jude nothing. He hadn't fulfilled the sweet promises he had made to her. He hadn't completed any of the plans they had made when they were children, when he was her father's student. Plans that were all his, but she had agreed to because she thought she would be his wife. Because she thought she adored him.

When he failed her, he had lied about it. How could he sit there, looking hurt, as if she had betrayed him by carrying Simon's child?

Chapter Eight

Heat traveled up from her belly, banishing the cold. Sarai vowed once again, this child was solely hers. Simon had no claim. He had forfeited the right to be father to her child, when he cast her aside. He had his chance to repent and make things right during those days of confusion after Jesus walked out of the tomb, but he hadn't come for her. Just as Jude hadn't come for her.

"I'm sorry," she said, getting to her feet with more speed than she had used in at least a month. Despite being so small, the growing baby did throw off her balance. Sarai had to remove Jude from her sight, or she would remain in the swirling prison of her thoughts. She didn't need the resentment to poison her blood, and in turn poison the child. "I am -- I need --" She fluttered her hand in a general direction of the kitchen and her room, her sanctuary on the other side of the wall, and managed to get to the stairs without stumbling. How she got down the stairs without falling, she wasn't sure.

She snatched a handful of raisins and a honey cake and a cup of goat's milk on the way through the kitchen. Her temper likely suffered from hunger. Her scattered thoughts needed something to settle her stomach. Sarai flung open the shutters of her room and sat on the wide sill to eat, looking down on the stream of humanity traveling the street a story below her. She prayed, but what exactly she prayed, she couldn't be sure.

~~~~~

Jude stayed at the inn. Malachi could not deny him hospitality. Unless Sarai said outright that his presence harmed her, what could he do? No one came to call on her for healing, so when her regular duties were finished, she walked to Istra's house, just to get away from the inn. She could help in compounding potions and pastes and powders, or discuss a new scroll of healing lore Istra might have obtained from a trader.

Ananias met up with her on her way home late in the afternoon that first day of Jude's stay. Sarai almost blurted the questions churning in her head, certain he had come deliberately to intercept
~~~~~

her. She kept silent and gratefully let him take her arm, to give her some support. The walk back to the inn felt three times longer than the walk to Istra's home that morning.

"You are troubled." Ananias patted her hand, tucked into the curve of his arm.

"Did the Spirit tell you, or did Norah ask you to intervene?" She could almost laugh.

"First our dear Norah, then the Spirit expanded my understanding. You fear, and you are perhaps right to fear. Not that you will lose your child to her father, but that you will lose friends and respect when the lies you tell are shattered, and the false wall that shields you is torn down."

"Lies," she murmured. "I am innocent, and yet …" She sighed. "I know I did right by holding fast to my faith in Jesus as the Messiah. I stayed loyal to my father's teachings, despite the condemnation of the Sanhedrin. Why am I wrong to refuse to wear the brand of shame that Simon put on me, because I did not choose him over the Messiah, over truth, and the fulfillment of Adonai's promises?"

A sense of weight lifted from Sarai's shoulders as her words seemed to linger in the air. An odd pressure squeezing the back of her head vanished. She hadn't realized those sensations were there until they vanished. She could almost laugh, and she stared at Ananias as a slow smile brightened his face. He squeezed her hand again.

"There, and that is perhaps the root of the oppressive spirit stealing the joy that is the birthright of all those who follow our Savior. It is unfair, I know, that we are hobbled and chained by the actions of our persecutors, and those who treat us unjustly. Unfair that we are not justified in telling lies to ward off the unjustified punishment and shame others would heap on us."

"Unfair that telling the truth would open my family, my defenders, to harassment and accusations of immorality, and damage the reputation of the inn? We had a difficult enough time as it was, the first few months here, with men walking through our gates and demanding that every bed contain a girl to entertain them. And me, with my belly … such as it is." She choked on a thickness in her throat that might have been bitter laughter. Her growing belly had seemed dangerously small, until Jude looked at her. Then suddenly it was large enough to eclipse the sun.

"I think enough of the truth of what happened in Jerusalem has reached Damascus. People will understand what happened, and why, and not condemn you immediately as an adulteress, when the truth is revealed."

"To whom?" She tried to tug her arm free, but Ananias held on. Despite that, his grip was gentle.

"Rabbi Amos has spent enough time with us, learning from our memories and the growing record of the Christ's teachings. He knows of the political maneuvering in Jerusalem. He will understand why Simon gave you the ultimatum, and why he had to follow through. If Amos supports you and says you are innocent of adultery, if not innocent of disobedience to your husband ... Yes, better the truth come out now than later. Now, people will still sympathize and consider you ill-used. And you must think of all your suitors. To defend yourself against them, if nothing else."

"Suitors?" Sarai stopped, only a few steps away from the doorstep of the house. "Why must I continue to worry about suitors?"

"Child ..." He chuckled and reached up with his other hand to brush her cheek with the tips of his fingers. "You are young, you are lovely, you are intelligent and gifted. A midwife and healer. This makes you greatly respected and highly valued in every district of the city, among every nation and the followers of every god, false and true. Plus, you are fertile. For consideration of your widowhood, and because of your coming child, all those who would pursue you as a bride have restrained themselves."

He gestured at the door of the house. Sarai nodded and let him lead her to the doorstep. Ananias waited until they were inside and sitting on the bench in the entry hallway. "The only thing protecting you from an onslaught of suitors once your daughter is weaned is the truth, that you are divorced. If the young men who only see a pretty young woman aren't halted by the stigma, their parents will be. I can name at least eight mothers, yearning to be grandmothers, who have been preparing their sons for the day that you are considered once again available for marriage. You need to halt them before the race begins."

Sarai moaned and hid her face in her hands. Her cheeks felt hotter than she had thought they could ever feel. Not since her days in the slave market.

Ananias was right. Why hadn't she thought that far ahead? She had ignored, or tried to ignore, the assessing looks from the older women, the mothers of eligible sons, when she went to the synagogue or encountered them in the marketplace.

"Do you want to marry again?"

"No!" A moment later, a sharp burst of laughter escaped her. She hadn't realized how much she hated the thought of marriage, remarriage, until he asked.

"Then you must use the truth as a shield. Those who are not repulsed and do not consider you unclean because you are divorced might just discourage their sons from seeking you as a bride because you are loyal to Jesus."

"And what of the young men who have chosen to believe Jesus is the Messiah, coming first as the Suffering Servant?"

"I shall deal with them." He squeezed her hands. A weary chuckle escaped him, ending in a sigh. "Ah, I did not look forward to having this painful talk with you. It has weighed on me. Perhaps it is a good thing your former suitor has arrived and caused you such turmoil."

"Jude." She sighed. "I can't."

"Can't what? Talk with him? Be honest with him?"

"Marry him. If that is what he wants. I pray to Adonai that is not what he wants. I pray he has only sought me to ease his conscience, because he did not rescue me the first time."

"What if he had rescued you?"

Sarai shook her head. There were too many other considerations fighting for her attention to play the game of "what if?" again. The sore spots in her soul were still there, from wondering what would have happened if Jude had followed through on all his sweet promises -- and wondering why he hadn't.

~~~~~

"Sarai?" Jude paused a moment in the doorway of the kitchen.

This late into the evening, there was no more cooking. Even the aroma from the stew that Norah had kept simmering all day had faded from the air. The last plateful had been served more than an hour ago. The faint aroma of the bread rising for tomorrow's baking would not perfume the air for hours to come.

Sarai had come to make her nightly infusion to help her sleep
~~~~~

and strengthen her blood. One of the first scrolls her father had bought for her had contained a recipe that would strengthen her against childbed fever and protect the newborn during the strain of labor. Sarai had used it often enough, when she assisted Huldah in Bethany, she knew the recipe by heart. She also had proof that it worked. It soothed her to know some things were reliable, even more than it soothed her head and helped her relax to sleep.

"Have you been out in the city all day, tending to your father's business?" She lifted the iron pot off the fire, to pour the almost-bubbling water into the clay cup holding the finely ground herbs.

"Yes, but -- you have been gone all day." He stepped over the threshold, but stayed in the doorway, blocking most of the light from the lanterns and torches in the courtyard.

"I am not a woman of leisure and wealth. I have duties to attend to." She put the pot back on the grid over the fire and continued the motion, to brush her hand over her belly. It was an unthinking gesture. She didn't do it to hurt him, though she caught the wrinkles gathering around his eyes and mouth, the momentary pained look.

"We will tell everyone the child is mine."

"What?" She held back an inexplicable bubble of laughter.

"We can be married immediately. We will tell everyone -- well, everyone believes you are a widow, but we can tell them I seduced you in your first days of grief."

"Everyone who can count knows that my child -- my daughter," she emphasized, "was conceived while I was still married."

"We need a story to explain things, to protect you, when we return to Jerusalem, or at least return to Judea."

"I am not returning to Judea. This is my home."

"Your home should have been with me all along."

"Jude, thank you, but there is no need for you --"

"Sarai, why won't you let me rescue you? Like I should have rescued you years ago."

"Is that why you are doing this? You feel you owe me some debt? Or because you don't like to lose?" She picked up the small plate to cover the steaming cup, and mentally slapped herself for delaying that step. Vital properties of the herbs could be lost from the potion through the escaping steam. Tonight, especially, she would need all the soothing in the cup.

"I fear for you." He took a few shaky steps and reached for her hand.

Sarai stepped back and picked up the pottery cup as a defensive measure. It was almost too hot for holding. If she had to, she supposed she could throw the hot mixture into his face and then start all over, making a new batch. The calmness of that decision helped her, somehow.

"I will not marry you, though I thank you for feeling you need to protect me."

"Sarai, don't you love me?"

"I --" She couldn't tell him no. She couldn't hurt him that way. She supposed somewhere deep inside she did have tender feelings for him, but she had changed from the innocent, idealistic girl with starry-eyed dreams of sweet love and devotion. "All my love is reserved for my child."

"Simon's child." Those lines around his mouth and eyes tightened to anger.

"*My* child. Mine alone. Her father has no claim on her, and if you ever truly ..." She took a deep breath, resolved not to use the same tactics he had been trying to use on her. "If you ever truly held any regard for me, you will not tell Simon about his daughter."

"How can you be so sure you carry a daughter? Don't you want a son, to hold against him and hold over him? A better son than Hannah could ever have given him?"

"A prophet spoke to me and told me I carried a daughter. He promised she would be a gift and blessing from El Shaddai." Sarai put the cup down and slid the covering off it, to test the aroma for strength.

"So you don't need me?" He tried to smile. "Not even a little?"

"Jude ... I am a divorced woman. Jesus taught that only immorality was justification for divorce, so in many ways, I am still married to Simon. I will not make myself unclean, and I will not make you unclean. An adulterer." She was glad she had put the cup down, because she felt a little breathless. Where had that come from? She had never considered the teachings of Jesus on divorce, not as it applied to her, not even as she wrote down the memories of those lessons other people shared with her.

Perhaps Adonai had answered her prayer for help and

guidance, and put the words into her mind, or even on her tongue?

"He cast you off. He betrayed you, turned against you. Doesn't that make you free?"

"I have not sinned, even though many would accuse me of betraying my husband because I did not put him above my devotion to Adonai. I have not sinned, but that does not mean I am free to marry again." She picked up the cup and brought it to her lips. "Please, Jude, leave me in peace? In this matter at least?" She turned partially away from him and blew on the surface of the potion, preparing to taste it.

Jude said nothing. She closed her eyes and sipped. Almost strong enough. She turned back. He had left the doorway. She couldn't see him against the torches and lanterns in the courtyard. Sarai took a deep, slow breath, and crossed the kitchen to pick up the pierced cup lined with cloth, to strain the potion for drinking.

~~~~~

Sarai did not see Jude again before he left the inn. If he went to stay at another inn before completing his business and leaving Damascus, she did not know. She chose not to ask, and none of her inn family offered the information. She was grateful for their discretion and protection.

Later, after she had given birth, she learned that Jude and Laila had argued. He had accused Laila of encouraging Sarai to hope that Simon would come for her. She had laughed in his face. Then he accused her of poisoning Sarai's heart against him. Laila responded that Sarai's heart was too hurt even now to belong to anyone other than Jesus and her child.

Sarai wished she had thought to say that to Jude. Why hadn't she put her devotion to Jesus and His teachings first? There was some truth in Laila's words, that her heart was still wounded. Perhaps the sore spots meant she still loved Simon, but that was a weak, useless kind of love. The kind that made her vulnerable to others and easily used and hurt. She prayed for strength and healing. She had her daughter to think about, and prepare for, and protect.

Before she lost her courage, Sarai agreed to follow Ananias' advice, and reveal the truth about her marriage and divorce, starting with Rabbi Amos. She was pleased and relieved when Ananias offered, as leader of their fellowship of believers, to
~~~~~

approach Amos in confidence.

The very next Sabbath, Amos came to join them for their worship and study time. After the psalm that ended the formal part of the evening, Sarai came outside with a basket of bread studded with apricots and dripping with butter, to feed their guests. She saw the two men in a corner of the courtyard, deep in discussion, and fumbled the basket when she guessed what they were discussing. She kept busy all through the evening and spent most of her time in the kitchen despite her growing sensitivity to the heat of the cooking fire. When she stepped out into the courtyard and Amos was gone, she called herself a fool and coward.

Ananias stayed after everyone else had departed for their homes. Sarai reluctantly joined him and Norah and Malachi on the roof to speak quietly, while the rest of the inn workers doused torches and lanterns, and swept the courtyard, and stacked benches on the tables.

"I do not know why I am constantly surprised by the providence of the Master," Ananias said, after telling them almost word-for-word what he had told Amos.

It was Norah and Malachi's right to know what had been revealed to the synagogue leader, because eventually the story would circle back around and affect the inn, one way or another.

"Our friend is a gift from Adonai, a shelter against coming storm. He revealed he was disturbed by many of the stories coming from Jerusalem, both the accusations being made by the religious leaders and the stories of abuses the believers are beginning to suffer. Small prejudices and injustices, but growing ..." He shook his head, his gaze going distant for a moment. "Amos understands why Simon cast you out. While he agrees that Simon has the law on his side, he does not believe Yahweh approves what was done to you. He brought up the teaching of a number of rabbis who condemn men who cast aside their wives for any reason other than the immoral actions of the women. Amos especially approves of the teachings of Gershom ben Phineas, of the tribe of Asher, who insists that such a man should be considered dead to the Hebrew community. Such a man has allowed his fleshly desires to overrule the law of the Spirit of Adonai. In such a situation, the woman is considered blameless, unjustly harmed, and free of all obligations and condemnations. Like a widow." Ananias nodded for punctuation.

"How ... convenient," Norah said, drawing the words out. "Did you ever hear of this rabbi, Sarai?"

She could only shake her head. A half-dozen retorts caught at the back of her tongue, some of them bitter. How many times had some of her father's more arrogant students retorted that she was just a woman and couldn't retain knowledge, even after she had proven them wrong by correctly quoting from Scriptures?

"Amos has only praise for Sarai, that she would hold to the story that she is a widow, rather than the victim of her husband's selfish actions. She proves the purity of her heart by protecting him from shame and mockery, even though he is in the wrong. Amos will reveal the truth ... as he sees the truth, I suppose ... gradually, to the leaders of the Jewish community." Ananias shrugged. "That is all we can do, and for the rest we must trust to El Shaddai for protection and blessing."

"Thank you," Sarai whispered.

She didn't know how she would be able to face Rabbi Amos when he returned to the inn. Perhaps there was something she could do to express her thanks for his support, understanding, and lack of condemnation? She wasn't sure what, other than finding another, more pleasant potion for him to drink, to ease the pain in his joints.

However, before Amos returned to the Inn of the Three Sisters, and before any response to the story he was telling could appear, Sarai gave birth to her daughter. The rain began softly when her labor pains made themselves felt in early afternoon, and the child took her first breath at sunset, as Sarai had been told months ago.

She named her Pearl, as Ananias had instructed in his prophecy.

Laila and Dorcas and Norah had a bit of fun, tallying the potential suitors and trying to decide, based on the reactions of their matchmaking mothers or aunts or grandmothers, which ones would give up and which ones would have to be discouraged further. A handful of women didn't wait for Sarai's ritual purification period to end, but came to visit her, hiding their intentions behind gifts of clothes and treats and caged pigeons to give as her purification offering. Sarai only needed two pigeons, so Norah had enough to make pigeon-stuffed pastries for the entire inn household. Those women were neatly divided into two categories. The ones who wanted fodder for gossip, and the ones who were so desperate for a granddaughter, they could overlook Sarai's questionable status as a divorced woman and a follower of Jesus. They were consistent in remarking on how small and delicate Pearl was, then stunned by the loud outcry from such a tiny body, when she was hungry or her swaddling needed to be changed.

Ebenezer and Nahum kept close to the women as they left the house, and often even followed them home, to listen to their real reactions and thoughts. Several expressed the belief that Pearl's smallness was a punishment for Sarai rebelling against her husband's authority. After all, as one said, Jesus was just another misguided rabbi and troublemaker. Other women were enchanted with the baby and declared she would be a beauty when she was grown. She would need a strong, clever father to protect her and make a good marriage for her. Those women's names were noted. Laila and Norah had fun planning how to discourage those women and their unmarried sons.

The day Sarai finished her time of isolation and went through the purification ceremony, Malachi held a celebration. After all, he declared loudly, after he made the toast of blessing, if Sarai was considered a daughter to him, then Pearl was by rights his first grandchild, and he was delighted with her. Norah managed not to respond, either in word or expression, until her father had gone to the other side of the courtyard to talk with some guests. Then she declared she was grateful he hadn't made her life miserable by pressing her to consider several wealthy or influential young men who had become nuisances. They expressed interest, but not enough that Malachi could outright tell them no. The women were all sitting under the canopy by the door into the kitchen, and they laughed at her words. Sarai had seen the look on Norah's face when she held Pearl and knew her friend wasn't averse to marriage and having children. However, the requisite husband who met her standards had yet to appear.

The relief Sarai felt at Pearl's birth, and the security of Ananias' prophecy faded quickly, when several members of the inn's household were questioned about the name of Sarai's husband. What did he do for a living? Where did he live? Who was his family?

"They don't have any right to know, they don't need to know," Laila fumed several days later, after yet another inquiry was reported to them. She and Sarai were on the roof, enjoying what might be the last of the warm, pleasant fall weather, before the cold rains began to bring in winter. "Mark my words, they're asking so they can have power over you."

"What kind of power would they want? What good would it do them?" Sarai kept her voice down. Pearl slept in her cradle on the far side of the roof, where an awning deflected the direct sunlight and the breezes.

"From my calculations, the ones who were asking belong to the families of suitors. The hard part will be determining if they've given up, and they want to punish you for being out of their reach. Or they want to threaten you. Or they want to determine what kind of trouble they'll have if word reaches Jerusalem that you married their son or grandson or nephew."

"I'm not marrying anyone."

"You and I both know that, but some men are like nasty little children with fingers full of honey. If they can't have the jar all to themselves, they'll either break the jar or spill it on the floor, so no one else can have it."

"They want to know about Simon, so they can contact him and tell him about Pearl? Maybe they think I'll be willing to marry if I don't have Pearl?"

"Or they'll only keep their silence if you marry their son."

"If I refused Jude, what makes any of them think they're a better choice?"

She was so infuriated, it took several days before she could offer a polite greeting to anyone who was even distantly related to a potential suitor.

Sometimes Sarai let herself wonder what would have happened if she had encouraged Jude. Would he have stayed in Damascus, or maybe taken her even farther from Jerusalem and people who might send news of her back to Simon?

She pondered the possibilities, until the night she woke up in terror, sweating, and stumbled across the room to Pearl's cradle, to make sure her daughter was there. In her dream, Jude had taken her back to Jerusalem, and Simon had pursued them with all the Sanhedrin's guards, claiming Jude had robbed him. He demanded payment, and when Jude insisted that he had paid for Sarai already, Simon tore Pearl from her arms and threatened to throw her from the roof of the Temple. The law made the child of his bondservant his property, and he would destroy her rather than let Jude profit from her. Sarai woke when in her dream she flung herself at Simon to snatch her baby from his hands, and they both fell.

"Adonai, Father of Lights, cleanse my mind. Free me from this fear. Forgive me for longing for what I cannot have. What cannot be good for me," Sarai whispered. She stayed on her knees next to Pearl's cradle, whispering psalms to comfort herself, until dawn light trickled through the gaps in the shutters.

Chapter Nine

Sarai braced herself for something to happen. She wasn't sure what, either good or bad. Passover came and went, and a full year had passed since Jesus died and returned to life. Her written collection of the memories of other believers in Christ grew. Ananias asked her to make copies, to add to transcribed memories others were collecting. Nothing changed in Damascus, other than a slow growth in acknowledgment from the Jewish community that the followers of Christ existed and were not madmen or rebels, but intelligent, hard-working people who were good neighbors.

Marakata chose to stay in the little house in the wall. She was a skilled seamstress and had a keen eye for the decorative little stitches and tucks that let clothes fall in flattering lines. Until her arm healed completely, she had limited herself to mending and assisting the inn's women who did simple sewing tasks. Then, when she had built up her courage to go out in the daylight, veiled, her face devoid of cosmetics, in dull colors, she wandered the city and listened and watched. She applied the cleverness that had kept her alive as a harlot, using it to learn what people found attractive in colors and decorations. Then she applied what she learned to make clothes for the poorer women in Damascus. The ones who couldn't afford jewelry. She embroidered flowers and fanciful designs into the sturdy, plain cloth these women could afford, and gave them a chance to feel pretty. Such women didn't generate much attention, so although Marakata's name became known for her clever stitchery, it didn't travel beyond the poorer classes. She earned enough to provide food and clothes for herself and was proud when she could give Eli a few coins to help with the household expenses.

Slowly, carefully, Laila and Marakata went about Damascus and offered shelter to other harlots. When they knew the women would not betray them, they told them about the house in the wall. No outcry was raised when one harlot vanished from the streets. Then a month later, another vanished. Again, without outcry. The girls who wanted to leave the life were not the alluring, popular ones who had men clamoring for their favors. Few people, except perhaps the brothel owners, cared if the girls had been killed by the last man who used them, which was usually the case. They did care, a little bit more, if a rival brothel owner had captured a girl and was now collecting what little profit she had been making for the previous man. No one thought long about the possibility that the desperate girl had run away. Where could runaways go?

In later years, Sarai remembered how the oddness and irony of her new life struck her at times. She who had looked down on harlots, if she ever thought about them at all, had nearly become one, and now had a ministry to help them. Adonai was still teaching her humility and compassion. She came to like most of the girls who hid in the house in the wall and tried to change their ways. To those who had the ability to learn, she taught simple healing potions and skills. Anything the girls could use to support themselves without trading their bodies and risking their lives, they gladly learned.

However, she couldn't bring herself to take Pearl with her when she went to the house, either on a regular weekly visit, or when someone came to take shelter, battered and bleeding. Someday she would take her daughter with her, but not now. She could not expose such innocence to the sorrow and pain that thickened the air when she stepped through the door.

Sarai made it a habit to pray aloud as she went about her healer duties. She gave a greeting and blessing in the name of Jesus the Christ when she entered a home, and she sang Jesus' name over newborns as she washed and rubbed them with salt and anointed them. The practice generated a reputation for her, and she wasn't surprised when some who were in more regular contact with the leading families and authorities in Jerusalem no longer requested her services. There was more than enough work for her to do helping Gentile families who relied on her skills. More Jewish families called on her for help than families who shunned her, and they seemed grateful when she spoke the name of Jesus over them.

The testimony and approval of the healers and midwives throughout Damascus served to protect the inn, as did the Roman soldiers. Only a fool irritated a healer, because there was no way of knowing if an injury or poison had killed a man, or the healer had deliberately made a mistake. Other healers might be able to tell, but healers stood together against those who threatened or bothered them. The Inn of the Three Sisters was known also as the Inn of the Healer, and it gained a reputation as a safe place for travelers with families, especially little children.

There were always a few brutes and bullies who tried to intimidate and take liberties with the women who lived and worked in an inn. The Roman soldiers, especially their officers, were always conveniently nearby to help. No one gainsaid them if they claimed the woman's attacker had committed more crimes than try to drag an unwilling woman into a room he hadn't paid for yet. If the man was bloodied and bruised before he reached the official who processed his sentence, he knew better than to complain or accuse the soldiers of brutality.

Jude came to Damascus every four or five months, traveling on his father's business. When he stopped at the Inn of the Three Sisters, he only stayed one night, each time. He always had a gift for Pearl. An Egyptian doll one time, a kitten another time, a necklace of shells taken from the cold waters of the sea north of Gaul. He never brought Sarai a gift, and she could always feel his sad gaze on her while she went about her duties. Sarai asked him about Hannah and Micah, and he rarely had any news other than gossip. Hannah had never recovered from childbed. She was an invalid, and Simon spent large sums on physicians. He earned some criticism from Caiaphas and other members of the Sanhedrin for seeking help from Gentile healers.

Sarai prayed for Hannah and thought often about Micah, but didn't tell Pearl she had a brother who was three months older than her. Perhaps she never would. There was no telling the future. She would trust El Shaddai for knowing the right time to tell her daughter about her family in Jerusalem.

Someday, she would have to tell Pearl. Someday, Sarai knew she would go home, if only once, to see her father's tomb.

~~~~~

Pearl was two-and-a-half years old when the news came that the small community of Christ-followers in Damascus had anticipated, but prayed would never happen. The pressure of enmity against the believers in Jerusalem had finally grown to the bursting point. Jealousy over the growing numbers and the sweet fellowship proved to be sufficient motivation to strike out at them,
~~~~~

just as the Sanhedrin had struck at Jesus. This time, the lies and liars were better organized, and false charges were brought up against a man who was a servant-leader in the growing fellowship. His name was Stephen, and he was stoned by an angry mob of religious leaders and officials. This time, there was no maneuvering and game-playing to trick the Romans into legitimizing the execution.

The backlash and confusion that had slowed the Sanhedrin in striking at Jesus' followers in the days after the resurrection did not appear. There was no pause in the collective mind and soul and heart of the city. Within weeks of Stephen's death, arrests scourged the city. Believers fled not just Jerusalem, but Judea. Many of them came to Damascus, seeking shelter with the small fellowship. Malachi sent regular customers to other inns, to make sure there was room for fugitives to take shelter.

Jude came, but he was not among the fugitives. He was simply on another journey for his father, this time returning to Gaul, to set up a clearinghouse for trading. He told them he would not be back for several years. Sarai asked about Hannah and Micah, as she always did.

"If she's lucky, this will be the final illness." Jude seemed not to notice Sarai's flinch of pain. He tore in half the fresh round of warm bread she had brought him, paying more attention to the herb-infused oil he dipped it in than his words. "She didn't deserve to have this happen to her, but I would not be surprised if Yahweh is using her to punish the entire family of Simon ben Micah."

"Jude, how can you say that?"

"It's only the truth. It balances out his wealth, his rise in prestige in the Sanhedrin. He didn't even suffer for giving Rabbi Nicodemus shelter when Annas condemned him and barred him from entering the Temple to worship. What is the fairness in that?"

Sarai pressed her lips flat together to hold back the dozens of words burning to escape. What about all the injustice that Simon and his father had suffered at the hands of Jedidiah and his father? Before she could respond, Jude said what she had feared hearing from the moment he stepped into the inn courtyard with such a determined look on his face.

"It's time, Sarai. Come with me to Gaul where you'll be safe."

"You know I can't."

Jude paused, holding still for five heartbeats she heard

thudding in her ears. Something shifted in his expression. His jaw tightened. Sparks touched his eyes. He threw down the bread and scorched her with the most furious look she had ever seen him wear. Then he turned and stomped away.

He didn't look for Pearl to give her the usual gift before he left the inn. Sarai found a little satisfaction in knowing her daughter didn't realize Jude had been there. She didn't miss someone she hadn't known was there. Perhaps this was the last time she would see him? She tried to be glad, yet her traitor heart wouldn't be quiet. As the news from Jerusalem and spreading outward across the land grew grimmer and darker with blood and fear, she had to wonder if she had made the wrong choice after all. What if Adonai had sent Jude to provide her a way to flee to safety, to protect her daughter, and she had wasted her only chance to preserve their lives?

~~~~~

A new flood of believers fleeing Jerusalem brought reports that yanked Sarai into a sea of memories. Saul of Tarsus was a name she knew well, back in the glory days before her father fell into disgrace. Saul was the prize student of Gamaliel, one of the most revered rabbis in Jerusalem. His family had sent him to study with the famous teacher, and he had come to Rabbi Eliakim's home numerous times, accompanying his teacher. Sarai had spoken to Saul, to welcome him to her father's house, but he never spoke a word to her. He was a "Pharisee of Pharisees," as Gamaliel had said, with a chuckle and a rolling of his eyes. He had come back after that first visit to apologize and explain his brilliant student's rudeness.

Saul had only looked at her once, when her father introduced her to him, and then had totally ignored her presence for the remainder of his visit. She made it a point to never come down into the courtyard, where her father entertained guests, when she knew Saul would be there. Joseph had teased her once that they should dress her up as a boy and let her debate the young man. Her brother swore she knew far more about history and law than Saul did. Of course, Joseph wanted to finish the intellectual thrashing by revealing that the clever boy was actually a girl. Gamaliel had laughed when, during a visit without Saul, Rabbi Eliakim had shared that bit of silly plotting. He had apologized again for the idealistic and elitist attitude of the young man, and assured Rabbi
~~~~~

Eliakim that someday, El Shaddai would get hold of Saul and slap some common sense and humility into him. Then, when he picked himself up out of the dust, he would truly be a great man and a worthy tool in holy service. Until then, they would all have to endure and practice patience.

Sarai heard the stories of Saul's zeal against Jesus' followers. She wondered if Gamaliel had been won over to support Caiaphas, or if he despaired of his student's eventual redemption. Saul was the loyal and determined, perhaps even fanatical, tool of the Sanhedrin. He scoured Jerusalem and the surrounding towns and villages, hauling believers from their homes with the full authority and approval of the Sanhedrin. He oversaw their scourging and imprisonment, the demands that they deny their faith in Jesus, and the confiscation of their homes and possessions if they did not comply.

Malachi prepared the Inn of the Three Sisters for a new flood of refugees. He called on several merchant friends he fully trusted and asked them to be ready to take the fleeing believers with them to cities even farther away. Rabbi Amos and other leaders in the Jewish community still came to the inn for fellowship and to enjoy Norah's specialty dishes, but there was less laughter and fewer smiles, and the visits were shorter. Sarai wondered how long before people would have to decide between their friends and the distant authority of Jerusalem. If the day came that they were ordered to name the Christ-followers in Damascus, to help a hunter pursuing the Sanhedrin's business, who would choose Jesus, and who would choose Caiaphas?

Jasper came one night to sit and drink wine with Malachi and share the newest gossip that had come through the eastern gate. He complimented him on the luck of having such a talented daughter, and the fame of his inn, dwelling a little longer than usual on Norah's many good qualities. Sarai heard the laughter of the serving girls, repeating the flattery when they came to the kitchen to fill the trays with more plates and cups and baskets of bread. Sarai didn't realize until much later, when she was drawing water for washing before going to bed, that she hadn't heard Norah laughing about Jasper's flattery, like she usually did.

Sarai decided she would ask her about that. Had Norah tired of Jasper's unsubtle hints that someday he would whisk her away from serving at the inn and surround her with servants so she would never have to work again? Or had she started to take the man's words seriously? Deciding how to approach Norah with her suspicions was the difficult part.

Before she came up with the right words to say, Absalom, an apprentice of a silversmith on Straight Street, came to request her help as a healer. Sarai gave the jar of water to Anna and asked her to check on Pearl. She gathered up her bag of healing supplies and followed Absalom into the night.

The silversmith's brother had a guest in his house who had been there two days already, suffering from blindness that had struck him on his journey to Damascus. After two days of praying and fasting, and no relief from his darkness, they had convinced the man to let healers see him. Absalom led her to the inner courtyard of the house that belonged to Judas, a leader in the Jewish community who was vocally opposed to the fellowship of believers. Sarai was surprised he had sent for her.

A man sat in the corner, out of the reach of the torches. The smell of herbs and lamp oil, heated wine and other aromas of the healer's trade hung heavy in the air. The boy hadn't said other healers had been sent for already. Sarai guessed none of them had been able to help. She wondered if she had been sent for to provide Judas and his friends a chance to speak ill of believers. They expected her to fail. She had the reputation of praying aloud for help from Jesus, and if she failed it would reflect badly on her Master.

Use me, Master. Work through me. Show Your power and Your mercy. Give me the right words. Do not let me be the road through which our enemies can find justification to harm all who obey and serve You.

"The peace of Adonai be on this house," she said, as she approached the man. "I come in the name and in the service of Jesus the Christ, the risen one, the face of the one true God."

"You --" the man jerked, halfway rising from the bench. "You are a follower of the Nazarene?"

"I am."

"I have prayed." His voice cracked, and he made a rasping sound that she realized was weary laughter. "You sound young. Please don't be frightened, despite what you may have heard about me."

"I have heard nothing except that you are in need of healing, and I am a healer. If I have any success, any good reputation, it is because Adonai graciously uses me as a vessel of His healing power." She looked around the courtyard. "Will you come into the light?" A sigh escaped her. "I'm sorry. That was not meant to be cruel."

"You are far kinder than I deserve." He stood and held out a hand and took several steps. There was no hesitation, and she guessed that he had moved around the courtyard often enough to become familiar with the obstacles. Nevertheless, she took his hand and led him over to the table, where enough torchlight fell to give her better lighting to examine his eyes.

Someone had prepared in advance for any needs she might have. A small brazier with glowing coals, several sizes of knives, a long wooden board for chopping, a mortar and pestle, a bowl and pitcher full of water, and towels. She asked the man if he would wash his face, and poured water into the bowl before guiding his hands to find it and the clean towel. She emptied her bag of supplies while he was washing and arranged everything neatly on the table. In a flat wooden box, she kept small, delicate items that had proven useful in the past.

The first step was to get a good look at his eyes. The torchlight was strong, but not intense enough. However, she had needed focused light before, and had found a mirror useful. This was a small, slightly concave disk of glass, coated with silver, which she used to bounce torchlight directly into the man's eyes. She warned him what she would be doing, and gently pulled back bottom and top lid with thumb and forefinger, checking both eyes several times.

"Your eyes are ... there is something thick and coarse-looking covering your eyes. I can barely see the pupil. The boy who fetched me said this came on you suddenly?"

"Yes." The man smiled, one corner of his mouth trembling. "The judgment of Adonai. Physical blindness, to reflect the blindness of my soul and spirit."

Sarai took another step back, really looking at his face for the first time, and nearly dropped the mirror. She clutched it to her chest, heart racing, and fought not to go to her knees on the courtyard tiles.

He had aged at least ten years since the last time she had seen him, a favored student, arrogant in his self-righteousness, sitting at her father's table. Yet she knew him.

Saul of Tarsus.

"Healer?" He turned toward her, cocking his head in the manner of other blind folk she had seen over the years.

"I -- I am sorry. All I can suggest is salve to soften the rind or scales or whatever is covering your eyes." She babbled, and knew she babbled, suddenly very aware of the knives waiting to be picked up and used.

Could a blind man find those knives and stab at her?

Was this a trap? Would all the believers in Damascus be lured here to Judas' house -- how appropriate that name suddenly seemed -- to be tested and attacked, arrested, or simply slaughtered?

"The other two healers called them scales. One suggested taking a knife and cutting them away. The other said it was the judgment of Apollo, that I had insulted his demi-god healer son at one time." Saul shrugged. "Healer, please do not be frightened of me. I swear to you on all that I hold sacred in this world, I encountered Jesus on the road to this city, and it was He who struck me blind."

Sarai shuddered. Somehow, she made herself move. She wanted to flee. His words were just sounds for a few heartbeats. "I have salve that I make for soothing and softening skin," she said, as she slipped the mirror back into the wooden box. "It is especially effective with skin that has been burned, and thickened, so that movement is difficult. That might help." She fumbled through the small pots and wax-coated and sealed jars among her supplies, searching for the small pot of salve. She got everything back into her healer's bag despite the trembling of her hands. "Here, this should help."

"You are afraid." Saul caught hold of her hands as she settled the pot among his fingers. "I am sorry. I will spend the rest of my life making up for the terror and pain and loss that I have inflicted on the followers of the Christ."

Sarai nearly yelped and leaped back a step. Had he said what she thought he said? Then his previous words seemed to puncture the thick veil smothering her mind.

"You … you met Jesus?"

"I have been fasting and praying since my traveling companions brought me here. I have had a vision from Jesus. A promise, I hope. If the man He is sending to me is not too afraid to come. I think only then will I have healing and a return of my sight. But I thank you for coming. I thank you for the hope you have given me, speaking the name of the One who has claimed me as His servant. Tell me -- you do not have to, if you do not wish it -- but is there a community of Christ-followers here, in Damascus? Do you think someday, when I have proven myself, they will allow me to sit with them and fellowship and learn?"

"When you can see again …" She cupped his hands around the pot of salve. Somehow, the shaking had left her hands and settled into his and she feared he would drop it. "Judas knows where the believers meet. All the Jews in Damascus know where we fellowship. He can take you to us. When you can see again, then we will know that Jesus has sent you to us." She stepped back, and she needed to take several breaths before she could speak her ritual blessing of departure on him.

"Wait," Saul called, as she turned to the door out of the courtyard. "Who are you? I would like to speak with you, when I can see again. How will I find you?"

"When you find the fellowship of Christ's followers, you will find me." She took a step backward, wanting to flee, yet she felt as if something caught at her feet, slowing her steps. A gentle touch nudged her, urging the words that caught in her throat. *Please, Adonai, must I?* Then a bit of humor touched her. "I am Sarai beth Eliakim ben Levi of Bethany."

Saul gasped as she stepped out of the courtyard. He did not call after her, and something like laughter filled her chest with a hint of lightness as she went in search of Absalom, to escort her home again.

~~~~~

When the Sabbath came, Ananias was noticeably absent, on the walk to the synagogue, at the synagogue during the worship, and at the fellowship meal afterward. That wasn't a common occurrence, because he was in many ways the leader of the fellowship of believers. However, there were occasions when he did not join them, and no one was worried. Not even with the
~~~~~

knowledge that Saul of Tarsus, the hunting dog of the Sanhedrin, had come to Damascus.

Sarai told no one but Malachi and Norah of her encounter with the devoted young Pharisee. She wasn't sure what to think of it. Somehow, she managed to put all thoughts of that odd evening out of her mind by the time she went out on visits that afternoon. There were several elderly folk whom she had met first as a healer, and then became friends. She tried to visit them at least once a week. Most of them appreciated hearing what the rabbi had taught during worship, so she tried to spend her Sabbath afternoons visiting them, when the homily was fresh in her mind. They adored Pearl, so she always brought her daughter with her when the visits were to bring treats, such as honey cakes or dried fruit soaked in weak wine. None of the men or women looked or sounded anything like her parents, but she liked to imagine that Pearl had grandparents just the same, and to spare.

They left the inn with Pearl toddling happily along beside her, carrying a tiny basket like Sarai's. They returned just before dusk with the little girl asleep in the sling across her mother's chest. Sarai found some humor in being grateful at times like this that her daughter was so small. Most of the time, especially since Pearl had learned to walk, the child's size made her hard to catch and stop. She could slip through narrow spaces and duck down out of the reach of all the adults in the inn family who tried to keep her out of trouble. Sarai sometimes laughed at herself, remembering how grateful she had been when Pearl learned to walk so quickly. Laila and others teased her that Pearl had never walked -- she had gone from crawling to running in a matter of days, and someday soon she would learn to fly. Sarai did not look forward to the day that some small tragedy, an injury or fright, would teach her daughter to look ahead and not dash through life. Yet the child needed to listen and obey when adults called for her to turn around, or just stop. She needed to learn the lesson before the kind of tragedy struck from which they might never recover.

Sarai recognized several members of the fellowship walking ahead of her as she turned onto Harvest Moon Street. The gates of the inn were visible beyond them. So, she wouldn't be arriving too late to help with some of the preparations for the fellowship and the meal. She took a deep breath, straightened her shoulders, adjusted her arms under Pearl's weight, and picked up her pace.

A handful of people stepped out of her line of sight as they went through the inn gates. She saw Rabbi Amos and several other members of the fellowship coming up to the gates from the other direction. He saw her and waved, gesturing toward her. Joab stepped away from the others and hurried to meet her. He was Amos' great-nephew, grandson of Amos' older sister. His wife, Leah, had died just eight months ago, at the premature birth of their daughter. Leah had lost three children in five years. She had been a good friend of Sarai's and had doted on Pearl, with an intensity that made Sarai fear there was something broken inside her heart and mind. Sarai liked Joab, but she feared that when the proper time of mourning had passed, he would ask her to marry him. Rabbi Amos had intervened for her with several suitors in the years since Pearl's birth, but she feared when it came to Joab, the only intervention would be to persuade her to join his family.

Still, Joab was just as much a favorite uncle as the inn's menfolk. When he reached for Pearl, silently offering to help, Sarai accepted. Her daughter woke up during the transfer, while Joab supported her and Sarai slipped the sling off over her head. The little girl sighed, yawned, and blinked several times, and her adorable, bright smile lit her face when she looked up at Joab. A fatuous grin softened his rugged, tanned face. Who didn't adore the little girl? Sarai laughed silently at herself. Maybe Joab didn't really want her; he just wanted to be able to claim Pearl as his child. He had to ache just as much as Leah had over the loss of their children, although in different ways.

Amos stopped short just a few steps inside the gates. The courtyard was far emptier than Sarai expected for that time of the day on the Sabbath. Most of those who came to eat and talk and carry on business at the inn on the Sabbath were Gentiles. The regular customers understood that when sunset came and the Sabbath ended, the followers of Jesus came here to worship. There were always a few who stayed to mock, and a few who were curious and had finally worked up the courage to stay and listen. After several evenings of listening to worship, they either moved closer to the table where the teachers and song leaders stood, or they avoided the Inn of the Three Sisters on the Sabbath altogether.

Sarai wondered if there was some news, some development in

Damascus that had made such a visible change in the Sabbath evening routine. She stepped around Amos, between him and the carpenter, Nathanael, and looked toward the canopy and the door to the inn. She saw Ananias, in earnest conversation with Malachi. Both men were focused on a balding man who sat quietly at a table entirely by himself, facing into the courtyard, hands folded in his lap and head bowed.

Sarai dropped the basket she had carried back, hanging in the crook of her elbow. Fortunately, it was empty of all the gifts she had taken to the elderly folks she and Pearl had visited. Every pot of salve and parchment envelope of powdered herbs to put in steaming water, to ease breathing. Staring at the man, she bent and reached blindly for the handle of the basket.

"What's wrong?" Joab asked, stepping up next to her. He half-turned away, shielding Pearl with his massive body. Sarai thought for a moment she could love the man, just for his unthinking defense of her daughter. "I don't recognize him. Who is that?"

"Saul of Tarsus," Sarai said, in unison with Rabbi Amos. She turned and locked gazes with the elderly rabbi.

"How do you know him?" Amos asked.

"He is the prize student of Rabbi Gamaliel and came to visit my father's house several times." She hung the basket on her elbow and thought about taking back Pearl. The clear path through the inn courtyard to the door into the kitchen lay right past the bench where Saul sat. She wished she had turned left at the gate through the inner wall, and gone to the house, instead of her usual habit of entering through the inn. The Sabbath evening routine was to come in here and put Pearl down for a nap in a large basket in the kitchen while she helped prepare the meal for the fellowship time.

Then again, she much preferred knowing Saul was here, warned before she encountered him, rather than being surprised when she stepped out from the kitchen. Did he remember her, from that evening in Judas' courtyard?

She looked around for Judas, but the man who had been sheltering Saul didn't seem to be visible. Perhaps he was inside the inn, talking with someone? Was he giving Norah orders, or just interfering advice on how to treat this most unwelcome, possibly dangerous, powerful guest? Why was Saul here? Was he looking for her? Why had Judas brought him here?

"Uncle?" Joab said.

"He came to the synagogue … most unwilling. His host seeks healers and prayers and anointing for him, to cure the blindness that struck him," Rabbi Amos said. He narrowed his eyes as he glanced back and forth between Sarai and Saul several times. "It seems he had a vision, instructions from the Almighty, for his healing."

"Who brought him here?" Sarai murmured.

Pearl chose that moment to wriggle and nearly slid through Joab's hands as she lisped her demand to be put down. He obeyed without thinking, just like most of the men who came under the child's influence. Before Sarai could stop her, Pearl scampered between the tables and the last few departing customers, darted past Saul's feet, and flung herself at Malachi. She wrapped one arm and both legs around his ankle and calf and held up her free hand, demanding that he look. Old Phoebe had given Pearl a bracelet of braided scarlet and purple threads and the child had been beside herself with delight over her new "pretty." Naturally she wanted her adoring slave, Malachi, to see and admire it.

Ananias looked down at Pearl and smiled, then raised his head and his gaze locked with Sarai's as she hurried forward to gather up her child. He held out his hands, beckoning for her to join them. The effort not to look back at Saul as she passed him made her neck ache.

Chapter Ten

"Child." Ananias clasped Sarai's shoulder as she bent to pick up Pearl and detach her from Malachi's leg. "All is well, there is nothing to fear now." He gestured with a lift of his chin at Saul. "You were very brave."

"I was caught entirely by surprise." She gladly clutched Pearl close, grateful that her daughter didn't resist her. Everyone assured her the child was good and obedient, but Sarai thought the little girl had an incredible talent for picking just the right time to protest, loudly, when she wanted to do something she shouldn't.

"You did not run, you did not cry out, you carried yourself as a healer and servant of God Most High and follower of the Christ, and you showed mercy to your enemy."

"I still need to be convinced," Malachi said, with a nod and a grunt for punctuation.

"Did you bring him here?" Sarai wanted to flee, but where could she go? "I told him that night, there was nothing I could do except give him some salve for his discomfort."

"That was mercy, and obedience. I must confess I was not as speedy in obeying the Master, when He sent me to bring healing to Saul," Ananias said. "But come, see, and testify. You saw the scales on his eyes?" He stepped back, gesturing toward Saul.

"Yes." She didn't want to go with him; she didn't want to take Pearl with her, but she couldn't let go of her daughter now.

At any moment, the soldiers of the Sanhedrin would burst into the inn and take all of them prisoner. They weren't in the Jewish quarter, and the authorities of Damascus might protest the Sanhedrin ordering the arrest of people who were technically not under their jurisdiction. Sarai doubted that would do them much good. By the time protests were registered and an investigation started, everyone captured tonight at the inn would be on their way back to Jerusalem.

Saul raised his head as they approached the table where he sat. New lines bracketed his mouth, and his cheekbones looked a little sharper, as if he had eaten nothing for days. Something about him had changed, but she couldn't put her finger on it, other than that he sat quietly. That vibration of earnest eagerness she had seen him display in her father's house had entirely vanished from him. He looked older, worn, and yet not defeated.

"The pearl of great price," Saul whispered, and raised his hand in blessing, gently touching the top of Pearl's head with the first two fingers.

"What did you say?" Her voice cracked.

"I told him nothing of you," Ananias said.

"No, but the Spirit has much to teach me." Saul turned his gaze to Sarai.

Now she could see his eyes, the pupils large and dark and clear. The crusty, gray, thick-looking covering had vanished.

"How?" she said, retreating behind her duties as a healer.

"The Master called me in a vision to go to Saul and pray for him, to receive his sight back," Ananias said. "When I put my hands on him, the scales fell from his eyes. We have spent nearly every hour since then together, as teacher and student."

"He claims this man is now a believer and has been baptized," Malachi offered, speaking over Sarai's shoulder.

"And now I must prove myself to all those whom I had come to persecute," Saul said. "Let me start here, because of all those I have wronged or intended to wrong, you I have harmed most."

"No, you haven't." Sarai felt suddenly as exposed as she had felt standing on the auction block.

"I have much to repent of, starting with arrogant self-righteousness. I despised you, and even if I did not speak the words, I thought them, mocking you in my heart when others scorned you for your scholarship. Your father was rightfully proud of your clever mind and your ability to memorize and understand scriptures. I was rude to you when I was a guest in your home, believing that as a man I was more righteous than you and Adonai loved me more. For that I repent. I ask your forgiveness, Sarai beth Eliakim ben Levi. I ask your forgiveness for my cruel thoughts when I heard and agreed with the condemnation spoken against your father." Saul slid off the bench as he spoke and went down on one knee. "I thank you for your kindness, even once you knew who I was."

Ananias intervened before Sarai could ask for more details of how Saul had been healed. This was a story that everyone in the fellowship needed to hear. To avoid confusion and mistakes in retelling, he and Malachi agreed they should wait until everyone had gathered for the evening's worship. Sarai gladly excused herself to go into the kitchen to help with the preparations. Malachi had sent word out to all the followers of Jesus, telling them simply that what they feared had been changed by the mercy of the Father, and they needed to come hear the story. She anticipated a large number of believers joining them, and they would need twice as much food as was usual.

When she stepped out into the courtyard a short time later with the first baskets of bread and spiced oil, she found some of the early arrivals had left. Fewer people than she anticipated joined them. Many stayed out of the reach of the torches, as if they feared being seen and recognized later. Sarai didn't blame them. She completely understood the inability to believe that the man whose coming had frightened them had become one of them.

As a result of the far fewer numbers that evening, she was able to sit close to front of the gathering. Saul and Ananias related how Jesus had intervened to heal blindness in the heart by inflicting blindness of the body, and turned the believers' enemy into their new ally. She understood fully Ananias' reluctance and fear when Jesus spoke to him and told him to go find Saul. She trembled when Ananias asked her to stand and testify to what she had seen as a healer, the change in Saul's eyes. There was some irony there, that they called upon her to give validity to his story. Women were not considered reliable witnesses in the courts. Pharisees especially disdained to put any value in what a woman said. Yet here was Saul of Tarsus, a Pharisee of Pharisees, lauded as a strict servant of the law, asking her, a lowly woman, divorced, a follower of Jesus, to attest to the miracle that had touched him.

The fellowship over food was subdued, even after Saul excused himself and Ananias accompanied him. Long after the gathering dispersed, Sarai felt as if she kept walking in circles, thinking over what both men had told them. How could she doubt Ananias' words? Yet how could she believe Saul's side of the events, especially to believe Jesus had spoken to him, in essence had scolded him?

"I know what the problem is," Laila said, long after midnight.

Sarai couldn't sleep, and Pearl seemed to reflect her mother's restlessness. In consideration of the other women in the house, who also seemed to be struggling to sleep, she went up onto the roof to walk in the cool of the darkness and think. As long as she kept moving, Pearl was content to sit quietly in her mother's arm.

Laila found them there. Sarai wasn't sure how long the older woman watched her, seated at the top of the steps, before speaking.

"My father would say this is as if we had found a scroll that someone had written on, after the previous writing had been damaged. Our challenge is to determine if the original writing has been restored or altered. If we do not know the author of the original writing, and what the scroll was supposed to say, how can we know if the new writing is faithful?"

"Hmm, I hadn't considered that." Laila came up the last few steps and crossed the roof to Sarai. "I suppose those questions might be troubling others in the household."

"What is my problem, then?"

"Envy?"

Sarai stared. The soft, warm weight of Pearl in her arms stopped the shout of denial deep in her chest. She took a few deep breaths, and then thought.

"You want to hear Jesus' voice. You want to know why someone so cruel, so self-righteous, so dangerous, would have that privilege, and not you, who have lost so much because you were faithful. You don't understand why he was given a chance to be forgiven." Laila spread her hands, palms up, in a gesture that clearly challenged Sarai to contradict her.

"You have faced that, haven't you?" Sarai whispered. "People have asked why you deserved to be freed from demons, to be healed by Jesus." She sat down on the bench without looking, trusting that it was where it had always been. "You might be -- no, you *are* right. I don't want him to be forgiven. I want him punished."

"Regret is the worst punishment of all, because it is a whip we use on ourselves." She wrapped her arms around herself. "I know."

~~~~~

Laila's words still churned through Sarai's thoughts when Saul came to the inn two days later. She watched him approach Malachi and shuddered. The fellowship of believers had divided over
~~~~~

whether to believe his story of the encounter with Jesus and his calling to spread the truth of the resurrection. It wasn't a simple division of belief and unbelief, but of what Saul hoped to accomplish if it was deception. Perhaps he wished to become leader of the believers in Damascus. Should they run the risk of sending him back to Jerusalem and to the disciples for questioning and judgment? Surely the leaders of the growing community of Christ's followers had the sensitivity and ability to hear the Spirit's leading, if anyone did. Certainly they could determine the truth of what Saul told them. Sarai had more experience with Saul than any of them, because of the few visits he had made to her father's home when he was Gamaliel's prize student. She reluctantly had admitted that Saul was not the sort of man, as far as she knew, to play such an elaborate deception. No matter how arrogant and self-righteous he had acted in the past, she didn't think he was capable of pretending to have such a drastic change of mind and heart for the sake of deceiving and trapping the believers.

Sarai disliked being considered the source of information. People kept asking her opinion even after the Sabbath evening meeting dispersed and all through the next two days. So now when Saul walked across the inn courtyard and bowed to Malachi, she needed to leave. His presence made her uncomfortable, but not through fear. At least, that was what she told herself.

She found Pearl sitting in a basket of linens waiting to be scrubbed and beaten clean in the stone trough on the far side of the courtyard. Her daughter giggled and tried to burrow into the layers of cloth when Sarai bent to retrieve her, thinking her mother was playing with her. Tears touched her eyes as she tried to force laughter and a smile and tugged the cloth over Pearl several times. When that shiver of apprehension grew strong enough to make her scalp prickle, she scooped up Pearl, settled the child on her hip, and turned to hurry into the kitchen and through, to the house. There were plenty of chores to tend to indoors, in the women's portion of the house. Where no one would have the audacity to intrude.

Saul stepped into her path just before she reached the semi-safety of the canopy and platform before the kitchen door. He bowed to her, and he smiled at Pearl, who was still giggling and wriggling in Sarai's arms.

"Could you spare me some time? To sit and talk here, where

everyone can see and hear us?" He gestured at the table in the shade of the canopy.

"To talk of what?"

"My education is ..." He shrugged and offered her what might have been called a bashful, embarrassed smile in someone a quarter of his age. "Unbalanced? Neglected? I sat in your father's presence and listened to him and my master discuss what he had learned from the scriptures, but I learned nothing. I must again confess and apologize for the scorn and mockery I spoke, about you and your father, educating you as if you were a son."

"You are not alone in such thinking." She was grateful to have Pearl to hold, to focus on and to anchor her.

"Yes, but agreement does not guarantee correctness. I have heard you spoken of as a compassionate healer and a trustworthy scribe. I must conclude that the earlier tales were truthful, calling you a clever, quick student."

"One whose only failing was to be a woman?"

"I believe at the time the criticism was that you were a girl-child." He rested his hands flat on the table. "Again, I apologize. The Spirit has much work to do in me, remaking my mind and my heart to make me a worthy servant. I am glad, in this instance, to be humbled. There is no one I can trust more to teach me what I refused to hear the first time, when your esteemed father tried to teach me the truth. Will you tell me what Rabbi Eliakim ben Levi learned and taught about the Messiah as the Suffering Servant?"

Sarai caught her breath. Her arms tightened around Pearl, making the child squawk a moment. She gladly fussed over her daughter, apologizing with kisses, until all was well again. At least, outwardly.

"This will be difficult for me," she finally said, after a struggle to meet his gaze.

"Because you do not trust me yet." Again that smile, which she decided later was apology and wounded spirit and a kind of cringing away from punishment. Saul had been knocked flat in body and mind and spirit, when Jesus spoke to him and he landed in the sand of the road to Damascus. He was justifiably unsteady on his mental feet, and cautious about the new foundation that had been thrust upon him.

"I trust Ananias, and he vouches for you, but ..." She offered a shrug.

The movement seemed to be a signal for Pearl, who loudly whispered that she wanted to get down. Sarai reluctantly let her daughter go. The child toddled away only a few steps before plopping down on the courtyard pavement to play with the string of heavy beads that was always in her grasp.

"It is painful in some ways, to speak of my father. It brings back the memories of the bad days, before his death, when he faced the condemnation of the Sanhedrin and his friends abandoned him."

"Including my master, Gamaliel." Saul nodded. "I do not know if it is any comfort, but he was not happy or at peace with his choice. In the end, he chose holding to scripture and the loyalty he owed our religious leaders over friendship."

"That makes sense," she said, nodding slowly. Sarai held back a longing to demand to know how anyone could ignore her father's reputation for orthodoxy, for wisdom, for loyalty to the scriptures, for standing up for the truth rather than what was expedient and safe. How could anyone consider his reputation and casually dismiss his teachings as heresy? Didn't anyone stop to think, to consider that perhaps the traditional teachings had been warped or even just neglected, and this wasn't new teaching, but *regained* teaching?

Such questions should have been asked and pondered years ago. It did her no good to bring them up now. She tried to find some satisfaction in knowing that one of the brightest and most exacting minds among her generation admitted to being wrong. Perhaps even more important, he had come to her to fill in the missing pieces in his education. To her, the despised daughter of the heretic.

"This will take many hours of talking. I know I will be unable to recall everything from memory, but will need to look in the scrolls, to refresh my memory."

"Thank you." Saul gave her a head-and-shoulders bow, and his big, dark, somehow sad eyes held a gleam of excitement and perhaps even relief.

In the end, Rabbi Amos joined them in their thoroughly non-traditional lessons. The best place to speak in guaranteed privacy and have room to spread out several scrolls at a time, plus have access to truly old, valuable scrolls of the prophets and laws, was to meet in the synagogue. The elderly leader of the synagogue spent most of their meeting times listening, but Sarai had learned early that when he spoke, his thoughts had been refined and polished before he shared them. His words were always worth listening to. Saul showed appropriate respect for the elderly rabbi and was suitably hesitant to disagree with him. Sarai enjoyed their long discussions, despite the painful memories that accompanied the resurrection of her long-ago period of scholarship.

They met every other day, late in the morning, when Pearl was ready for her nap. After only two weeks, Sarai became comfortable with both men, who doted on her daughter. Often, Pearl would climb up into Rabbi Amos' lap, lean back against his ample belly, and promptly fall asleep. Even when one of them forgot themselves and raised their voices in the excitement of discussion, she never awoke. The comfort and ease in each other's company grew to the point that Rabbi Amos didn't hesitate to hand her a message in front of Saul, as they were settling down for the day's studying time. He had received it the evening before, he explained.

"As your spiritual guardian, I have kept in touch with those left behind in Jerusalem," he explained. "Not directly with them, but with those who know them and are aware of their lives. Malachi agreed with me that if there was any change in attitude, if you were mentioned, if your husband gave any indication of taking action to find you, it would be wise and kind to provide you warning."

"Action? To find me?" Sarai held the folded, wax-sealed bit of parchment between thumb and forefinger, like she would hold Pearl's soiled wrapping. She didn't want to open it. She needed to. How much faster could a messenger travel than a man coming to Damascus with the authority to arrest her, perhaps? Had Simon found out about Pearl, and he would come soon to demand possession of his daughter? Or was he like some men in old, unreliable history scrolls, who had demanded the deaths of children conceived through adultery? Had he refused to consider or admit that Pearl was his child, conceived during lawful marriage? After more than three years, she couldn't say she knew Simon at all, to predict his actions.

"Peace, daughter." Amos rested his hand on hers, gently pressing the hand holding the message to the surface of the table. "They do not know where you are, and if anyone speaks your name in that household, only the servants hear it and care."

Saul stayed on the other side of the room, making no pretense that he wasn't listening, but he didn't watch them. He turned around now, putting his back to them, and neatened the rack holding the many scrolls.

Pearl had been sitting on Sarai's lap. She half-climbed up onto the table and reached for the packet. Sarai muffled a little gasp of laughter and turned it over and broke the wax seal with her thumb. Then she thought of something.

"How do you know what is in it, if the message is still sealed?"

"My friend has grown to care about some members of the household, and when he learned about the woman's sad circumstances, he sent his daughter to speak and offer help. That message is specifically for you."

"The woman?" Something squeezed her heart. "Hannah?" She thought of Jude's words, that Hannah had never fully recovered after giving birth to Micah.

She unfolded the packet. Pearl climbed down off her lap and toddled over to Saul. Sarai watched as he went down on one knee and produced a length of cord, which he offered to her to play with. Then she read. The message was short.

Hannah had had long spells of being an invalid since giving birth. She rarely left the house. Deborah was good friends with Bernice, the sister of Bartholomew, Amos' friend. Deborah had nearly wept when Bernice admitted that they had been charged to watch over the household, as a kindness to Sarai. Deborah had grown worried enough for Hannah to ask that Sarai would come. If not to heal her, then to give Hannah a chance to say goodbye.

"To say goodbye?" Sarai nearly crumpled the piece of old, much-scraped and bleached parchment. She trembled at the thought of making that long trip to Jerusalem. How exactly was she to get into the house to see Hannah without Simon knowing? How could she leave Pearl behind, even knowing everyone in the inn would take good care of her?

She inhaled sharply when she realized that in just a few heartbeats, she had accepted the idea of going all that distance. For Hannah, first. She missed the woman, who had been like a sister to her, never a rival. It was truth now, she realized, and not bitterness speaking: leaving Hannah, and then Deborah, were greater reasons for sorrow than the sense of betrayal and rejection when Simon divorced her.

Sarai wanted to see Micah. She wanted Hannah to see Pearl. She wanted her daughter to meet her brother. She wanted to see Deborah. Perhaps she even wanted the childish thrill of walking into Simon's house without his knowledge, without his approval, and walking out again without any consequences.

How can I say I am a follower of Jesus, a student of His teachings, when I think this way? Jesus would not approve these thoughts, this hope, this need to slap back at Simon.

"Thank you," she finally said, after smoothing out the parchment and then folding it back into its original creases. "I need time to think."

"Go in peace, child." Rabbi Amos made the sign of Shaddai over her. "May Adonai hear your prayers and grant you wisdom and courage."

Sarai nodded her thanks, as she gathered up Pearl and left the small studying room in the synagogue. She held back the words that want to burst out: she would only need courage if she were to go to Jerusalem.

~~~~~

"What do you fear more? That Simon will take Pearl, or that he will try to take you back?" Laila said, after Sarai had told her and Norah about the message.

The three women sat on a corner of the roof in the quiet and cool of evening, as the day's busyness faded from the inn courtyard below them.

Sarai had told no one else about Amos' words and her own uncertainties. She wasn't sure it would be wise to let anyone know, especially if she decided not to go.

Yet the thought of Hannah needing her, of suffering, of dying without being able to say goodbye -- it troubled her. Hannah was her family, her sister. Sarai had looked forward to helping to raise Hannah's child. She thought about Hannah doting on Pearl, and nearly wept with longing.

"You don't need to worry," Laila continued, mischief sparkling in her eyes, when Sarai couldn't find words because she couldn't find an answer. "Don't you know that you're impure? Tainted? You're a healer, and who comes to you for help more than anyone in Damascus? Who depends on your reputation for compassion?"
~~~~~

Norah gasped and some of the worry wrinkles bracketing her mouth softened. She caught hold of Sarai's hand and whispered, "Harlots."

Sarai didn't understand for a few heartbeats, then a giggle escaped her tight throat before realization bloomed through her mind like a lamp brightening a room. Of course, Simon couldn't take her back no matter how much he wanted to, if he knew that she had regular contact with harlots. She tended the ones brutalized by cruel customers and gave potions to ease the suffering of the ill and dying. She and Laila tried to help the girls who wanted to leave the life. Simon would be scandalized if he knew -- when he knew. He would live in terror that the Sanhedrin would find out the truth. Nothing could be so important to him that he would risk the loss of his reputation and the approval of those he admired and obeyed.

That night, Sarai dreamed of Hannah, frail and emaciated and shivering on her bed in a darkened room. Sarai saw herself standing in a lighted hallway, with a closed door between them. All she had to do was pull on the latch and shove on the door. She could take light and warmth into the room, and free Hannah from the cold and darkness.

She woke from the dream before she could move her arm to take hold of the latch. That bothered Sarai. When she slept again, she dreamed again of Hannah, this time calling to her through a thick mist. Her dreams shattered and warped each time, just before she could reach Hannah. When morning came, she was more weary than when she had stretched out on her bed.

Were her dreams guidance from God, telling her to go to Hannah? Or just her own heavily guilty conscience?

Sarai went to Ananias. If anyone had experience with guidance from Adonai, especially in matters that were difficult to consider, he had the most. He didn't seem surprised when she told him about her dreams. He played with Pearl, tossing a soft cloth ball back and forth with her as he listened. When Sarai finished relating the last dream, Ananias caught hold of both her hands in his and looked into her eyes, and his smile was sad.

"You already know what you need to do, to ease your soul more than anything else. Yes, it is always wise to seek guidance from Adonai, especially when going back to a place that holds such painful memories."

"And yet?" She suspected the tight ball of pressure in her chest would turn out to be bitter laughter.

"What reasons do you have for *not* going? If you had no fear of encountering Simon, no fear that the Pharisees would accuse you of enough crimes to justify stoning you --" An odd little smile twisted his mouth when his words wrung a gasp from her. "You did not consider that possibility? Anyone with any sense would realize that you would be with followers of the Christ. The Sanhedrin has given itself not just permission, but a duty to torment and accuse and punish us. So if any of them recognized you, yes, common sense says you would be standing before them, facing accusations true and false, fast enough to make you dizzy."

"I didn't consider that danger at all. My only real fear was facing Simon." She took a deep breath. "And if that were removed, all I fear is ..." She nodded at Pearl, who sat at their feet, chattering nonsense to herself now that she had lost Ananias' attention. "How can I leave her behind for all the time it will take me to return to Jerusalem, ensure Hannah is well, and come back here?"

Chapter Eleven

"Take her with you." Ananias shrugged, as if the solution were simplicity itself.

"All that distance?"

"You carried her in your belly all that distance with no harm. And you said yourself, you want Pearl to meet her brother, you want Hannah to see her. How are you to accomplish that, without taking Pearl with you? Won't you feel better about her if she is with you?" He chuckled. "I'm sure everyone at the inn will be relieved that she is with you."

Sarai knew he was teasing to make her feel better. She wanted to hug him, but she couldn't move, feeling frozen inside at the idea of taking that long trip. Making Pearl face the long journey. Not just the dangers of the road, but entering Jerusalem again. Encountering hundreds of people who might recognize her after all this time. All it would take was one person who would have reason to raise the hue and cry …

And do what? If Simon had made no claim on her in all these years… If he made no effort to find her… If no one who traveled between Damascus and Jerusalem had told him the woman he divorced was alive and well and working as a healer, and had a daughter with his curly ebony hair and bright eyes … was it possible he would make no move against her now? He had his son, after all. He had his child born to a free woman. Why would he want the daughter born to the slave woman? Why would he make the effort to find out the age of the child? Why would he care to determine if Pearl was his, conceived within their marriage, or conceived through fornication, even harlotry?

Could she take the accusations of harlotry, if anyone recognized her and learned about Pearl? What would it matter? Simon had cast her off, cast her aside. He had no claim on her. With her father and brother both dead, there was no one with the legal or moral right to punish her.

"Child, your thoughts are tangled and you harm yourself." Ananias gripped her shoulders and made her look him in the eyes.

"Go home and pray. Beg Adonai for guidance. Ask the rest of your household to pray, and I will do the same. The answer, the path to take, will come."

~~~~~

Sarai went home. She tried to pray. She wished Ananias had not put those new fears into her mind, even as she was grateful that he had made her face them. Better to be prepared than to be surprised and frozen and terrified at the worst possible time. Such as turning a corner in the marketplace in Jerusalem and coming face-to-face with Menahem or Andrew or another Pharisee who had come as a guest to her home.

She told Laila and Norah, and then later told Malachi and Eli, and the other men who were like uncles to her. She tried to pray silently as she helped with the cooking, and then as she bathed Pearl and put her to bed. Her struggles to pray so occupied her, she wasn't startled when Saul approached her, stepping out of the thickening shadows as evening turned to night. He asked if she was all right, and brought apologies from Rabbi Amos, who feared he had perhaps harmed her with the news he delivered.

"Oh, he shouldn't feel any guilt. This is something I think I have always known I should do. Or feared having to do." Sarai tried to laugh, but that choking feeling tightened around her throat again.

"I wish I could help you, to repay a small part of the debt for all the help you have given to me. I know little about Simon ben Micah's household. He has advanced very little in the ranks of the Sanhedrin. I only know the gossip I have heard. Much of it cruel, mocking, so I cannot know how much to believe. Simon does not entertain. Some criticize him for letting the ill health of his wife deter him. Others commend him, for showing her kindness. You can guess who says what."

"Indeed, I can." Sarai shook her head, feeling as if she were emerging from deep water, as if she had been wading and stepped into a hole so she went in over her head. "I'm sorry. Please, let me bring you something. Are you here to see Malachi?"

Saul thanked her and said he was expected. Ebenezer and several other men their age were waiting for him in an upper room of the inn. He nodded respectfully and headed for the stairs. Sarai returned to the task of carrying emptied baskets of bread back to
~~~~~

the kitchen. Saul's words added to her thoughts and considerations.

Praying became easier when she was finished with her work for the day and the inn fell quiet and she could be alone on the roof of the house. Sarai settled on a bench that backed up to the higher house next to them. She wrapped a cloak around herself against the growing cool of the night and prepared to wait until she had an answer.

When she fell asleep, she wasn't sure, but she had evidence that someone was watching out for her. Sarai woke in her own bed, still wrapped in the cloak. She had an ache in her neck, likely from leaning over crooked.

She also had an answer.

Malachi insisted that they talk to Saul to determine just what danger she might face, the current mood in Jerusalem toward followers of Jesus. Ananias came with him, and Sarai sat quietly while the three men discussed how to keep her safe. They all laughed, a little chagrined, when Sarai asked them where they thought she should stay. Malachi's inn on Spindle Street in Jerusalem had been taken over by someone who had Caiaphas' approval. However, he had been a stingy host and unpleasant to work for, and had let the building itself be badly used. There were other inns, but the owners were rivals of one kind or another.

"How is Rabbi Nicodemus?" she asked with a shiver. Sarai had the oddest feeling Nicodemus had been in her dreams the night before. "I know that he lost his home, and he sheltered for a time with Simon and Hannah. I know he still lives, and he remains in Jerusalem, but nothing else. If anyone, I would feel safe with him."

"Surely if he is still in Jerusalem, he has fallen greatly in standing, perhaps even isn't part of the Sanhedrin any longer," Malachi said. "Would that mean he is ignored, and therefore a safe shelter? Or are our enemies watching him, looking for the last proof that will justify destroying him?"

He and Sarai both watched Saul, waiting for him to respond. His frown indicated deep thought, and his gaze was unfocused. Sarai found some comfort in the fact that he took time to think. A quick response, she had learned over the years, was usually either negative, or unreliable.

By the end of the day, their plans were settled. Malachi sent a message to Nicodemus, courtesy of Jasper, who could ask favors of the couriers between the different Roman outposts. Saul assured them that while he was no longer active in the leadership of the Jewish people, Nicodemus still held too much respect throughout Jerusalem and Judea to be endangered by his support of Jesus. If anything, his involvement in placing Jesus in the tomb after the crucifixion had earned him respect, even from the Christ's enemies. The elderly rabbi was still visible in the Sanhedrin, but rarely spoke. He lived quietly and had sent away most of the servants who had stayed loyal to him when he faced a short period of persecution. He had lost his home, but still retained his vineyards, so he had been able to re-establish himself. His home was much smaller, and far from the prestigious quarter of Jerusalem. Anyone who stayed with him would be safe from scrutiny.

If Sarai could not stay with him, there were several old friends of her father who might give her shelter. Saul said they had also withdrawn from being vocal and active and even visible in the Sanhedrin. If Adonai had given Sarai permission and guidance to go to Jerusalem, then He would watch over her and shield her steps.

Ananias knew who to contact to arrange for safe passage to Jerusalem. Sarai would ride in a wagon with a canopy and curtains, to shield her from view as well as the blowing sand and sun. They agreed that speed was essential, especially if Hannah was indeed in need of Sarai's healing skills. They would have to step out in faith that she was indeed being sent and that El Shaddai would prepare the way before her, not just in keeping her from being recognized, but that Nicodemus' home would be her safe haven.

~~~~~

Sarai was grateful for the shelter of the wagon and the kindness of Ananias' friend, Heru. He and his three children -- two sons and one daughter -- were broadminded folk who found nothing unusual or worthy of mockery in a Jewish woman who could read and write. The daughter, Nefret, was as confident and strong as her brothers, and Sarai rode in her wagon, for propriety's sake first, and then because the slightly younger woman made instant friends with Pearl. When she wasn't driving the wagon herself, Nefret spent the long hours carving animals no larger than her thumb, for the little girl's amusement. She had the ability to talk and carry on
~~~~~

intelligent conversation while she carved, and plied Sarai with dozens of questions about healing. By the second day on the long road to Jerusalem, they had a pattern established. Every time they encountered another merchant caravan or stopped in a small village, Nefret took Sarai to the most likely shop for healing herbs, or took her to the village healer, to confer, to trade. By the time they arrived in Jerusalem, Sarai had twice as many herbs and compounded mixtures and flasks of potions and oils and salves as she had started with, and more possibilities for offering some relief to Hannah.

Heru and Nefret went on foot with Sarai, once they had passed through the outer gates of Jerusalem. They left the rest of the traveling party and the wagons at the caravansary they always used. Sarai kept her face covered, because she knew several people at that caravansary, all friends of Malachi and Norah. Or rather, they had been friends, but had cut off contact after the capture of the Zealots and the confiscation of Malachi's inn. Malachi had never been sure if the family who ran this caravansary had left him in silence because of fear of the Romans or because friendship would no longer profit them. Sarai didn't want to take the chance that they were fearful enough of the Sanhedrin to report her presence in hopes of a reward. Even after more than three years, gossip lingered in a city as large and as full of political churning as Jerusalem. Someone out there would find profit from knowing she had returned, if only to cause Simon discomfort and embarrassment. That would not be an auspicious beginning to what she hoped would be a quiet visit of blessing for Hannah, and for the comfort of Sarai's heart and soul.

Father and daughter walked her and Pearl to Rabbi Nicodemus' door late in the afternoon, when the shadows visibly stretched out before them a little longer every time they turned at a street corner. Sarai carried Pearl, who whimpered in weariness and clutched at her and only raised her head to ask for dinner. Heru pushed a small one-wheeled handcart with her small bags and the precious wooden box jammed full of healing craft.

Sarai nearly cried out that no, they had come to the wrong place, when Nefret knocked at the door. She shook her head and took a few deep breaths, and looked around. Yes, they were at the right door, on the right street. This matched what Saul had told them, and what Rabbi Amos' friends had confirmed. The street was narrow and crooked, not wide and well maintained and decorated to befit the wealthy and prestigious people in the quarter where Nicodemus had originally lived. The homes here showed signs of having declined from a higher level of prosperity. Paint and other decorations had faded and weathered and not been replenished. Yet when she looked a little longer, a little closer, she saw signs that someone did care. The street was clean of debris, the walls maintained, the mortar replaced. That was more important than decorations. She took a deep breath and allowed herself to relax. This street felt safe. Perhaps it was safe because it was so quiet and neglected.

"Welcome, and may the peace of Adonai rest on you," Rabbi Nicodemus said, as he pulled the door open.

His mouth stayed open for a few heartbeats as his gaze rested on Nefret. That reaction made sense, because the merchant girl was a little unexpected, in her clothes of several different styles, with her hair in a mass of short Egyptian-style braids. Then he glanced past her, to Heru, and then to Sarai. He inhaled sharply.

"Child. Welcome." He smiled and bowed and spread his arms before stepping back.

Sarai wanted to throw herself into his arms and cling to him and weep. Not just for herself and her weariness from the journey, but because Nicodemus had visibly aged at least ten years in the few she had been gone. His beard was stark white and thinning and the lines around his eyes and mouth that had given him dignity had multiplied. However, she couldn't do that. She had Pearl in her arms and her friends to thank and her bags to bring into the house.

Nicodemus earned a sleepy smile from Pearl, rather than the fear Sarai had half-expected. That pleased and surprised her, because her daughter did not go easily to strangers. That had always been a comfort to her, because of the constant flow of people in and out of the inn. She put her child down and walked with Heru and Nefret to the gates, thanking them again. They confirmed the length of their stay at the caravansary before they planned to leave, when they would return, and their expected return to Damascus. When she had shut the gate behind them, the walk across the small courtyard to the door into the house seemed like a mile. She stepped through the door into the small greeting room and found

Nicodemus sitting on a bench, listening to Pearl chatter and show him all the carved animals she carried in a pouch fastened to her belt.

"El Shaddai bless you, child." Nicodemus held out a hand to her and drew her down onto the bench with him. "You refresh my spirit. You are well? Yes, I know you wrote to tell me about the inn, and friends of Malachi have kept me informed, to ease my old heart and the duty I owe your father, but ..." He sighed and nodded at Pearl. "Such joy and encouragement, seeing you and this precious little one." Another sigh, and his smile faded. "I could wish she did not favor Simon so much. Yes, she is your mother as a child, but who else alive today remembers her? They will see him, first."

"Do you think that will be a problem?" Sarai swallowed back the words she didn't want to say, because they would make her fear real: Would the resemblance give Simon reason to take Pearl from her? Would others seeing the resemblance force him to act, when he wouldn't care about a daughter, otherwise?

"The wise course of action is to avoid being seen, as much as you are able. Her face *will* protect you from those who would insist that you be punished for adultery. Why risk such accusations at all?"

"I am not the same dreamer I was."

"None of us are." He caught hold of her hands. "You give me such joy, and you ease my heart." A rusty little chuckle escaped him. "Perhaps you give me courage. I might accompany you back to Damascus."

"Has the situation grown so bad?" Sarai restrained herself from complaining that those who said Nicodemus was safe had either lied or had a false interpretation of his situation.

"Not enough to fear for my life, but how long did they take to destroy your father?" He shook his head and released her hands and slowly got to his feet. "Enough. My faithful Hephzibah is likely flying around in her kitchen, preparing our meal now that you are here. We need to get you and this little one settled before we eat."

~~~~~

Their plan was simple enough. As soon as Simon had left the house for the day, Sarai would go to see Hannah. Nicodemus assured her that faithful Deborah had stayed, even if the other servants had left in the wake of the tumult after the resurrection.
~~~~~

Sarai was surprised to learn that Simon had let Saul go, after all the things the manservant had done, siding with him against her. Simon had taken up the habit of rising early, to join other, older, and more conservative members of the Sanhedrin for prayers. They shared a time of meditation and reading scripture in the Temple courtyard before the day of work officially began. That meant Sarai was able to leave Nicodemus' house while the morning shadows were still thick, traffic in the streets was light, and chances of being seen and recognized were small. Simon usually stayed in his room in the Sanhedrin, studying or conferring until late in the afternoon. Usually he left to time his journey home before the streets grew thick with workers heading to their lodging and meals. If Sarai left between the ninth and eleventh hours, then she would never have to risk encountering Simon in his home or on the streets.

Sarai carried her healer's bag. Offering help and healing to Hannah was, after all, the largest reason for this trip. This first morning in Jerusalem, however, Sarai went to visit Naomi, the midwife who would have helped Hannah when she gave birth to Micah. If anyone could give her the most accurate information on what was wrong with Hannah, what she needed, Naomi was the surest source.

However, Sarai learned after only a few minutes she was wrong on many levels. Naomi recognized her and welcomed her with outstretched arms, but that was the only joy in their short meeting. The news was grim and disheartening. Simon had forbidden Naomi to come into their house, once Sarai had left, because the old midwife had chosen allegiance to Jesus and His teachings. Most members of the Sanhedrin had taken their frustrations out on the common people who would not renounce their belief in the Christ, forbidding their wives and children and servants to have anything to do with them.

Simon had called in an older midwife who was a relative of Annas to tend Hannah through the remainder of her pregnancy. Bithia had a bad reputation, passed along in whispers because everyone feared Annas' anger. The worst rumors were that she practiced witchcraft and discarded common sense practices of cleanliness when tending mothers in labor. Nothing could be proven. Hannah gave birth with no company but Bithia, so there were no witnesses to prove or disprove the rumors. The old woman wouldn't let even Deborah attend Hannah during her long labor. The new mother was so terrified of the midwife, Simon didn't let her back into the house. However, neither did he complain to Annas or Caiaphas. He was rude to Naomi when she came to the house to offer her help, when Hannah hadn't been seen for more than a month after the birth and her time of purification. The man who took Saul's place at the door refused to let Naomi in.

Sarai thanked her and promised to bring Pearl to see her, and then she prayed on the long walk from the midwife's home to Hannah's. She had to think of this as just Hannah's home, not Simon's, and certainly not her former home. She was here first as a healer, and then as a friend. That was the only way she could keep up her courage and walk in the love and generosity that all followers of Christ needed to bestow on the world.

The door of the house had a fresh coat of pale blue paint, and the whitewash on the wall surrounding the house was fresh as well. Sarai wasted several moments, wondering what that boded about the people living behind those walls. A fresh coat of paint on the Inn of the Three Sisters meant very different things from the upkeep and decorations of a home. Was it a sign of prosperity or an attempt to cover over decay and misfortune of the spirit?

Finally, after the sun peered over the tops of the houses, Sarai knew she had wasted too much time. She shook her head and silently scolded herself for being afraid, then crossed the cobblestone street to knock on the door. Sarai waited, listening through the momentary quiet. No one walked on the street in either direction, but she heard the rattle of wooden and metal-rimmed wheels on the uneven paving of streets nearby, the hum of voices, the thud and bang of doors. A door creaked nearby, and she thought the sound came from the other side of that white wall and blue door. Her heart thumped a few times in her ears and she nearly laughed as she realized she had been holding her breath. Sarai took a few deep breaths, and the sighing in her ears muffled the sound of someone pulling on the latch and then the creak-scrape of the iron hinges. The door swung open.

Old Deborah took a shaky step backwards and both hands went up to cover her mouth. She stared at Sarai.

"The peace of the Messiah be on this house," Sarai said, and gripped her healer's bag with both hands because they were trembling. She refused to show fear now.

"Sarai." Deborah's voice cracked, then she lunged and caught hold of Sarai by one wrist and drew her into the courtyard. The door had barely thudded closed, the latch clattering into place, before she wrapped her bony arms tight around Sarai and burst into tears.

The tears didn't last long. Deborah cast glances at the door, as if she expected someone to come bursting through, then she wiped her face on her veil and urged Sarai to come inside the house. She explained that the manservant, Lemuel, had gone to the marketplace and would be back quickly because he didn't have any friends to see while he was there. That comment prompted Sarai to think of Ruth for the first time in years. She didn't ask about her former friend. Even if she still cared about Ruth, she didn't dare go to such a public place and risk the uproar the other woman would create, and then being seen and recognized by the wrong people.

"I'm here as a healer," Sarai said, when Deborah gestured toward the kitchen. A great wave of weariness washed over her. There was nothing she would like more than to sit in the kitchen and talk about silly, little, meaningless things, and pretend the intervening years hadn't happened. "I'm here to help Hannah, if I can. I believe Adonai wants me to be here. How is she?"

"Bless you." She patted Sarai's shoulder and turned, still moving with grace despite her years and the aches in her joints. "Today is a good day. They're in the inner courtyard. Did you know she --"

"She has a son, Micah. Yes." Sarai tried to smile, and took a few deep breaths as Deborah led her down the long hallway to the inner courtyard.

Her first impression of Hannah was that her friend and sister had grown smaller. She sat in the sunshine, eyes closed, slumped slightly in the high-backed, cushioned chair, face tipped to the sun. Sarai felt a little bit of relief that Hannah was outside. Several healers had written their firm belief in the benefits of sunlight for the mind as well as the body of an invalid. Hannah sat with her feet propped up on a footstool, with a blanket across her lap, and a cup and pitcher sitting on a small table next to her chair.

"Mama!" A browned little boy, his legs long, his face round, and his hair a riot of glistening black curls, darted from the far side of the courtyard. He held something in his outstretched hand. "I caught it. See?" He was only a few steps away from Hannah when he seemed to notice Deborah and Sarai. He stopped so quickly his sandal-shod feet slid on the smooth paving stones.

"That one bids fair to rivaling Nimrod the great hunter," Deborah said with a sniff and shudder. That earned a giggle from the boy. "What is it this time?"

"I hope it's a mouse and not a lizard." Hannah's voice was light but rippled with laughter. That loosened several knots of worry that had formed in Sarai's belly since her talk with Naomi. She still had life and strength in her spirit, if not her body. Hannah opened her eyes and went very still as her gaze met Sarai's. Then her eyes glistened, and she spread her arms.

Laughing, fighting tears, Sarai ran the dozen steps across the courtyard and into Hannah's arms. She barely remembered to let her healer's bag slide to the pavement before going to her knees and wrapping her arms around her sister. They clung to each other, rocking a little, and wept silently. Until a little hand touched Sarai's arm. She loosened her hold on Hannah and sat back on her heels. Sighing, she wiped her face on her veil and turned to regard Micah. He had his father's hair and chin, but his mother's eyes and mouth.

"Is Mama sick again?" he asked.

"Oh, no, sweetheart," Hannah said. "I'm just happy to see Sarai. She's been gone since before you were born. Do you remember what I told you about her?"

"You told him about me?" Sarai struggled upright and settled on the bench just a few steps away from Hannah's chair.

"Aunt Sarai." The little boy nodded, still giving her a big-eyed, solemn look.

"Aunt?"

"You are more my sister than anyone who remains of my father's family." Hannah sniffed, her mouth flattening with irritation, so uncharacteristic of her that Sarai nearly laughed aloud. "The groveling, greedy cowards would have taken everything when Jedidiah died, but I was protected there. They tried just once to ingratiate themselves with Simon after ..." She sighed. "Oh, my sister, I am so glad to see you. Where have you been? Are you back in Jerusalem to stay?"

"I am sure this will take a long time, and we will all be hungry before the tale is finished," Deborah said. "I will be just a moment. Come, rascal, help me." She held out her hand. Micah grinned and dropped what he had been holding in his cupped hands all this time. She shuddered when the boy reached to take her hand, and that earned another giggle from him as they hurried into the house.

Chapter Twelve

"A mouse?" Hannah asked, as a small, dark object wriggled a few times and then darted into the shadows.

"A lizard, I think," Sarai said.

"What blessing has brought you back?"

"This, first of all." She picked up her healer's bag, set it on the bench and dragged it closer to Hannah's chair, so their knees almost touched when she sat down again. "I heard you were ill, and ..." She shrugged. "I had dreams. Of you. And someone I believe Adonai sent told me, or gave me His blessing, to come and see if I could help you. There are so many healing practices from other lands, other peoples, that I have learned since going to Damascus."

"Damascus! Of course. I should have guessed, after all that Norah and her father said." Hannah sighed. A weary smile lit her face. "Do you know, I learned to read and write? If I had known where you had gone, I could have written to you."

"We shall write to each other when I return to Damascus." Sarai patted the healer's bag. "Tell me, how are you? Truthfully?"

She didn't want to speak of her own life. Not yet. Not until she had a better idea of how things stood in Hannah and Simon's household. Despite being welcomed with tears and smiles and embraces, Sarai could not be sure of her safety. The less anyone knew of her, the safer she would be if she had miscalculated and misunderstood the guidance she thought had come from God. If no one here knew about Pearl, if no one knew she had come to stay with Nicodemus, and they didn't know about the Inn of the Three Sisters, then that would make hunting her down harder.

Micah and Deborah returned with bread, figs and apricots, sweet new wine, and honey for the bread. The boy returned quickly to his hunting game in the courtyard once he understood the women were talking about why his mother was tired all the time. The conversation took all morning, discussing Hannah's eating habits, her sleeping habits, the cycle of weakness and energy plaguing her. Sarai examined her eyes and the beds of her nails, examined her skin in several places, studied her teeth and looked in her mouth. She asked Deborah for oil and wine and a small brazier, mortar and pestle, and honey.

When she spread the contents of her healer's bag out on the long table in the courtyard, the activity drew Micah's attention. He climbed up on a bench and then sat on the end of the table, watching her, asking questions she found quite intelligent for a boy of his age. Hannah told her then that she had learned to read so she could teach Micah, and he was nearly as good as her now, so young. The little boy grinned proudly, making Sarai laugh. He eagerly helped her by running into the house for a wax tablet to write down the instructions for preparing and using the healing potions and powders Sarai made for Hannah.

Sarai kept watch on the progress of the shadows across the courtyard, to be sure of the time. She trembled a few times at brief images that struck her without warning, of Simon coming home and finding her still there.

"You are coming back, aren't you?" Hannah asked, after Sarai and Deborah had prepared the first mixture for her to drink.

This, to be taken every afternoon, was to strengthen her blood. Another mixture was a paste, heavy with honey, to put on her bread in the morning to aid her digestion. A third mixture, using poppy and mixed with warmed wine, would help her sleep at night.

"My work isn't done," Sarai said with a smile.

"No, that's not what I meant."

"But it is what I meant. I came here to help you. I can't be settled in my spirit until I have spent many days with you."

Deborah chuckled softly and patted Sarai's shoulder, then scooped up the jars of the different mixtures to take into the house.

"Good. I missed you, Sarai."

"And I have missed you. I must confess, I haven't prayed for you as much as I should have, but I have prayed."

"Then your prayers helped me when no one else could spare a thought for me." Hannah shook her head and made a brushing motion with her hand. "No, I don't mean things are that bad with me. I have friends, but you were my first true friend. Someone who saw me, and not my father's daughter or my husband's wife or the influence I could use for or against them among merchants or the landowners or ..." She shrugged. "I wish sometimes I had the courage to go with you."

"Do you believe Jesus is the Messiah?" she whispered.

"I don't know. There is so much I need to learn. Simon refuses to speak of the disciples and all the things being done to silence them, but I still hear whispers. Even here, cut off from the air and the rest of the world." She gestured around the courtyard. "When I'm strong enough, Deborah and I go to the marketplace, and I hear the whispers. No one says anything to me directly, because they know who my husband is, but I still hear … stories. You are with the disciples, aren't you? Some of them fled to Damascus?"

"Yes, there are many of us." Sarai thought for a moment she couldn't breathe. Was this the sign, the certainty of safety that she had prayed for?

"You are with Norah, yes? Is she safe? Did her father buy a new inn?"

"Tomorrow." She tucked the last box of herbs into her healer's bag and yanked it up onto her shoulder. "We have many days to talk, and to make sure my potions are helping you. Then I must be sure you and Deborah can continue making them properly when I must return home."

"Home." Hannah blinked a few times and her smile went crooked. "I used to hope that someday, Simon would soften and admit he was wrong, and come fetch you home and we could be a family again."

"That is contrary to the law. A man who puts aside his wife cannot take her back again."

"Only if she has taken another husband, and only if he put her aside for adultery." A tiny snort escaped her. "I have asked quite a few people who know more about the law than me. I'm sure Simon gained a reputation of being a brute or a bully, because people thought I feared I would be next to be cast off. I noticed that the law says nothing about the husband putting his wife aside because he was committing adultery, and he wanted to make the second woman his wife and be free of her. Oh." Hannah flushed. For a moment Sarai thought she might be having a bad reaction to the first draft of blood-strengthening potion. "I didn't ask -- you haven't told me anything -- are you married?"

"No. Though I have had some hopeful suitors. Malachi considers me a daughter, and he protects me."

"Why haven't you? Certainly there are many men who would have gladly married you, no matter what people said about you."

"Yes, I'm sure of that. Several rabbis in Damascus are sympathetic and have declared me clean. I am considered a widow in Damascus, and I have earned enough respect for my healing skills that I have many defenders. I have no need of a husband." She took a breath. "And my daughter has many uncles and grandfathers who will stand for her, and many aunts who will take care of her, if anything should happen to me."

"Daughter?" Hannah's eyes shone. "Oh, I suspected, I hoped, before … Did you know before you left, that you carried Simon's child?"

"Like you, I suspected. But I ask you, please, do not tell him."

"Did you bring her with you?" Deborah asked.

"Yes, and if you will promise not to tell anyone, I will bring her tomorrow." Sarai tried to smile. "I wanted her to meet her brother, to meet you, if nothing else."

"Yes, yes, please." Hannah's eyes gleamed with happy tears.

~~~~~

Micah met them at the door, when Sarai and Pearl arrived the next morning. He gleefully announced that his mother was feeling much better, so Sarai had to come every day to make sure Hannah felt good all the time. He and Pearl spent less than half an hour watching and studying each other, while the women settled down in the courtyard to talk and tend to small tasks like mending. Then Micah announced that he would teach Pearl how to catch lizards.

"But Mama," Pearl began, her forehead wrinkling.

"Perhaps they do things differently in Jerusalem." Sarai fought not to burst out laughing, so she wouldn't hurt her daughter's feelings. "Let him show you how he does it, and then you show him how we do it in Damascus, all right?"

That brought a grin and a happy nod from her daughter. Pearl ran off after him to the opposite corner of the courtyard. The women waited and listened for a few minutes, as Micah showed her how to hold the stick and where to dig among the plants and loose tiles.

"Do you have a lizard problem in Damascus?" Deborah asked.

"Not at all. Several of the people who work for us bring their children with them, and there is always a competition among all
~~~~~

the children to catch rats and mice and lizards and any other creatures that might travel to the inn on the wagons and carts or in bales or jars. Malachi pays them quite handsomely to always be on the hunt, and the smaller the vermin are, the happier he is. It means they aren't breeding faster than they can be killed."

That day, she learned more about the events in Jerusalem after she had left with Norah, and she shared much about the activities and people at the Inn of the Three Sisters. Sarai wasn't ready yet to tell about the fellowship of believers who met in the inn. She certainly wasn't ready to tell them about Saul of Tarsus, and how the hunter had joined the band of rebels condemned by the Sanhedrin. Sarai wondered how long he could safely stay in Damascus, learning from the teachers and reading the recorded memories of Jesus' teachings. How much reprieve would he have before Caiaphas and the authorities in Jerusalem learned what he had done, and reached out to punish him?

The children got along well, once Micah got over his dismay that a little girl, a full head shorter than him, was much more skilled at catching the lizards and mice that hid in the shadows and holes in the courtyard. He quite admired Pearl's skill in holding up a small pot and staying as still as the wall itself, waiting for the prey to emerge from its hiding place. When the creature was far enough from its hole, she dropped the pot down on it. Then it was a matter of waiting until the prisoner wore itself out from scratching and racing about its dark prison. Micah enjoyed building a wall of broken tiles and bricks around the pot, so when it was lifted, the lizard or mouse had nowhere to go except forward, straight into the bag waiting to hold it.

Sarai was grateful that Hannah and Deborah had thought further ahead than she did, and they agreed not to tell Micah that Pearl was his sister. Simon doted on his son and made sure to spend some time with him every evening. The last thing they needed was for Micah to blurt out news about his new sister, or worse, ask his father why she didn't live with them. Hannah had referred to Sarai as Aunt Sarai when she told Micah about her, so it was easy enough to let the children think they were cousins. Sarai ached a little, when Pearl called Hannah "Aunt Hannah," bringing tears to the woman's eyes. Deborah glowed, when the child decided she was her granny, and easily fell asleep on her lap.

The five of them enjoyed quiet, blissful fellowship for three days. Hannah responded well to the potions and pastes Sarai made for her, and they had hope she would continue improving. Then the Sabbath arrived. Sarai and Pearl spent the Sabbath evening quietly, enjoying the solitude of Rabbi Nicodemus' home. Despite the growing disapproval of Caiaphas and his supporters, Nicodemus still had the respect of many, and he was always an honored guest at Sabbath gatherings. He could not decline an invitation, even though it meant leaving his guests alone. Someone might remark on it, and the wrong person might hear and ask the wrong questions.

After noontime the next day, when the heat of the day had begun to dissipate, Sarai covered her head and went to the marketplace. There were more non-Jewish shopkeepers in Jerusalem now, and it showed how little influence the Sanhedrin held, that the marketplace was open and active on the Sabbath. Sarai's chances of being recognized were much smaller here, among Gentiles, although she didn't doubt that many Jews came out on the Sabbath to seek merchandise when there was less competition and the crowds were easier to navigate. Sarai found more than she had allowed herself to hope for, more herbs and spices and purified lotions and oils. Even better, two shops were owned by healers. She found several scrolls of healing texts, but the price was too high. She had to be careful of her funds. If she needed to leave before Heru's merchant caravan returned, or she decided to stay behind for a while longer when they left again, she would need to have enough money to pay her and Pearl's way back to Damascus.

Sarai walked back to Rabbi Nicodemus' home, her head full of memories and regrets, and longing for her lost trove of scrolls. For the first time in years, she thought of the merchant, Ebed. He had been the source of most of the scrolls her father bought for her. He had tried to save her from the Romans. She had thought about Ebed a few times when she was married to Simon but had refrained from finding him. If her father had been condemned for being friends with the big Nubian merchant, then she couldn't risk Simon's future among the Pharisees by finding the man. Sarai wished she had done so now.

She reached Nicodemus' home in plenty of time to help

Hephzibah with preparations for the evening meal and pleased the kind old woman with the treats she had bought in the marketplace. Honeyed dates and imported vegetables and roasted garlic paste were luxuries now. Sarai spent the evening in the courtyard, making several new mixtures to help Hannah and listening to Nicodemus talk about the people he had seen and talked with, the news he had heard. He delighted Pearl with a simple, somewhat noisy game he had thought up for her. It consisted of a handful of sturdy clay flasks he had found, which he set up in a cluster again and again, while Pearl stood several steps away and rolled -- or tried to roll, rather than throw -- a wooden ball at them to knock them over. He didn't have to set up the flasks very often, because it took more rolls than there were pins for Pearl to knock them over. The little girl grew weary long before she grew bored with the game. Finally she was so tired she wobbled when she walked and could barely keep one eye open. Sarai gathered up her daughter and carried her back into the house, to put her to bed. Pearl insisted on kissing Nicodemus goodnight, and that brought tears to his eyes.

He was still pensive and sitting quietly, rolling the wooden ball between his hands, when Sarai came outside again.

"Are you all right?" she had to ask.

"I am a coward."

"Surely not." She offered a smile.

"A coward. A little lazy. A little too much set in my ways. Selfish. Yes, all those things. I am alone, and it is so sweetly easy to think of you as my daughter, and Pearl as my granddaughter. And it struck me that I don't want you two to leave, when the time comes."

"How does that make you a coward, or selfish, or all the other things you called yourself?"

"I think about going to Damascus with you, when you return home, and something in me recoils at the thought."

"Perhaps that is the Spirit of God speaking to you, guiding you in what to do?"

"If only." He shrugged. "No, it is the discomfort of the journey that worries me. And the turmoil of making a new home for myself. And not wanting to change. And those thoughts lead me to wonder what kind of life I honestly have here, living in the shadow of the

Sanhedrin and fearing what I could lose if I spoke up more often on behalf of the followers of the Christ. I am quiet, and I fool myself into thinking I am doing more good than harm. I tell myself that as long as I am free and living under no threat, I can help all those who brought the wrath of Caiaphas down on themselves."

"You do, don't you?"

"Yes, I am a shelter for a few days at a time, until we can find them safe passage out of Jerusalem and disperse them to other strongholds of believers. I have retained most of my wealth, and I still retain some influence, but how much good do I truly do for other believers? How much are profit for myself, security, and fear my true concerns?"

"You will be welcome in Damascus. You will be honored as one of those who spoke with Jesus when He walked in flesh."

"Child, I do not want honor. I want to be useful." He patted her hand, then hauled himself to his feet. "Thank you for listening to a foolish old man."

"You are not --"

"Allow me a night to wallow in self-pity, will you?" A twinkle touched his eyes that had been so dark and introspective just a moment ago. "In the morning, the world will be a kinder place once more. And perhaps Adonai will speak to me in my dreams, or my morning prayers, and I will know what is both brave and wise and what to do."

Nicodemus nodded to her and crossed the little courtyard to the house.

~~~~~

The next three days passed as the first three had, in sweet conversation and watching the children play together. Sharing household tasks and seeing Hannah improve a little bit every day. Sarai remembered Naomi's words, about the rumors that Bithia mixed witchcraft with her healing practices. She asked Nicodemus what he had heard about the old midwife, and he grew grave. Yes, he had heard such rumors, too, but as long as she had the approval and protection of the High Priest, no one could do anything to have her investigated. Until the wife or child of a much more powerful and influential man than Simon ben Micah died in childbirth, no one dared to complain. Sarai was pleased to hear that Bithia was angry with Simon when he didn't let her come back to tend the
~~~~~

newborn. She had grown angry enough to declare that she could have ensured that Hannah quickened again and gave him more sons. Without her help, she promised Hannah would never have more children. How could someone ensure such a thing, unless they resorted to witchcraft?

All that mattered to Sarai now was that Hannah was safe from further harm at that woman's hands. She told herself her satisfaction didn't have anything to do with the black mark against Simon's name, because he had insulted someone Annas favored.

Sarai talked with Deborah about what she had heard, and the old woman confirmed that yes, Bithia had blocked her from attending Hannah while giving birth. There had been odd, unpleasant smells in the room and dark smoke, and none of that was normal for the healing and cleansing and strengthening herbs and other mixtures used by midwives. Sarai spent time in prayer for the safety of Hannah's household. Once an evil spirit had been invited in, could it linger even after the one who invited it had gone away? She walked through each room of the house, praying, and gathered up her courage to command evil spirits, in the power of the name of Jesus of Nazareth, to leave. She didn't know if she was being silly, but several people who had given her memories to record agreed that Jesus had given power to His followers, if they asked in His name. If they believed, if they trusted in Him. She had to believe, for the sake of Hannah and Micah and Deborah. If her prayers and rebuking the spirits of evil did any good, only time would tell.

Time, however, ran out. The fourth morning of that second week, Sarai went into the kitchen to fetch the mortar and pestle. She had remembered a recipe for a soothing drink and Deborah had found the ingredients when she went to the marketplace the day before. The women intended to work on the drink now that Hannah had taken her morning dose of medicine. Sarai heard a door open and only paused a moment in her errand. The manservant, Lemuel, was not due to return until long after the noon meal. She supposed he had finished whatever errand Simon had given him that morning when he left, and had returned early. Holding the mortar and pestle close to her chest, she hurried back out to the courtyard. Micah came running to her, giggling with excitement. She gasped when he ran full tilt into her legs, afraid she would drop the mortar on the boy. He grabbed her skirts with both hands and pulled.

"Come out, Aunt Sarai! Come see!" Then he turned and ran.

"See what?" She laughed as she followed him.

The laughter caught in her throat, choking her, when she stepped into the courtyard and there stood Simon, only a few steps away from her. She dropped the mortar and the stone bowl hit the courtyard tiles with a *thud-crack*. Later, she thought to look, and saw the tile had broken, not the mortar.

"See?" Micah ran to the corner where Pearl had been sitting, playing with the rag doll Deborah had made for her. He caught hold of her and tugged her to her feet. Both children were laughing, completely oblivious of the disaster that had struck them. "See, Abba! My friend."

"Yes," Simon said, glancing down at the boy. Then he went utterly still as his gaze rested on Pearl. The world seemed to hold its breath. Then he shuddered and closed his eyes and turned his head away.

Something inside Sarai tore and she thought she tasted blood. Her eyes ached from her determination not to cry.

Simon took a deep breath and opened his eyes. His gaze touched her and his mouth twisted in an attempt at smiling. "Sarai, you look well. Are you well?"

"Yes." Her voice sounded like sand.

"Micah says you are the healer who has been helping Hannah."

"She is my sister. When I heard she had need, I came to see what I could do."

Had she seen him flinch, when she said Hannah was her sister? Did that hurt him? Or was he relieved that she didn't make a foolish mistake and call him her husband?

Forgive me, Lord. Help me to forgive him. Help me to be kind. Please … Sarai choked and held still, when she wanted to snatch up Pearl and flee the house as swiftly as the wind. *Please, don't let him take my daughter.*

"Micah." Hannah sat up stiff and straight and held out a hand. The very calmness of her voice broke through the little boy's excitement. He trotted over to her chair. "What did you tell your Abba?"

"He told me that you had a surprise for me, and his Aunt Sarai was making you all strong again." Simon finally tore his gaze free of Sarai and walked over to Hannah's chair. "He wants Aunt Sarai to stay with us always, so you will always be well." He bent and gently caught hold of Hannah's hand.

Sarai blinked hard against more tears, but these weren't from fear. That gentle, simple touch told her so much. Simon loved Hannah. She thought she could breathe again, and some of that freedom came from relief, maybe even joy.

"Son, you need to learn that a surprise isn't a surprise if you tell the person who is supposed to get the surprise." Simon caught a bench with one foot as he spoke, and dragged it over, and sat down.

"I'm sorry, Abba." Micah pouted for a few seconds, then that irrepressible grin of his broke out. "Don't like waiting!"

Simon's little chuckle allowed Sarai to bend down and pick up Pearl and put the child astride her hip.

His smile stiffened and his gaze flicked away from the girl.

I can't do this.

"Will you go find Deborah for me?" She put Pearl down, facing the door into the house. Her daughter didn't hesitate but toddled off quickly on her errand. Sarai went down on her knees and saw the damage the mortar had done to the tiles. She gathered it up, and the pestle, and stood, clutching them close. "Let me put these away and then …" She couldn't even make herself meet Hannah's eyes. She would know what Sarai intended before the thought was even clear in her mind. The years and her suffering had made her perceptive.

Sarai's shoulders hunched with anticipation of Simon's voice behind her. The mortar and pestle seemed to weigh nothing. Deborah was in the kitchen when she returned there.

"I'm sorry," the old woman whispered. "I didn't know he had returned so early until I saw him, already facing you. How did he know? Who could have seen you?"

"Micah told him." Sarai thought she might be able to laugh in a little while. Not now, though. She had taken to leaving her healer's bag in the kitchen, rather than have it sitting out in the courtyard where she and Hannah and the children spent their days. Pearl knew not to touch her mother's bag, but Micah tried every day to see what was inside. In a matter of moments, Sarai had the strap over her shoulder.

"Mama?" Pearl stopped, eyes big, her little mouth dropping open in surprise. She looked at the little plate of fruit tarts in her hands.

"I'm sorry." Sarai held out her hand and held her breath, silently pleading, until her daughter put the plate down on the table. She let Deborah hug them both, she caught hold of Pearl's hand, then they were out the kitchen door, taking the back ways between houses.

Chapter Thirteen

Hephzibah was out on an errand when Sarai reached the house. Nicodemus hadn't returned from the long list of planned visits and consultations he had told her about last night. Sarai was glad. The fewer questions she had to answer, about why she had returned so early in the day, the better. She needed time to think, to settle her mind, to pray. Yet she doubted she could do any of that, even with no one talking to her. Especially someone expressing concern.

She settled Pearl in the courtyard with the little lap loom the elderly cook had given her and oversaw the child's efforts to learn the new skill. Her thoughts and her attention were as scattered and full of holes as the little square of cloth Pearl proudly showed her more than two hours later. Sarai hugged her daughter and praised her, grateful the child had been so absorbed in what she was doing. Indeed, they had spent as much time taking the tangled threads out of the weaving as Sarai spent struggling to pray, or casting aside the different ideas that came to her.

She could barely put three or four coherent thoughts together in her mind without a need to wail rising up in her throat. Sarai tried not to cry out in her heart, demanding an explanation from Adonai. Or worse, accusing Him of betraying her. Pearl's constant interruptions for help were a blessing rather than irritation. When Sarai slid the little girl onto her lap, that seemed to provide some steadiness for both of them. Pearl's little fingers grew more sure as she guided the thick thread through the warp threads, and her weight and warmth gave Sarai comfort that drove away the tendency to shudder and leap up and pace.

By the time Hephzibah returned to the house, Pearl had produced a ragged bit of cloth that would serve better as a sieve for making cheese than a scrub rag or a patch. More important, Sarai had the beginnings of a plan. She was grateful Pearl was tired, and put the child down to take a nap. Hephzibah asked Sarai if she would mind going to the marketplace to find a few items for that night's meal.

Mind? Sarai was glad of the legitimate reason to go, to move, to have something to do and occupy her mind. She didn't even consider the possibility of Simon finding her until she had stopped at the first stall for three handfuls of almonds. The idea of him searching for her made the basket she carried shake in her grip, so the nuts rattled around in the bottom. Sarai clutched the basket against her chest and hurried on to the next merchant, to find the apricots Hephzibah wanted. Why, she sternly scolded herself, would Simon come after her? Certainly not out in public, where there would be witnesses. If he were angry with her, he would hunt her down carefully, discretely, and scold her in private. Maybe threaten her. What were the chances he would bring a soldier with him, to arrest her and punish her? He might accuse her of infidelity after all this time, with Pearl as proof of immoral behavior. Yet wouldn't he hesitate and put consideration for his own humiliation and embarrassment first?

She could almost laugh, if it weren't so hard to breathe. She slowly rewove her sense of self-control and calm and saved her breath to deal with the merchants to obtain the few items Hephzibah needed. Yes, she supposed by the time she returned to Damascus, she would find it amusing that she hadn't thought of Simon's reaction to seeing her until now. He was probably terrified she would make some claim on him. Pearl was so small for her age, people thought she was a year younger than she really was. At least, until she opened her mouth and spoke, her voice so clear, her words and thoughts so coherent. Rabbi Eliakim would have been so proud of his clever little granddaughter. No, there was no way Simon could even begin to guess that Pearl was his daughter.

At least, he wouldn't think that unless Hannah told him.

She wouldn't do that, would she?

"No, she won't betray me," Sarai whispered, after that question came clear in her mind. Hannah was too grateful for the healing she had brought, the help and health and strength.

Hannah hadn't betrayed her at all. Simon might never have known. He certainly hadn't noticed Hannah's growing strength and the bloom of healthy color in her cheeks, had he? At least, he had said nothing to Hannah or to Deborah, if he had noticed. Simon might never have known about Sarai's visits if Micah hadn't told him. And what, exactly, did the little boy know? Nothing, other than that Aunt Sarai came and made his mother feel much better. And yes, her little girl was a fun playmate, and he wanted them to stay forever.

Sarai and Pearl could not stay forever. She intended that they would leave Jerusalem as quickly and quietly as possible. Her final stop in her errands, her reason for gladly helping Hephzibah, was to visit the shop where she and Heru had agreed to leave messages for each other. The merchant running the shop served as a clearinghouse for many traveling bands, leaving messages and payments and information for each other. He was polite and distant, asking no questions, showing no real interest in Sarai or her reasons for being there. He remembered her because Heru had made sure Sarai met him. No, he hadn't heard from Heru or Nefret or her brothers. Yes, he would let Sarai leave a written message for them. He didn't show any surprise that she could read and write. He offered her papyrus, ink, pen, and sealing wax to ensure the message would be unread by anyone until Heru opened it.

Her message was short and simple: she would be ready to leave Jerusalem as soon as Heru and his traveling party wished. She would come to the shop every other day in the morning to find out if there was any word from them, or about them.

Nicodemus returned to the house before Sarai. She sat with him a long time on the roof, though it took very little time to tell him what had happened at Simon's house. Both were silent for a time. Then Nicodemus held her hand as he led her in prayer, asking El Shaddai for guidance and protection and peace. He didn't scold her or praise her, when she told him about her decision, but he did look sad and shake his head.

"Am I a coward? Or have I been mistaken, believing this was by Adonai's guidance that I came here?" she finally said.

"How is it foolish to want to be safe? Or to fear danger and harm?"

"Would he harm me, do you think? If he knew the truth about Pearl?"

"Simon and I have spoken very little in the years since that world-shaking Passover. Not as the friends, teacher and student, we once were. As his prestige rose and mine fell, we shifted to different paths, in life and in the city. I think sometimes he would like to return to our former roles. There is a shadow of sadness in his eyes. However ..." He sighed and shook his head.

In the silence, Sarai heard the sounds of life traveling on the evening air. The voices of parents calling to children. The clinking of plates as families gathered to eat in their courtyards. The creaks of ropes and scraping of jars and splashing of water. The groans of hinges, the lowing or whinnies of animals as servants tended to tasks in the larger houses. The shuffling of sandals on the paving stones and the queries of late travelers, hurrying down the streets to reach their destinations before full dark fell. The tromping of metal-toed boots and the thud of spears from the foot patrols as soldiers headed out into the city. Night settled in over Jerusalem.

"There have been several times when he did not speak in support of something Caiaphas and his circle advocated," Nicodemus said after a while. "That is not the same as speaking in support of me, and those who distrust the political games played to keep Rome friendly toward us. Or simply speaking in support of those who have earned Caiaphas' disapproval because we are known to be sympathizers, if not Christ-followers ourselves. Still, it makes me think there is some softening in his heart, some doubts growing stronger in his mind."

"What good -- what effect can that have on me?" she corrected quickly, pitching her voice to be soft simply because there was an ache to voice the words she hadn't said: What good did this change of heart in Simon do her?

"Hmm, perhaps none. Except perhaps give you some peace?"

Hephzibah called up to them, asking Sarai to help her with the last preparations for dinner. Nicodemus smiled and nodded to her. He squeezed her hand one last time before she hurried down the stairs.

Nicodemus did not pursue their discussion further, when they settled around the low table in the courtyard. He very gravely praised the unraveling bit of cloth Pearl so proudly showed him, and didn't laugh when she explained, very seriously, that she had taken it out of the loom too soon. Would he help her put it back on? He asked why she wanted him to do it. His eyes watered with the visible effort not to laugh at Pearl's response. Mama had told her Rabbi Nicodemus was the wisest man in the world, so of course he knew how to fix everything.

Sarai and Hephzibah laughed quietly together in the kitchen, while Nicodemus and Pearl stayed in the courtyard after dinner and struggled with the loom. The two took turns going to the courtyard to fetch the dirty dishes and uneaten food, and left long gaps in between their trips. Sarai wished she had some way of preserving forever the images. The elderly man struggling with the thick threads and knots. The sweet-voiced, patient, believing little girl who encouraged him despite his increasing frustration.

At last she took pity on the old man and told Pearl it was time to go to bed.

"Tomorrow, we will learn the very valuable lesson of discarding a hopeless cause and starting all over again," she said, after her daughter had kissed Nicodemus goodnight and toddled off into the house to her room.

"Very wise," he said on an exhausted sigh that turned into a groan. He slouched a little in his chair, and his second sigh turned into a chuckle. "How I wish your father were still alive. He would be utterly her slave. I am grateful you brought her with you."

Sarai managed a smile and hurried after her daughter. Her throat ached with unsaid words. How grateful would Nicodemus be when they left him and his house in peace once more? Perhaps more important, how quickly did they need to leave? She stumbled when she wondered for the first time if perhaps her presence endangered him.

Hannah had told her the little she knew about the discussions in the Sanhedrin, the concerns that the Christ-followers gave the Jewish leaders. Simon kept his home separated from his work, but there were still times when he spoke about it. He needed to tell someone about the things that concerned him. It helped him to release the pressure among people who wouldn't be affected by his concerns or fears or what angered him. Maybe it helped him to tell Hannah for the simple fact that he thought she didn't understand. Or, more accurately, she didn't reveal that she understood far more than Simon thought she did.

Nicodemus and other religious leaders who had expressed some respect for Jesus' teachings had been living under a shadow ever since the events of that Passover and crucifixion. They hadn't been driven out of Jerusalem after the death of Stephen like many of the believers, but their lives had been restricted, their influence had decreased. How much punishment could Nicodemus face, if anyone found out that he had given shelter to Simon's cast-off wife? Worse than that, a woman who had been divorced because she refused to renounce her belief in Jesus as the Messiah. Even worse than that, the daughter of disgraced heretic Rabbi Eliakim ben Levi.

Sarai scrubbed Pearl's face and hands and sat with her daughter while she lisped her innocent, sweet prayers, asking for blessings for everyone she loved. The list was long, because her world was enormous with all the people who were part of her life. Sarai was grateful that Pearl didn't ask for a song or a story before she closed her eyes. She didn't think she could force out a sound. Quietly, she went around their room, gathering up clothes and small possessions and packing them in the baskets they had brought from Damascus. The moment Heru or Nefret came for her, she and Pearl would be ready to go. Just pick up their baskets and put on their outer clothes, and leave. She put away everything but the clothes that needed washing, or that she and Pearl would wear the next day. Sarai thought there was enough wash water in the large jars in the courtyard to give the clothes a good scrubbing and rinsing. She would lay them out on the roof, to dry overnight. Yes, it was a wise plan to be ready to leave. For Nicodemus' sake, if not their own.

She heard the low murmur of men's voices coming from the roof, when she stepped into the courtyard. Sarai hesitated a few moments. The days when she let curiosity lead her were long gone. Wisdom said to go back to her room and lie down on her own pallet. Still, she needed to get the washing done. Better tonight than hoping to rise early to wash and hang out the clothes. The sound of scrubbing would be enough to keep her from overhearing whatever Nicodemus and his visitor were discussing. At the same time, she was sure she could keep the sound of washing soft enough they wouldn't know she was down there in the courtyard.

In the end, she was both right and wrong. Sarai had just taken the long washing trough to the gap in the wall, that would let water run out and downward, to the street outside. She tipped it to drain the dirty water out when she realized she didn't hear men's voices coming from the roof any longer. The low murmuring had been just loud enough to be heard over the soft splashing and wringing of cloth, without any words clear enough to be understood. That had stopped. She flinched and tipped up the trough higher than she planned. Some of the water spilled out over her feet. Muffling a gasp, she took a step back.

"Sarai?"

She flinched again, nearly dropping the trough, and looked up. Two men were coming down the inner stairs from the roof. The second man had spoken. Not Nicodemus.

"I'm sorry," she said, and tipped up the trough to dump all the water. Her feet were already wet, so what did it matter? "I will not trouble your house again."

"Trouble?" Simon's foot caught on the last step and he stumbled before he had both feet on the ground. "You have been a blessing. I was blind not to realize how much better Hannah is." He glanced at Rabbi Nicodemus, who still stood several steps above him. "I came to thank you."

"There are no thanks necessary. Hannah is my sister." She choked, wanting to say she loved Hannah, but fearful of Simon's reaction. Did she want to hurt him? Did she want him to say he loved her? What did it matter? She was no longer his wife, so it was not just foolish, but wrong to want those words.

Besides, he had never really loved her, had he?

"You will come back tomorrow, won't you?" He tried to smile. At least, she thought so. The lanterns in the courtyard were far apart, so he was mostly in shadow. "I promise, I will stay away all day, if that will convince you to come back."

"Hannah is well now, or at least she will soon be well enough not to need me."

"In the body, yes, but can you be sure of her heart?"

She turned the trough over to let the last drops of dirty water drain out, and stepped away from the wall. Her knees wobbled a little. She resented him in a brief, hot flash, for making her take a wide circle around the courtyard to get to the pile of wet clothes, and beyond them the door into the house.

"I did what I came to do. There is no need for me to return."

"Sarai …" Simon reached out, as if he would catch hold of her arm.

She gasped and flinched away and the pain that flashed across his face startled her.

"I would never hurt you." He wrapped his arms around his middle and watched her pick up the clothes and put them in a basket.

She bit her bottom lip to keep silent, determined not to remind him of the times he had struck her. Yet the wounds to her heart were far deeper than any bruises to her flesh. Why hadn't they healed after such a long time?

"You know she can't entirely believe you," Nicodemus said, his voice a soft rumble.

"Everything has changed. Sarai, please believe me." His voice stopped with a crackle as she turned her back on him and tried to wring out the worst of the wet before settling the clothes in the basket.

The thought of climbing those steps to the roof made her want to weep. Not for the effort to get to the top, but the fear that Simon would still be there in the courtyard, waiting when she came down. Or worse, he would follow her up to the roof, and perhaps keep her from escaping him until he had said or done whatever had brought him to Nicodemus' house.

"How did you know I would be here?" she blurted, dropping Pearl's little dress on top of the pile of wet clothes. "I didn't tell Hannah."

"Where else would you be?"

She turned back to him. He had such a sad little smile on his face. She remembered again the eager boy who tried so hard to please his teacher and to be liked by his fellow students.

"I never wanted you to know I was here. I didn't come for you. I came for Hannah."

He flinched at her words, and she didn't know if she was glad she had hurt him, just a little. The arrogance of the man! Did he think she had come all the way from Damascus to help Hannah for love of him?

"I know," he said. "I'm grateful. I will do whatever you ask, if you will come back tomorrow. For Hannah, and for Micah. He's in tears, thinking he did something bad and made you leave."

"Now that's cruel, Simon. How can you let that sweet little boy feel such guilt?"

"It's true, though, isn't it?" He held out a hand again to her, and took a step closer. "If he hadn't told me, I wouldn't have come back and you wouldn't have fled."

"Perhaps."

"He adores you."

She swallowed hard, wanting to say she adored Micah too. She loved how he shared with Pearl without being told to. She would miss hearing the two children shriek and laugh together and chase each other around the courtyard. How they snuggled down together to take their naps in pure innocence and affection. Tears touched her eyes, knowing Pearl would cry when they didn't go back tomorrow and see Hannah and Micah and Deborah.

"I will come back in the morning. Will that -- will that be enough?" She barely caught herself in time, to keep from asking if that would make him happy. Simon's happiness was none of her concern or her duty.

He seemed happy enough, as he thanked her and promised again that he would be gone by the time she arrived. He would stay away until late afternoon, his regular schedule. He bade her goodnight, and Nicodemus accompanied Simon to the door. Sarai climbed the stairs to the roof with the wet clothes, and she listened hard for any sounds of conversation that drifted up from the street. Her heart pounded so loudly, it drowned out all other sounds, so she didn't even hear the creak-thud of the door closing. She went over the conversation in her thoughts as she laid out the clothes. One detail made her go quiet inside and seemed to validate her resolutions. The last bit of shaking had left her hands and legs and she walked down the stairs steadily enough with the basket on her hip.

"Are you well, child?" Rabbi Nicodemus asked, when she reached the door into the house. He sat on the bench next to the door, a dark, quiet shadow just outside the spill of soft, fading lantern light.

"He didn't ask about Pearl." She shifted the basket to her other hand and reached to push the door open. "Or did he ask you, before?"

"No, he didn't. Perhaps he was afraid to ask."

"Perhaps." The quiet settled in deeper inside. "That's always been his problem, hasn't it? Fear."

"Hmm, but some fear is good for you." He groaned softly as he got to his feet and followed her into the house.

~~~~~

Hannah said nothing about Simon when Sarai returned to the
~~~~~

house the next morning. The children greeted each other with delight. They threw themselves into their games, and Sarai sensed an odd kind of desperation in their exuberance. Perhaps they both feared not having another day together? She doubted the children would even be conscious of such ideas, but it made sense to her.

The day passed pleasantly enough, as all the previous days had. Sarai and Deborah conferred over the preparation of the different brews to be used to treat Hannah's discomfort, and when to resume different potions for strengthening her blood, if her pallor and weakness returned. When everyone else had gone into the kitchen to make their noon meal, Sarai walked slowly around the courtyard, praying for protection. In the name of Christ, she commanded the evil spirits and influences the old midwife had brought with her to stay away. Sarai had discussed her prayers and her thoughts about Bithia with Nicodemus several times. He agreed with her, much to her relief. If necessary, he would ingratiate himself into Simon's household once again, to come and pray protection over them regularly. Sarai hoped Simon's visit last night had rebuilt some of the relationship between the two men. It would be nice to know her visit to Jerusalem had brought some benefits to others that would last.

She tried not to think about how long that renewed friendship would last, if Caiaphas and his followers learned of it, and levied their disapproval on Simon as well.

Hannah did mention Simon when Sarai was preparing to leave, but only to say she hoped eventually, all of them would be able to share a meal. Simon wanted to express his gratitude for what Sarai had done. Hannah managed to laugh a little, when she said he was stunned and a little ashamed, when he finally realized that she had been improving.

More stunned that it was at my hand, through my efforts, and not whatever prayers or advice his friends offered? Sarai knew better than to speak her thoughts. She managed to avoid responding to Hannah's suggestion by calling for Pearl to hurry, they needed to be on their way.

She worked hard over the next three days, to ensure everything was prepared and Deborah could tend to Hannah. More than making sure she took regular doses of the strengthening potion, Deborah needed to ensure that old midwife and the evil that followed her did not return. Sarai thought about enlisting Simon in the effort, warning him, presenting him with what she thought had happened when Hannah gave birth to Micah. The problem was that she had no certainty he would believe her. He might get angry that she would accuse Annas of endangering people by his patronage of the old woman. He might accuse her of spreading marketplace gossip, maybe even report this to Annas, in an effort to get further into his good graces. He might just laugh at her. Sarai let herself hope Simon would believe her, and he loved Hannah enough to keep old Bithia away. Both Deborah and Hannah said the old midwife came every three or four months, to try to leave charms to ensure more sons would be born. Now that the evil influences had been driven away and Hannah was healthy, perhaps she would give Simon another child. Micah needed a brother or a sister. After all, he was such a good brother to Pearl.

When she grew aware of that particular path of thought, Sarai knew it was time for her and Pearl to leave. How much closer could the children grow before Micah got more ideas in his head? What was he telling his father already about the daily visitors? Sarai couldn't ask Hannah without worrying her. Or worse, putting ideas in her head, too.

She prayed hard about the dilemma on the walk back to Nicodemus' house that night. So hard, she nearly laughed aloud when Hephzibah gave her a message written on old, much-scraped and bleached parchment, when she stepped into the kitchen to help prepare dinner.

Nefret was in Jerusalem, only overnight. She would leave early in the morning with five of her father's wagons, to travel to Bethany and south, and then curve north again, reaching Damascus in three weeks. If Sarai wanted to leave right away, there was room in the wagons for her and Pearl. Otherwise, she would have to wait more than a month before Heru came through with his half of the caravan.

"Of course, it is the wise choice," Nicodemus said, after he had read the message. "I shall miss you both greatly. You have brought such light and joy to this house. Another house will miss you even more, I think."

"My work is done. It is better that I leave and let them get on with their lives." She tried to smile, but she only felt unutterably weary. Sarai told herself it was just anticipation of all that needed to be done before going to bed. Then she needed to rise earlier than normal, to reach the caravansary on the outskirts of Jerusalem in time to join Nefret. She felt nothing else. Maybe later, when she was on her way home to Damascus, she would feel something else. Hopefully, just relief.

Chapter Fourteen

A psalm of thankfulness hovered on Sarai's lips as she wrote a letter to Hannah, which Nicodemus promised to deliver in the morning. She was grateful that Hannah knew how to read now, so she could say farewell and leave a few last instructions. They would remain for Hannah and Deborah to refer to. This was better than waking the household before sunrise to say goodbye. Sarai told herself that several times as she struggled to write the letter. She paused nearly as many times, considering leaving the name and the street of the Inn of the Three Sisters, but in the end gave Hannah no way to find her. It was better this way, Sarai reasoned. Simon would have no guilt, no sense of duty driving him if he didn't know where she had gone. She just wished she didn't have to disappoint Hannah, who had so looked forward to being able to exchange letters, once Sarai had gone home.

"It is better this way," she whispered the next morning, as the wagons jostled down the road, heading for Bethany, and the sun peered over the horizon, sending brightness into her eyes.

Pearl was excited to be riding in the wagon again. She didn't realize she wouldn't see Micah and Hannah and Deborah that day. Not until they had reached Bethany and the wagon drivers started to unload the barrels and sacks and amphorae in the marketplace. The noise and new surroundings distracted the little girl easily enough, so she didn't cry until much later that evening, when she finally understood they weren't going back.

~~~~~

A package from Nicodemus was waiting when Sarai returned to the Inn of the Three Sisters. He had passed on a message from Hannah, who wanted them to write to each other. Since Sarai had not told her the name of the inn, or where it lay in Damascus, Hannah proposed sending their letters to each other through Nicodemus. Would that be all right? Hannah wanted to know about Pearl, and she thought Sarai would like to hear about Micah as he grew up.

Sarai wept, but not because of the request or that she wished
~~~~~

she had thought of that simple little bit of protection. Hannah had sent her the shawl she had embroidered during the long, sleepy, peaceful afternoons sitting and talking in the courtyard. Then there was the ball and the little horse on wheels, pulled on a string, which Micah had insisted on sending for Pearl. Sarai knew they were among his favorite toys, but he wanted the little girl to have them. She smiled through her tears, imagining the little boy's consternation when he realized, after a few days, that he would never see those toys again. Did children truly understand the great sacrifices they made only after it was too late to change their minds?

She agreed to Nicodemus' and Hannah's plan, and took four days to write a long, carefully detailed letter that told much about her home, her daily life. She left out any names that might lead anyone who found the letter to suspect she lived in Damascus. She sent a small chest to Nicodemus, with the letter, honey-coated figs for Deborah's sweet tooth, a pale blue, sheer veil for Hannah, and a set of toss rings for Micah.

Two days later, Jude came to the Inn of the Three Sisters. Sarai nearly didn't recognize him. Gone was the travel-worn, grim, weathered man he had been the last time he came to see her and plead with his sad eyes. He was once again a rich, happy young merchant with a comfortable future. He reminded her so much of the man who had filled her dreams, Sarai trembled. A cold weight settled into the pit of her stomach. What had happened to change Jude from the somber man he had been, to this slightly swaggering, overdressed man who smiled at her?

Jude bowed to her and inquired, formal and proper, about her health and her healing work, and about Pearl. Then he went through the inn to greet everyone he seemed to consider a friend. Sarai went back to her duties, working on tallying the records. The taxes were due in four more days. Rumors were going around the city that the new official over the tax collectors had a reputation for creating trouble, just so he could levy fines and take more than Rome's fair share. Before Jude could return to the table where she sat at her work, Phoebe came to fetch her. Istra wanted her help dealing with a difficult childbirth. The mother was too old to be having another child, and multiple births ran in her family line. Istra feared for her life. Sarai gathered up her healer's bag, told Laila where she was going, and followed the girl.

More than a full day later, she returned to the inn, exhausted, carrying gifts from the grateful father and grandfather of the triplet boys. The most important part of the long day of struggle and prayer was that the mother had survived the birth. Sarai's throat was sore from singing psalms and praying aloud through the long hours, and from the incense the mother's aunts insisted on burning. It clashed horribly with the healing herbs Istra had steeping in pots of water all around the room. There was nothing Sarai wanted more than to wash, hug her daughter, and dive into her bed for a full day. Perhaps not in that order. It didn't matter.

"Sarai? You're back?" Jude seemed to appear out of nowhere.

Her vision was cloudy around the edges. Her dry eyes ached from exhaustion. Every part of her ached, now that she thought about it.

"I'm sorry," she began, then sighed as he took the basket full of dried fruit and expensive skeins of thread dyed in multiple jewel tones. The relief of having that weight out of her arms made her feel light for a few moments. Then her exhaustion pressed down on her again. She saw a bench only a step away and sank down into it. She couldn't remember stepping through the inn gates and crossing the courtyard.

"This isn't right." Jude dropped the basket down on the cobblestones and went down on one knee in front of her. "You shouldn't be working this way. Like a slave. You should be taken care of like a queen."

"Jude, please --"

"It's all right, Sarai. You're free now. I know you've hesitated because of all those silly rules of the law, about divorce and purity and remarriage, but you're free."

"Silly rules?" She blinked at him. Why did his smile seem too wide, too bright? He reached for her hands and she pulled back, her nose burning from the fumes of wine. It was far too early in the day for Jude to reek of strong wine. "Why do you say I am free?"

"Simon is dead. You can be my wife now."

Sarai couldn't breathe. She looked into his eyes, so bright, so different from the last few times she had seen him over the years. Jude had returned to the boy he had been, when she had thought her future was bright and bound to his. Yet not that boy. A strange, wine-soaked, blurred image of that boy. He frightened her; the change was so drastic. Where had he been, what had he done in his distant travels? When had he soaked himself in wine?

Her head ached with questions. She shuddered, as Jude's words rang through her head again.

How could Simon be dead, when she had heard from Hannah so recently? If he had fallen ill, wouldn't Hannah or Nicodemus have told her? Granted, it had taken nearly two weeks for the letter to reach her from Jerusalem, but that was a short period of time, compared to the long silence that had lain between them.

If Simon was dead, Nicodemus would have sent her word by the fastest courier. He would have sent for her to come and tend to Hannah and Micah in their grief. How could Jude have heard and reached her before Nicodemus' courier?

"How?" she asked.

"What does it matter?" Jude's smile widened. "He's not a problem anymore."

"How did Simon die?"

"I'm not sure." He shrugged. "Don't tell me you care, after all he did to you."

Sarai's stomach twisted, and a strange pain settled in behind her eyes. How could Jude insist Simon was dead and yet not know how he had died? How could he be sure?

Only two possibilities lay before her, and the world seemed to spin around her as she stared into Jude's bright, smiling eyes. Either he was lying, or he had killed Simon and claimed he didn't know how he had died to try to appear innocent. Yet, she couldn't believe that Jude had the strength of will to kill anyone.

So that made him a liar. She could easily believe Jude would lie. Hadn't he been lying to her all these years?

"My darling. My treasure."

"No," she whispered, and struggled to her feet. Jude reached for her. He was going to try to kiss her. "No!" she shouted, with all the strength she had left in her, and swatted at his hands.

"Sarai, what's wrong?"

"Go away. Never come to see me again." She caught up the basket and swung it at him when he reached for her.

"Sarai?" Eli appeared from the murmuring crowd slowly gathering around them.

"Send him away."

"No, Sarai, you don't mean that. She's just tired. It's a shock -- she's had a shock. Simon is dead and she's stunned. She's not thinking clearly." Jude turned to face the other inn folk who stepped up through the crowd. "It's good news. Sarai is free to marry me now."

"I will not marry you!" Her throat hurt from the force of her cry.

"But Sarai, this is what your father wanted. Don't you remember?"

"I remember many things. I remember that I have told you again and again that I will not marry you. Eli, please --"

Eli stepped up, putting himself between Jude and Sarai.

"She's tired, that's all. It's a shock. You'll see. Tomorrow, everything will be fine. I'll come back tomorrow, and we'll plan our wedding feast!" Jude spread his arms and turned, beckoning to everyone in the inn courtyard. "You're all invited! This will be the greatest celebration Damascus has ever seen."

"No," Sarai whispered, and headed at long last for the kitchen, and through it to the house. She stumbled and nearly cried out in terror when a strong arm wrapped around her back, partially lifting her off her feet.

"Peace, little one." Eli lifted her up onto the threshold and guided her through the door. He shouted for Laila, for Norah, for anyone, as he half-carried her down the hallway to the common room of the house.

Sarai gratefully sank down onto the cushioned bench along the wall and let the basket slide to the floor. She didn't even care when the contents spilled out. Eyes closed, she exhaled deeply and shuddered. All she could hear was the uneven beating of her heart.

"Here, this will help," Eli said.

Before she could open her eyes, he guided her hands to hold a pottery cup. The biting, resin aroma of the inn's strongest wine filled her nose. Sarai took a large mouthful, but only let a little trickle down her throat. She didn't need to choke and spill it on her clothes or the floor.

Laila and Malachi came in then, one from upstairs and the other from the caravansary. Sarai nearly burst into tears when Eli told them what happened and insisted something was wrong with Jude. She couldn't cry with her mouth still full of that strong wine.

She swallowed hard and managed not to cough. Laila held her hands, until Norah joined them and had to hear everything again, then she took hold of one of Sarai's hands.

"He told me Simon was dead, so now I was free to marry him." She told them what Jude had said, and then what she had thought.

"No fear." Malachi patted her shoulder. "I will post orders with the gatekeepers. He is not allowed inside."

"We had better put that bar on the house door that you were talking about when we first settled here," Laila said, her tone dry. "If he would tell such lies, then what's to stop him from breaking in and trying to take Sarai against her will?"

"Pearl. Where's Pearl?" Sarai tried to stand, but her two friends tugged her down onto the bench and assured her that her child was safe, sleeping in her own bed. Norah had seen her just before she heard Eli's shout.

She fell silent then, praying in her heart for her safety, her child's safety, and what made her laugh a little when she thought about it later, praying for Simon's safety. If Jude would be so determined, even desperate enough to try to trick her into marrying him -- if Eli and Malachi both thought he had become dangerous enough that they would forbid him to enter the inn -- wouldn't it be possible that he would attack Simon? Or was she just overtired and letting her imagination turn to fear? Sarai listened as her friends, her family, discussed the situation, and how to protect her and Pearl and everyone who lived in the inn. She wept a little, later, in gratitude and some small amount of shame. Laila scolded her for that, when she had slept and felt better and confessed some of the things going through her mind.

"The world since the beginning of time has always found it convenient to blame women for every bit of misfortune. And to make the weak and defenseless responsible when the strong and arrogant and selfish hurt us in some way. And then to condemn us when we take the only path left open to us to create shelter and put bread in our mouths. You have never wavered in telling Jude no. It is not your fault that he thinks he can somehow change the world to suit him and get what he wants. It is not your fault, whatever evil thing he chooses to do next. It is his choice. You have no responsibility to give him what he wants. You are not his wife; you are not his property. You remember that. Simon threw his coins back at him, when he tried to purchase your freedom." Laila snorted. "What sort of freedom is there, when a man holds a bill of sale over a woman's head?"

Just two days later, Sarai thought about Laila's words and shuddered when her friend remarked that perhaps she should see if Adonai had given her the gift of prophecy. It was meant as a joke, to try to lighten everyone's spirits, but Sarai felt ill.

Jude's next step was to go to the local synagogues and try to persuade their leaders to order Sarai to submit to him. The stories that came back to the inn in the days and weeks that followed were by turns frightening and pitiful. Even taking into account how news tended to become warped with gossip.

Sarai blamed Jude and the ruckus he generated for the increasingly negative attitude the synagogue leaders had toward the inn's household. First, he went to the synagogue on Marketplace Street. Perhaps because it was the largest and most prosperous, he expected them to have the most influence in Damascus. The leadership there considered themselves offended when Malachi made no overtures to gain their friendship and support. They were more offended when the surrounding craftsmen and merchants laughed at them for making no effort to make friends with the innkeeper.

Then the news about Jesus reached Damascus, and they learned that the Inn of the Three Sisters harbored Christ-followers. With some evident relish, they declared the inn's family unwelcome even before the first edict against the disciples reached them from Jerusalem. The moment Jude mentioned the inn to the synagogue leaders, they told him he deserved all the frustration he suffered for being associated with Malachi and Sarai. He stomped away, making threats, before they could send him away.

Next, Jude went to the synagogue on Kiln Street, because people in the Jewish quarter told him the leading families there had strong ties with the Roman authorities. He told them that Rabbi Eliakim had promised Sarai to him, and the Romans had taken payment from him for her freedom and then sold her in the Decapolis anyway. He added to his lies, saying Simon had offered to help him, took money, and bought Sarai in the slave market. Then he kept her for himself. Jude insisted that Simon had confessed his sins, and repented, and made him guardian of Sarai's daughter when he died. The synagogue leaders declared they had no authority over Sarai, and they would not take the time and expense to verify his story. Jude then insisted that Malachi ran a brothel and used his profits to help other Christ-followers to evade the punishment decreed by the High Priest in Jerusalem.

The synagogue leaders again refused to help him. They laughed at him, but there was evidence that some believed his stories. Jude's lies triggered a drastic change of attitude toward the Inn of the Three Sisters from that portion of the Jewish quarter where the members of that synagogue lived. No one confronted Malachi directly, but there were fewer requests for Norah to arrange celebrations. Fewer of the men who owned businesses met at the inn to discuss contracts over meals. The call for Sarai's healing skills declined among those families as well.

Jude then found the synagogue in the Court of the Phoenix Fountain. Rabbi Amos let him tell his entire twisted, false story without interruption. Then he went through the tale, piece by piece, and refuted everything Jude had said. Jude interrupted multiple times, shouting it was all lies. He fell silent when Rabbi Amos replied that he was only repeating what Sarai had told him years ago. If she was a liar, why did Jude want such a deceitful woman as his wife?

That evening, after his meeting with Rabbi Amos, he lay in wait in the shadows near the synagogue door, and he attacked when the elderly man started his walk home. Three other synagogue leaders and their students emerged in time to see Jude leap from the shadows, and they were able to subdue him. Soldiers were patrolling within hearing of the ruckus, and they hauled Jude away. He resisted them, fighting and cursing and shouting threats. He was left in the jail cell, ignored and unfed, until he grew too weak to shout and bang on the door.

By that time, the inn where he was staying had him declared dead or missing. They confiscated his possessions to pay the cost of the most expensive room and to stable his cart and horses. When Jude finally persuaded someone to go to the inn to obtain money to pay his fines, and heard what had happened, he swore out a complaint against the owners, accusing them of theft. They added to the bill, for trying to harm their reputation. The owner, who was a friend of Malachi, heard what Jude had said, lying about the Inn of the Three Sisters. He added more to the tally against him. The city officials who heard the charges and counter-charges agreed that Jude had no right to expect anything returned to him.

Jude had no funds to pay the steep fines and penalties exacted by the magistrate and the jailer, and the advocate representing Rabbi Amos and the synagogue. When Malachi declined to press charges against Jude because his actions and words threatened the good reputation of the inn, others stepped in and spoke in his and Norah's and Sarai's defense. The expenses mounted with each day Jude had to stay in jail. His actions and the mounting tally of threats against everyone who thwarted him did much to destroy the good reputation he and his father and grandfather had established throughout the region, and along the main merchant routes. People he sent to for help declared they didn't know who he was, or declared he was an imposter. No one was willing to stand with Jude and loan him money to pay his fines. The final insult was that he had to borrow money at an exorbitant rate to pay to send a messenger to his father, for money and an advocate to gain his freedom.

The entire tangled mess took weeks to unfold and for the kernel of facts to emerge from the gossip and speculations. When Sarai heard Jude had attacked Rabbi Amos, she was horrified and sickened with guilt. She wept when Rabbi Amos and the other synagogue leaders agreed that she was innocent, and even read a declaration in the synagogue that she was clean and had acted honorably.

Rabbi Amos approached Sarai and Malachi while the storm of rumors was still reaching its peak to discuss several concerns Jude's actions had raised. By necessity, refuting his claims had brought Sarai's situation and the truth of her divorce out into the open again. More people knew about Simon, that Sarai was a Christ-follower and had been cast aside because of her loyalty to Jesus. While Sarai would always have protection because of her reputation as a healer, Pearl's future was another matter. Malachi's claim to stand as Sarai's guardian and speak as her father was no longer adequate protection. Pearl could be harmed by the gossip as the years passed. She could be considered illegitimate, and while she was entirely innocent, she would suffer for her parents' choices. Her acceptability in the Jewish community might be tainted, at best, if not lost altogether. Plus there was the added weight and stain of growing up in an inn.

Rabbi Amos suggested that Sarai seriously consider finding a husband. Marriage would wipe away the risk of future accusations of immoral behavior on her part. A father for Pearl would give the child a name and the shelter of legitimacy, and ensure safety of both body and reputation, as she grew to womanhood.

Sarai listened to his advice. She loved the elderly man for his sincere concern for her welfare. His words crystalized thoughts she had been considering from time to time since Pearl's birth. A pool of calm surrounded her while Amos talked, and a sense of distance from the entire situation, as if she listened to a story told about someone else. Then he finished by adding that he understood any reservations she had, so he would not encourage her to consider Joab as a husband. Sarai laughed quietly, with tears in her eyes, kissed both his cheeks, and thanked him.

She shared what Rabbi Amos had said with Laila and Norah and Istra, the three she considered her wisest mentors and friends. All three agreed that there was merit in the advice, but they could not decide if there was enough merit, enough danger to ward against, to encourage her to follow it. When Sarai went to Ananias, he thought long, his gaze distant.

"Such a choice is sensible and moral and a sacrifice of great love for your daughter. If we asked a hundred men and a hundred women what you should do ..." Ananias shrugged and squeezed Sarai's hands, which he had been holding since she gave all the details of her conundrum. "I cannot predict what they would say. The question, daughter, is what the Master would have you do. What would please Him? What would serve Him, and the fellowship of believers?"

"How can I know?" Sarai nearly choked on the need to shout the question.

"Ask. Spend time in prayer. Then prepare to wait until the answer is made clear. Adonai exists in a different concept of time and necessity from what we frail mortals experience. Wait and trust ..." He smiled. "And continue with your life; do what you already know is wise and right. That is always pleasing, even when specific instructions do not come. Yes?"

She had to agree. Sarai went home and prayed. Her family in

the inn prayed for her. And they went on with their lives.

There was the continuing swirl of gossip and unpleasantness resulting from Jude's actions and words to deal with. The days passed and Sarai tried not to feel guilty whenever his name came up, such as someone asking if his lies were true. The Inn of the Three Sisters had detractors, even a few enemies. People who would enjoy seeing them suffer inconveniences and loss of business. That was a given, in a city the size of Damascus, with people from so many different lands visiting and living there. Jude's actions simply gave those detractors an excuse to speak against them, and new weapons for their ongoing, petty nastiness.

All anyone at the Inn of the Three Sisters cared about, at first, was that Jude didn't return. When they didn't see his face, and their friends in the surrounding streets reported they saw nothing of him, they were all grateful. Jude's lies changed with the gossip, so more and more he came across as a fool and madman. Eventually, their friend Gaius, a court official, gave them a copy of the records of what Jude had said and done, and the fines levied against him. Before they knew the true story, he and his advocate had fled Damascus.

The damage he had done, blackening the reputation of the followers of Jesus, did not fade away. Saul had been living quietly, studying and learning and praying under Ananias' leadership. As the rumors from across the Roman Empire grew darker, Saul walked through the city and confronted the stories and those who told them. Accusations spread that those who celebrated the sharing of bread and wine, obeying Christ's commandment to remember Him, were actually using the flesh and blood of children. More strangers appeared on the Sabbath evening when the believers gathered at the inn to worship. Sarai feared some were spies from the Sanhedrin, or authorities of the government, come to interrupt their worship and arrest them all. Two or three times, someone did upset the common cup holding the wine, spilling it, or swept the basket with the loaves of unleavened bread to the pavement, when no one was looking. Anyone who took the time to investigate could see it was plain wine and bread. The rumors should have stopped, but the accusations of such vile practices simply moved from Damascus to other cities where enemies insisted flesh-eating and blood-drinking were practiced.

Saul displayed the intelligence and sharp thinking and prodigious memory that had made him Gamaliel's prize student. He used the Scriptures to refute the false accusations and wild imaginations of the believers' enemies. Then he went on to prove that Jesus had fulfilled the prophecies about the promised Messiah. He pointed out and addressed the needs and fears of the Jews at the times those words came from Yahweh. Sarai marveled at the bits of Saul's teaching that others repeated to her. On the rare occasions when he taught on Sabbath evenings, she tried to write down everything he said. Her hands ached and she usually had ink spattered on her fingers. The scraps of papyrus she used were always messy from the effort to be quick and capture every word. Saul praised her for her efforts and always gave her time after every meeting, to ask questions and fill in the holes in what she was unable to record.

He didn't come to the Inn of the Three Sisters as often as the believers gathered there would have liked. Every day, Saul met with someone, either individually or in small groups, to teach and to reason. Also, he stayed away simply as a courtesy to those who had come to Damascus to find sanctuary against increasing oppression. His reputation as a follower of Jesus instead of the hound persecuting the believers did not spread as quickly as the marketplace gossip denouncing the believers. New exiles only knew of him as the one hunting for them, to arrest them for heresy and send them back to Jerusalem for sentencing.

Chapter Fifteen

The months passed, and relief came as some of the rumors and gossip faded. More business came to the Inn of the Three Sisters from Gentiles than from Jews. Several times, soldiers attached to the governor's household came into the inn in the middle of a Sabbath evening worship time. They walked among the tables and benches, always studying the faces of the men.

Ananias reported that Saul had left his household and stayed with a different student of his every night. The governor hadn't sent out an official arrest warrant, but the word from sympathetic officials was that it would be signed, as soon as the governor gave in to the demands or bribery or both from the authorities in Judea. Not just the Sanhedrin, but Roman officials were in support of them. Nearly every synagogue in Damascus had a proclamation from the Sanhedrin nailed to their front door, condemning Saul for his heresy and betrayal. They urged all good Jews for the sake of their souls to reject him, and to report his whereabouts to the authorities.

Just short of a year since Sarai had gone to Jerusalem, Nicodemus walked through the gates of the Inn of the Three Sisters. He looked whiter and frailer and older than he should have in that amount of time. In the interim, Sarai had received two letters and small gifts from Hannah; a dress and ball for Pearl, an alabaster jar of perfumed ointment, a stack of papyrus and pot of ink and a pen carved of marble for Sarai. She had sent three letters, and gifts of healing powders and ointments and toys Pearl had chosen for Micah. Sarai was expecting the next package from Hannah by way of Nicodemus, and she immediately feared for the worst when she recognized the elderly rabbi.

Malachi saw him first. He called his name in greeting and hurried to meet him. Sarai released a long, shuddering breath and started across the courtyard to join them. Her head ached with a deluge of questions. There were many reasons why Nicodemus would have come all this distance, and she didn't have to think long to know all were bad to some degree or another. She stumbled, halfway across the courtyard, at the sudden suspicion that she could be responsible for the dread circumstances that had driven the elderly teacher from his comfortable home.

"Healer?" Rhoda, the granddaughter of Miriam, one of the leading women in their synagogue, intercepted Sarai before she could reach Nicodemus. Miriam's cough had become worse, and she needed Sarai's help.

Sarai turned to see Nicodemus and Malachi settling down under the canopy by the kitchen door. Reluctantly, she counseled herself to patience. The elderly woman's cough was more important than her guilty curiosity.

Sarai took Pearl with her because Miriam doted on the little girl. Just as she hoped, the request for a healer's visit was more a social call than any dire concern or need, but she didn't mind. Sarai was glad to spend time in a household where she was welcome as a friend, not an unpleasant necessity. When she and Pearl returned to the inn, evening was slipping into nightfall. She had to carry her daughter who was sleepy-full from the treats Miriam had given her.

Sarai put Pearl to bed and went down to the kitchen to get her own dinner. Tabitha was scrubbing the massive cauldron that had held that day's spicy lentil stew. She smiled when Sarai walked in and nodded at a smaller, covered pot sitting on the edge of the cooking fire, then tipped her head toward the door out into the inn courtyard. That was easy enough to understand. When she had gotten herself something to eat, someone was waiting for her outside. Sarai counseled herself not to hope, but her heart skipped a beat.

Nicodemus and Malachi were sitting together under the canopy, looking tired but relaxed and at peace. Sarai nodded to them and sat down at the end of the table where she could see both their faces. They waited while she made her silent prayer over her food. Malachi got up and fetched a wineskin and brought back a cup for her.

"I am expected at your synagogue in the morning, to meet with Rabbi Amos ben Ezra. We have corresponded over the last few months, and I am glad to consider him a friend." Nicodemus smiled when Sarai paused, a piece of bread laden with lentils halfway to her mouth. "He very kindly kept silent on my plans to make my home here in Damascus. It is far easier to make a graceful, peaceful exit from one home and go to another if those who don't wish you well don't know your plans."

"Has Jerusalem grown so dangerous for believers?" she had to ask.

Sarai shuddered, wondering if Saul's arrest warrant had finally been signed, if the governor had given in to the mixed scolding and begging and demanding and threats from Jerusalem.

"Consider the idea that Satan will only persecute those he considers a threat. When we do not face danger from those who deceive and are themselves deceived, then perhaps we are not living as our Master requires of us." His soft chuckle eased a few knots of apprehension trying to settle in her chest.

Nicodemus spoke of his intention to join the synagogue, find a home near the inn, and become a teacher again. He revealed some of the correspondence that he and Rabbi Amos had exchanged ever since Sarai's visit the year before, and the respect and friendship the two had woven between them. He waited until Sarai asked before he spoke of Simon, Hannah, Deborah and Micah. They were all well, especially Hannah.

As the political temper of Jerusalem had shifted, Simon had separated himself from more actions and declarations in the Sanhedrin. The more extreme and stringent of his friends among the Pharisees had demanded choices and decisions from him that he could not in good conscience make. They had cut him off before he had to take the step to separate himself from them. He had made no move to ally with the moderate voices in the Sanhedrin, but that wasn't good enough for the loudest voices. Simon didn't actively condemn those they considered heretics and disobedient to the laws of Moses and to the traditions of the patriarchs. That nullified much of the respect he had gained over the years.

Simon had withdrawn from the Sanhedrin. Several months ago, he had sold the house in Jerusalem and moved his family to the ancestral property that lay north of Bethany. Hannah had mentioned in her last letter that Simon had moved her, Micah and Deborah to the estate for her health and safety in the increasingly tense atmosphere of Jerusalem. If she had known the other reasons, she had not said so to Sarai.

"So Simon has been living as a farmer and landowner,

returning to the ways of his ancestors. He has quite enjoyed teaching his son the first lessons in woodworking. He says the boy has the soul of an artisan." Nicodemus sighed, looking a little more weary than when Sarai had sat down at the table with him more than an hour ago. "They are safe, for now."

"Safe?" Sarai clutched the wooden cup in both hands. "Do you think his former friends are so angry at him for not standing with them, they will hunt him down?"

"Child, I have learned that nothing is impossible in this cold, darkened world, poisoned by our sin and rebellion." He narrowed his eyes at her a moment. "Do you care for him?"

Her tongue wouldn't move for a moment, her brain clogged with multiple responses, none of which could be called either truth or lie. Sarai finally shrugged. "I don't know. There will always be gratitude that he saved me, and I do have good memories of our first year together. I don't hate him, and I don't wish him evil, but to care for him…"

She shivered, remembering several dreams she had had, nearly identical, of Simon coming to take her back as his wife. He had not demanded but *asked* her to choose him. Each time she had awakened before her dreaming self could decide.

The first time she had the dream, Sarai had blamed Rabbi Amos' advice to marry again, which had been heavy on her mind. She had prayed often in that first month, over whether she should consider marrying to protect Pearl's future. Her prayers had faded slightly, to be renewed whenever she had that dream. She had not dreamed of Simon coming to her for nearly two months now. Sarai could almost laugh at the thought that perhaps that was the answer to her prayer. Yet how could she be sure? She had never heard Adonai's voice, like others had. She had reasoned with herself that to hear the voice of God would mean terrifying and momentous decisions and events. Let others enjoy the bliss and risk and pain and blessings of walking close in the Master's footsteps. She would be very happy to live just as she was now, with no changes, no choices, no danger.

"He is your child's father," Nicodemus continued, after they both sat in thoughtful silence for several moments. "Surely there is some affection there."

"He cast her off when he cast me off."

"He did not know you had conceived."

"I did not know!" She flinched when her voice rose. Sarai feared for a moment she would blurt the truth, that she had begun to suspect, but had been distracted by the turmoil of Passover, crucifixion, and resurrection.

"If Simon were to come to you and declare you innocent. To confess he was in the wrong and had wronged you. If he were to ask you to come back to him as his wife, and allow him to be a father to Pearl and give her a name … would you?"

"The law forbids it," she said, almost in a whisper. "The land will suffer from the uncleanness of it."

"Ah, you know better than that. If you had been unfaithful, if either of you had acted immorally, if you had gone to another man, then yes, to return to Simon would make you both unclean. But you know better."

"What does it matter? Simon is in Jerusalem. Yes," she hurried on, when he opened his mouth, most likely to contradict her. "He has gone to his family's estate, but that is just as good as Jerusalem, just as far away. I am here in Damascus. Pearl has many fathers in the men who work here at the inn. Each one of them, I would trust to guide and guard her. There is nothing she doesn't have that only the father who sired her could give her."

"Hmm. Perhaps."

"Perhaps?" She fought down the urge to fling her empty bowl at him. Something in Nicodemus' eyes made her think, just for a moment, that he was laughing at her. If not laughing, then he knew something that pleased him. Something he refused to share with her.

"I am sorry, my child. There is so much to do, to learn, things I must investigate before … I have overstepped my duties and come close to breaking my promises. Will you forgive an old man who loves you like a daughter? Believe me, I want only the best for you. I want you to find shelter and safety, comfort and peace, rest and healing. I want you to be not just content, but to have joy in this life."

"Yes." Sarai sank into the heavy wave of exhaustion that swept through her. "I know you care. You're simply too much of a scholar to speak clearly or act openly. Everything has to be riddles and puzzles and tests, just like my father."

Nicodemus chuckled and held out a hand to her. She went to him and let him kiss her forehead in blessing. That was as good a time as any to make her departure for the night.

The moon was at the right angle to spill through the loose weave of the cloth over her window and softly fill the entire room. Not enough to keep her or Pearl awake, but enough to see her child sleeping. Sarai lay in that curious, half-awake state, and watched Pearl, marveling at the tiny perfection of her every feature. Nicodemus' words swirled softly through her thoughts as she drifted closer to sleep but never quite fell into the gentle, ebony warmth. She had never thought to apply the word "joy" to her life. There was a difference between happiness and joy. Happiness was momentary, but joy was deep and quiet and part of contentment. A sweet kind of satisfaction, she supposed. Pearl was her joy. She found joy in her healing work, and in her studies. Happiness came when she found a new scroll of healing lore. Or made a new friend and ally among the city's healers. Or located a rare herb or root or seed that would allow her to experiment with a healing compound she had read about. They were momentary spurts of brightness, like sparks from the fire. Joy was like the deep, dim light of the coals that lingered and were difficult to quench without tearing the fire apart and drowning it.

She tried not to remember, but Nicodemus' other words softly spun through her mind as she slid further down toward sleep. If Simon came to her and acknowledged the wrong he had done her, acknowledged the bad choices he had made … If he acknowledged that Jesus was indeed the Messiah and had conquered death and prophecy had been fulfilled in His coming … If Simon wanted her as his wife again, and to give their daughter a name, a defender … would she? Could she?

When Sarai woke in the morning and remembered all the questions that had followed her into sleep, the only honest answer she could give was unchanged from what she had said to Nicodemus. She didn't know.

~~~~~

The day laborers had come for their morning bread, cheese, and hot, spiced wine, and left again. The inn courtyard was nearly empty. Sarai paused a moment to watch Pearl and laugh, as her daughter struggled with a broom that was taller than her. Today
~~~~~

she insisted on helping Obed and the other boys who worked on the caravansary side of the inn. They had the task of sweeping out the courtyard in between the regular tide of customers. The children were far enough away that she couldn't hear what they were saying, but close enough she could see Obed smile down at Pearl, and her daughter smile up at him. She wiped her hands on her apron and picked up two empty pitchers to carry back into the kitchen for washing.

When she came out with a bucket and rags to wash the tables, she saw Obed walking toward the inn gates, where a man was just stepping through. Pearl trotted after him, his shadow, dragging the broom behind her. Sarai went to the first table and wrung out the rag and got to work washing. Sometimes it amazed her how the men who came here for their morning meal could cover the tables with crumbs and water and wine, and yet leave with their stomachs full. A tiny snort of laughter escaped her, as she remembered Daniel's remark several months ago, when she voiced the same question. Perhaps it was slightly blasphemous, but it was still a little funny. He had said something about a large number of Christ-followers among the day laborers, trying to duplicate the miracle of the loaves and fishes, when Jesus had taught along the shore of the Sea of Galilee.

"Healer Sarai?" Obed called, and she looked up to see him weaving among the tables to reach her. The chubby, red-haired boy gestured back behind himself. "This man is new-come to the city, and his wife is ill from traveling; he needs a healer. Can you help him?"

She tossed the rag back into the bucket, wiped her hands, and turned to look past the boy. The man had gone down on one knee and seemed to be talking to Pearl. As she watched, he reached into the pouch hanging from his belt, brought something out, and handed it to Pearl. Whatever it was, her daughter needed both hands to hold it. Sarai shivered, though she didn't know why, as Pearl dashed toward her.

"Mama? Please?" the little girl called, as Sarai moved between the tables to meet her. "Can I have it?"

They met between two tables, at the edge of the open area of the courtyard. The man had stood up again and was slowly walking over toward them. Sarai went down on one knee and held out her hand for what turned out to be a wooden apple.

No, not a wooden apple, but a box carved in the shape of an apple.

Her hand trembled, so she almost dropped the box when Pearl gave it to her. Sarai knew that box. Right down to the butterfly carved into the side, where the pale golden and red streaks of stain rubbed into the wood were darkest. Where they hadn't worn away with much handling.

Simon had made that box for her, on that long, weary, happy walk full of dreams from the Decapolis to Jerusalem. If he had accepted the woodworker's offer that night, to stay in the village … where would they all be right now? Would she have Pearl? Would she be here in Damascus? Would Simon be standing before her, his face creased with a decade of concerns and a few silver threads woven in his hair and beard, but shining in hope?

"Please?" Simon stopped a few paces away from them.

Sarai had left the box behind, just like everything else Simon had given her. She had ached for the sweet memories and the promises and the dreams that had seemed to be embodied by the simple gift. She remembered what Nicodemus had said last night, about Simon teaching Micah woodcarving. She remembered everything he had said, especially the questions he had asked her.

This was why he had asked her those questions. He knew Simon was here. He had told Simon where to find her. Sarai struggled to stand before her legs lost all their strength. She refused to stay kneeling. Standing, she could breathe again. She knew she could fight the aching, drowning sensation that she would burst into tears at any moment.

She didn't know how she felt beyond the questions and shock. There was too much to think, to understand, to feel. She tried to be grateful Nicodemus had done a little to prepare her, rather than angry at what some would call a betrayal. He hadn't warned her, but hadn't he said that he had come close to breaking promises?

"Is Hannah truly ill?" she said instead, and let Pearl slip the apple box from her hand.

"Exhausted, but more healthy and strong than she has been in years." Simon took a breath. Licked his lips. "Thanks to you. We owe you … I owe you so much. Sarai," he said on a whisper. "Yes, I do," he hurried on, when she shook her head. He reached to take hold of her hand, and only then did she realize she had taken a step back.

"How long are you visiting Damascus?"

"We intend to live here. Hannah and Micah and Deborah and I." He glanced down at Pearl, who had dropped down to sit nearly on Sarai's feet, and had figured out how to pry the top off the apple to look inside. "Help us find a home?"

"I ... what do you want of me?" she asked finally, when so many words clogged on her tongue and she couldn't look into his big, dark gleaming eyes any longer. And yet couldn't look away.

"Hannah wants, she needs her sister. Micah needs his aunt, whom he loves dearly. I need -- I want to be a good father to my -- to our daughter." His hand trembled, gripping hers. "I need your wisdom. I need your forgiveness."

Wood clattered on the cobblestones. Sarai tugged her hand free and went down on one knee before she realized that Pearl had dropped the two pieces of the apple box. She picked up the bottom half, while her daughter scrambled on hands and knees to catch the top before it rolled away. Pearl giggled and handed it to her, then watched Sarai fit the two pieces together. Simon went down on one knee, just within arm's reach, but didn't try to touch either of them. The reprieve from the prison of his gaze let her breathe again.

"Please? Just come see Hannah. For her, for Micah, if there's nothing in your heart for me."

"Mama?" Pearl leaned into Sarai and clutched at the front of her dress. "Does he know Aunt Hannah?"

"This is Micah's father. He's married to Aunt Hannah. Micah and Aunt Hannah and Granny Deborah have come to Damascus to live. What do you think of that?"

Pearl clapped her hands, which meant she dropped the apple box. The lid stayed on. It rolled and bumped across the cobblestones, and this time Simon caught it. He held it out to Pearl, and his hand trembled just enough to be visible, as she took it.

Sarai didn't have all the answers to the questions Nicodemus had asked her, and she didn't have the answers to the dozens of questions now spinning once again through her mind. But for Hannah and for Micah and for Deborah, she would consider all that Simon had asked her, and all the things he hadn't said but she could read in his gaze. To give her daughter a name, to erase the questions that would always follow her through life, the doubts that would pull her down like weights tied to a swimmer in deep water ... yes, she thought she could willingly return to Simon's home.

Would it be enough for her, to take what he offered and let go of the pain and the wounds from their past? Would there be joy enough to reward her and heal her?

Savior, speak to me. Guide me. Help me choose wisely.

For now, she would do what she knew was right, and would pray for the answers to come as she needed them.

"I will fetch my healer's bag, and then we will go to Hannah." She smiled down at her daughter. "And Micah, and Deborah."

Pearl ran ahead of her to the door through the kitchen and into the house. Simon walked with Sarai, head bowed. She noticed more threads of silver at his temples, in his beard. He was no longer the determined boy who had fought against mockery and injustice to obtain his dreams ... and her. He didn't follow her into the house, but waited outside, just beyond the shade from the canopy.

When Sarai and Pearl came outside again, Simon held out his hand. She hesitated. Pearl giggled and reached up to take Simon's hand and hers. They crossed the courtyard and went out the gates of the inn with their daughter walking between them.

END

About the Author

On the road to publication, Michelle fell into fandom in college and has 40+ stories in various SF and fantasy universes. She has a bunch of useless degrees in theater, English, film/communication, and writing. Even worse, she has over 100 books and novellas with multiple small presses, in science fiction and fantasy, YA, suspense, women's fiction, and sub-genres of romance.

Her official launch into publishing came with winning first place in the Writers of the Future contest in 1990. She was a finalist in the EPIC Awards competition multiple times, winning with *Lorien* in 2006 and *The Meruk Episodes, I-V*, in 2010, and was a finalist in the Realm Award competition, in conjunction with the Realm Makers convention.

Her training includes the Institute for Children's Literature; proofreading at an advertising agency; and working at a community newspaper. She is a tea snob and freelance edits for a living (MichelleLevigne@gmail.com for info/rates), but only enough to give her time to write. Her newest crime against the literary world is to be co-managing editor at Mt. Zion Ridge Press. Be afraid ... be very afraid.

www.Mlevigne.com
www.MichelleLevigne.blogspot.com
@MichelleLevigne

Also by Michelle L. Levigne

Guardians of the Time Stream: 4-book Steampunk series
The Match Girls: Humorous inspirational romance series starting in 2020 with **A Match (Not) Made in Heaven**

Tabor Heights: 20-book inspirational small-town romance series.

Quarry Hall: 11-book women's fiction/suspense series

For Sale: Wedding Dress. Never Used: inspirational romance

Crooked Creek: Fun Fables About Critters and Kids: Children's short stories.

Do Yourself a Favor: Tips and Quips on the Writing Life. A book of writing advice.

Killing His Alter-Ego: contemporary romance/suspense, taking place in fandom.

The Commonwealth Universe: SF series, 25 books and growing

The Hunt: 5-book YA fantasy series

Faxinor: Fantasy series, 4 books and growing

Wildvine: Fantasy series, 14 books when all released

Neighborlee: Humorous fantasy series; re-releasing in 2020; 8 books and growing.

Zygradon: 5-book Arthurian fantasy series

* 9 7 8 1 9 4 9 5 6 4 8 1 5 *